"You're a beautiful woman, Alixe Burke."

She stiffened. "You shouldn't say things you don't mean."

"Do you doubt me? Or do you doubt yourself? Don't you think you're beautiful? Surely you're not naive enough to overlook your natural charms?"

She turned to face him, forcing him to relinquish his hold. "I'm not naive. I'm a realist."

Merrick shrugged a shoulder as if to say he didn't think much of realism. "What has realism taught you, Alixe?" He folded his arms, waiting to see what she would say next.

"It has taught me that I'm an end to male means. I'm a dowry, a stepping stone for some ambitious man. It's not very flattering."

He could not refute her arguments. There were men who saw women that way. But he could refute the hardness in her sherry eyes—eyes that should have been warm. For all her protestations of realism, she was too untried by the world for the measure of cynicism she showed.

"What of romance and love? What has realism taught you about those things?"

"If those things exist, they don't exist for me." Alixe's chin went up a fraction in defiance of his probe.

"Is that a dare, Alixe? If it is, I'll take it."

* * *

How to Disgrace a Lady
Harlequin® Historical #1104—September 2012

Introducing a deliciously sinful and witty new trilogy
from

Bronwyn Scott

Rakes Beyond Redemption

Too wicked for polite society...

They're the men society mamas warn their daughters
about…and the men that innocent debutantes
find scandalously irresistible!

The notorious Merrick St. Magnus knows just
HOW TO DISGRACE A LADY
September 2012

The untameable Ashe Bevedere needs no lessons in
HOW TO RUIN A REPUTATION
October 2012

The shameless Riordan Barrett is an unequalled master
in
HOW TO SIN SUCCESSFULLY
November 2012

Be sure not to miss any of these sexy men!

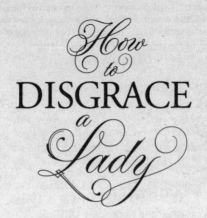

How to
DISGRACE
a Lady

BRONWYN SCOTT

entertain, enrich, inspire™

Recycling programs
for this product may
not exist in your area.

ISBN-13: 978-0-373-29704-7

HOW TO DISGRACE A LADY

BRONWYN SCOTT

is a communications instructor at Pierce College in the United States, and is the proud mother of three wonderful children (one boy and two girls). When she's not teaching or writing, she enjoys playing the piano, travelling—especially to Florence, Italy—and studying history and foreign languages. You can learn more about Bronwyn at www.nikkipoppen.com

Chapter One

Merrick St Magnus did nothing by halves, including the notorious Greenfield Twins. Even now, the legendary courtesans were delectably arranged in varying degrees of dishabille on the drawing room's long Venetian divan. His eyes on the first Greenfield twin, Merrick plucked an orange slice from a silver tray and gave it an indolent roll in powdered sugar, in no way oblivious to the charms of her lovely bosom pushed to the very limits of decency by the dual efforts of a tightly laced corset and a low décolletage.

'One sweet temptation deserves another, *ma chère*,' he said in liquid tones, his eyes meaningfully raking her body, noticing how the pulse note at the base of her long neck leapt in appreciation of his open seduction. Merrick skimmed the orange slice across her slightly parted lips, the tip of her tongue making pretty work of licking the powdery sugar, all the while suggesting she'd be quite apt at licking more than her lips.

He was going to enjoy tonight. More than that, he

was going to enjoy winning the bet that currently filled pages of White's infamous book of wagers and collecting the winnings tomorrow. He stood to make a respectable sum that would see him through a recent bad run at the tables. Certainly men had 'had' the lovely Greenfield sisters, but no man had obtained carnal knowledge of them *both* at the same time.

At the other end of the divan, twin number two gave a coy pout. 'What about me, Merrick? Am I not a temptation?'

'You, *ma belle*, are a veritable Eve.' Merrick let his hand hover over the fruit platter as if contemplating with great deliberation which fruit to select. 'Ah, for you, my Eve, a fig, I think, for the pleasures of Eden that await a man in your garden.'

His literary references were for naught. She pouted again, perplexed. 'My name isn't Eve.'

Merrick stifled a sigh. Think about the money. He flashed a rakish smile, popping the fig into her mouth and giving her a compliment she would understand. 'I never can tell which of you is the prettiest.' But he definitely could tell which one was smarter. He dropped a hand to the expanse of twin number two's exposed bosom and drew a light circle on her skin with his index finger, winning a coy smile. Twin one had her hands at his shoulders, massaging as she pulled the shirt-tails from his waistband. It was time to get down to business.

That was when it happened—his manservant began banging on the receiving room door.

'Not right now,' Merrick called, but the banging persisted.

'Maybe he wants to join us,' twin one suggested, unfazed by the interruption.

His man of all work would not be deterred. 'We have an emergency, milord.' He pressed from the other side of the door.

Damn it all, he was going to have to get up and see what Fillmore wanted. Between lost literary references and intrusive servants, this could be going better. Merrick pushed to his feet, shirt-tails loose. He placed a gallant kiss on the hand of each twin. 'A moment, *mes amours.*'

He purposely strode across the floor and pulled open the door just a fraction. Fillmore knew what he was doing in here, of course, and Fillmore probably even knew why. But that didn't mean Merrick wanted him to witness it first-hand. If he thought too much about it, the whole scenario was a bit lowering. He was broke and trading the one thing he did better than anything else for the one thing he needed more than anything else: sex for money, not that anyone else realised it.

'Yes, Fillmore?' Merrick managed a supercilious arch of his eyebrow. 'What is our emergency?'

Fillmore wasn't the normal manservant. The arched eyebrow affected him as much as the Miltonesque reference had affected twin not-so-smart. Fillmore puffed himself up and said, 'The emergency, milord, is your father.'

'Fillmore, you are aware, I believe, that I prefer my problems to be shared.'

'Yes, milord, as you say, our emergency.'

'Well, out with it, what has happened?'

Fillmore passed him a white sheet of paper already unfolded.

Merrick had another go at the arched eyebrow. 'You might as well tell me, clearly you've already read the message.' Really, Fillmore ought to show at least some slight remorse over reading someone else's post; not that it wasn't a useful trait on occasion, just not a very genteel one.

'He's coming to town. He'll be here the day after next,' Fillmore summarised with guiltless aplomb.

Every part of Merrick not already in a state of stiffness went hard with tension. 'That means he could be here as early as tomorrow afternoon.' His father excelled at arriving ahead of schedule and this was an extraordinarily premeditated act. His father meant to take him by surprise. One could only guess how far along the road his father had been before he'd finally sent word of his imminent arrival. Which meant only one thing: there was going to be a reckoning.

The conclusion begged the question: which rumours had sent the Marquis hot-footing it to town? Had it been the curricle race to Richmond? Probably not. That had been weeks ago. If he'd been coming over that, he would have been here long before now. Had it been the wager over the opera singer? Admittedly that had become more public than Merrick would have liked.

But it wasn't the first time his *affaires* had been conducted with an audience.

'Does he say why?' Merrick searched the short letter.

'It's hard to say. We've had so many occasions,' Fillmore finished with an apologetic sigh.

'Yes, yes, I suppose it doesn't matter which episode brings him to town, only that we're not here to greet him.' Merrick pushed a hand through his hair with an air of impatience. He needed to think and then he needed to act quickly.

'Are we sure that's wise?' Fillmore enquired, 'I mean, based on the last part of the letter, perhaps it would be better if we stayed and were appropriately penitent.'

Merrick scowled. 'Since when have we ever adopted a posture of penitence when it comes to my father?' He wasn't in the least bit intimidated by his father. Leaving town was not an act of cowardice. This was about being able to exert his own will. He would not give his father the satisfaction of knowing he controlled another of his grown sons. His father controlled everything and everyone that fell into his purvey, including Merrick's older brother, Martin, the heir. Merrick refused to be catalogued as another of his father's puppets.

'Since he's coming to town to cut off our allowance until we reform our ways. It's later in the note,' Fillmore informed him.

He'd never been the fastest of readers. Conversation was so much more entertaining. But there they were at the bottom of the letter, the words so curt and glaring he could almost hear his father's voice behind them: *I am curtailing your access to funds until such time as your habits are reformed.*

Merrick scoffed. 'He can curtail the allowance all he wants since "we" don't touch it anyway.' It had occurred to him years ago that in order to be truly free of his father, he could not be reliant on anything his father offered, the usual second-son allowance included. The allowance lay tucked away in an account at Coutts and Merrick chose instead to live by the turn of a card or the outcome of a profitable wager. Usually it was enough to keep him in rent and clothes. His well-earned reputation for bedroom pleasure did the rest.

His father could halt the allowance for as long as he liked. That wasn't what bothered Merrick. It was the fact that his father was coming at all. The one thing they agreed on was the need for mutual distance. Merrick liked his father's jaded ethics as little as his father liked his more flexible standards. Coming to London was a death knell to his Season and it was barely June. But Merrick wasn't outmanoeuvred yet.

He needed to think and he needed to think with his brain as opposed to other body parts. That meant the twins had to go. Merrick shut the door and turned back to the twins with a short, gallant bow of apology. 'Ladies, I regret the emergency is immediate. You will need to leave.'

And so they did, taking his chance at two hundred pounds with them at a point where money was tight and his time was tighter.

* * *

'Fillmore, how much do we owe?' Merrick sprawled on the now significantly less-populated divan. He ran through the numbers in his head; the boot maker, his tailor and other sundry merchants would need to be paid before he left. He wouldn't give his father the satisfaction of seeing to his debt. It might create the illusion his father had room to negotiate.

Damn, but this was a fine pickle. He was usually an adequate steward of his funds and usually a fair judge of character. He never should have played cards with Stevenson. The man was known to cheat.

'Seven hundred pounds including this month's rent on the rooms.'

'How much do we have?'

'Around eight hundred to hand.'

It was as he'd thought—enough to clear the bills with a little left over. Not enough to survive another month in the city, however, especially not during the Season. London was deuced expensive.

Fillmore cleared his throat. 'Might I suggest that one way to cut expenses would be for us to stay at the family town house? Rent for rooms in a fashionable neighbourhood is an extravagance.'

'Live with my father? No, you may not suggest it. I've not lived with him for ages. I don't mean to start now, especially since it's what he wants.' Merrick sighed. 'Bring me the invitations from the front table.'

Merrick searched the pile for inspiration, looking for a high-stakes card party, a bachelor's weekend in Newmarket that would get him out of town, anything that might assuage the current situation. But there was nothing amusing: a musicale, a Venetian breakfast, a ball, all in London, all useless. Then at the bottom of the pile he found it: the Earl of Folkestone's house party. Folkestone was hosting a party at the family seat on the Kent coast. Originally, he'd not considered going. It was three days to Kent on dry roads to even drier company. But now it seemed the ideal locale. Folkestone was a crusty traditionalist of a man, but Merrick knew Folkestone's heir, Jamie Burke, from their days at Oxford, and he'd attended a soirée hosted by Lady Folkestone early in the Season, which explained where the invitation had come from. He'd been a model guest, flirting with all the wallflowers until they had bloomed. Ladies liked a guest who knew how to do his duty and Merrick knew how to do his superbly.

'Pack our bags, Fillmore. We're going to Kent,' Merrick said with a finality he didn't feel. He didn't fool himself into believing a house party in Kent was an answer to his woes. It was merely a temporary salve. London was expensive, yes, but his freedom was proving to be more so.

The road to Kent was clearly *not* to be confused with the road to Hell, Merrick mused grimly later after three days of riding. For starters, there were no good intentions in sight. But there were apparently two highwaymen in broad daylight. Merrick slowed his horse and swore under his breath. Damn and double damn, he'd been a short two miles from the salvation of Folkestone's bloody house party. His hand reached subtly for the pistol in his coat pocket.

It was deuced odd for highwaymen to attempt a robbery at three in the afternoon when the polite world was ready to settle in for tea. But given the state of the current British economy, he wouldn't put it past anyone. It was unfortunate he was alone just now, having ridden on ahead of Fillmore and his luggage.

'Is the road out, my good fellows?' Merrick called, wheeling his horse around in a flashy circle. Their horses looked sleek and well fed. Great. He'd run into a set of the more successful brand of highwayman. Merrick's hand tightened on his pistol. He'd paid his bills and his last pound notes were tucked safely in his pocket. He wasn't about to surrender what financial surety he had left.

The two bandits, masked below their eyes with black scarves, looked at each other. One of them laughed and parodied his politeness. 'It is to you, good sir.' The man waved his more obviously displayed pistol with the casual flourish of a man long accustomed to handling firearms with ease. 'We don't want your money, we want your clothes. Be a good fellow and give us a quick strip.' The green eyes of the second bandit flashed with humour.

The sun caught the glint of the pistol butt. Merrick's hand eased on the grip of his weapon, a slow sure smile of confidence taking his face. Merrick stilled his horse and faced the two 'bandits'. 'Why, Ashe Bedevere and Riordan Barrett, fancy meeting you here.'

The green-eyed man with the pistol yanked his scarf down. 'How did you know?'

Merrick grinned. 'No one else in England has emeralds embedded in the butt of their pistol.'

'Damn it, it was a good prank.' Ashe gave his gun a rueful glare as if the weapon alone were to blame for ruining the gambit. 'Do you know how long we've been sitting here, waiting?'

'Waiting in the sun is dusty business,' Riordan put in.

'What were you doing, waiting at all?' Merrick pulled his horse alongside his two friends and they continued down the road three abreast.

'We saw your horse outside the inn last night and the ostler said you were headed over to Folkestone's for the party,' Ashe admitted with an impish grin. 'Since we're going, too, we thought we'd plan a little reunion.'

'We could have reunited over a pint of good ale and rabbit stew last night,' Merrick put in. Accosting friends with pistols was a bit demented even for Ashe.

'There's no fun in that; besides, we were busy with the barmaid and her sister.' Riordan pulled out a pewter flask and took a healthy swallow. 'There hasn't been any fun all Season. London's been an absolute bore.'

So boring that even a house party in Kent held more charm? It seemed unlikely. Merrick peered closely at his friend. Riordan's face bore signs of weariness, but there was no time to pursue that avenue in the wake of Ashe's next pronouncement.

'How about a bathe?'

Merrick's head swivelled in Ashe's direction.

'What? A bathe?' Had Ashe finally gone around the bend? He'd long suspected Ashe wasn't as sane as the rest of humanity, always the risk taker.

'Not in a tub, old chap,' Ashe replied, easily reading his mind. 'Out here, *before* we get to the house party. There's a pond—a small lake, really—over the next rise and off the lane a bit, if I remember this stretch of road right. It will be a chance to wash off the grime of the journey, a last chance to exist in nature before we embrace the unnatural formality of a country party where...' Ashe paused for effect and went on with great exaggeration '...everything should be natural, but most unfortunately is not.'

'Splendid idea, a bathe is perfect. What say you, Merrick? A bathe before high tea and the ladies?' Riordan voted with his heels, spurring his chestnut hunter into a canter, letting the light breeze ruffle his dark hair. Riordan called back over his shoulder, 'Race you! I've got the flask!'

'But you don't know where you're going!' Ashe and Merrick yelled in unison. This had always been the case; even at Oxford, Riordan had been heedless of the details, seizing the pleasure of the moment, ignoring the consequences. Merrick exchanged a knowing look with Ashe.

'All the better to race me....' The words floated back over the pounding of hooves on packed dirt. They needed no further encouragement to kick their horses up to speed and follow.

They found the pond as Ashe remembered it: a cool, shady oasis fed by a quick-flowing stream and perfect for the odd summer bathe. It was hidden from the casual eye by leafy willows and Merrick raced the others, wasting no time in divesting himself of his clothes, suddenly overcome with a desire to feel the cold water on his hot skin. He dived in, refusing to cautiously test the waters first.

The water closed over his head and he felt absolution. He reached out into the water with long strokes and began to kick, every stroke taking him further from London, from his father, from his ongoing battle for the freedom to be himself even if he didn't precisely know who that was. In the water he was clean. Unfettered joy took him and he surged to the surface, shaking the water from his hair. Ashe was watching him, posed gloriously naked on a rock like a sea-god. Merrick reached up, grabbed Ashe's leg and pulled. 'Come on in, the water's fine.'

Ashe gave an undignified yelp as gravity and Merrick took him sliding into the pond. 'Riordan, get in here and help me!'

There was a swift movement on the banks as Riordan grabbed for a sturdy vine and swung into the mêlée. Chaos ensued—the good kind of chaos that washes away years and trouble. They wrestled in the water; they scrambled up the banks, making the dirt into mud with their dripping forms; they ran the perimeter of their sanctuary with loud whoops of pure exuberance, only to jump back in and start all over. For all the sophistication of London and its entertainments, Merrick hadn't had this much uncontrived fun in ages. London's *haut ton* would cringe to see three of their members behaving with such careless, naked abandon. But why not? There was no one to see.

Chapter Two

Thank goodness no one could see her now. Dressed in a loose, serviceable gown of drab olive and scuffed half-boots, Alixe knew she didn't look at all like a proper earl's daughter. The family would have a fit. *Another* fit. The family wanted to have as few fits as possible. Which was probably why they'd let her go out wandering in the first place, despite guests arriving for the long-anticipated midsummer house party.

At the moment, Alixe didn't care if the king himself was scheduled to arrive. She had a precious afternoon of freedom entirely to herself. The weather was fine and she was enjoying her tramp to the furthest edges of the family property, perhaps a bit beyond because she was feeling a little naughty. She had a destination in mind—an old summer house on the nebulous fringes of the estate, where she could settle in with her books and her work, all carefully packed in a cloth bag looped over her shoulder.

She was getting close to the summer house. The

path was increasingly overgrown with fern and nearly obscured from plain view as she ventured further into the wooded area. She smiled and pushed aside some of the rampant undergrowth. It was cool here beneath the trees. Ah, there it was. She quickened her pace, taking the crumbling steps to the entrance two at a time.

Alixe opened the door and sighed. The old place was perfect. She should make a retreat out of it. She could scavenge odds and ends from the attics. Alixe put her bag down and surveyed the open-air room. It was more like a gazebo than an actual house, but it had infinite possibilities—a place where she could be alone, away from the family's odious neighbour Archibald Redfield, away from everyone and all their expectations for her life. Alixe closed her eyes and breathed deeply. Ah, yes, she was blessedly alone.

Then she heard it: the sound of not being quite alone. Alixe turned her head towards the sound. A bird call? It came again—distinctly *not* a bird. It sounded like a human shout.

Oh, dear.

The lake.

Alixe was galvanised into action. Someone might be in trouble. She tore through the woods, running towards the shouts.

Alixe crashed into the lake clearing and came to an abrupt halt too late to rethink announcing her presence once it became patently obvious the only thing in risk of drowning were her sensibilities. Three men cavorted—really, that was the only word for it—*ca-*

vorted in the water. They dove, they wrestled, they noticed her.

Oh, lord, they *noticed* her.

She didn't want to be noticed. This was not what she deserved for playing the good Samaritan. She'd run pell-mell to the aid of three men swimming nude in a hidden lake. Someone could at least have the decency to actually be drowning.

'Hello, are we making too much noise? We didn't think anyone was around,' one of them said easily, unfazed by her sudden appearance. He separated from his comrades and waded towards the shore, the receding water revealing him inch by marvellous inch until Alixe was sure of two things: first, she'd never seen such a finely made man in her life and, second, the finely made man was undoubtedly naked.

She should look away. But where to look? His eyes? They were too mesmerising. The sky wasn't even that blue. His chest? Too well-sculpted, especially the tapered muscles at his abdomen.

Abdomen!

Oh, lord, she hadn't meant to let her gaze or the water get so low. He was still moving towards her, unbothered by his nudity. She had to put a stop to it or she'd be seeing more than the firm muscles of his abdomen.

All her supposed good breeding failed her utterly. Her eyes remained riveted on the stranger's midsection. It would only be a matter of seconds now before all was revealed. She should say something. What did one say to a naked man at a pond?

She opted for a casual response and tried to sound as if she ran into naked men all the time. 'Don't get out for me. I'll just be going. I heard the shouts and thought someone might need help.'

Good. She sounded mostly normal.

Alixe took a step back from the lake and promptly fell over a log half-buried in the mud of the lake side. She landed hard on her backside. She could feel her cheeks burning. So much for normal.

The man laughed, not unkindly, and kept advancing. He was fully revealed now, his manly parts entirely visible. All she could do was stare. He was so magnificent that for a moment she forgot to be embarrassed, her curiosity unleashed at the sight of him. He was beautiful—*that* part of him was beautiful in a wild, primitive way. She'd not expected it.

'Seems as though someone might need help, after all.' The nameless, *naked* man stood over her with a hand held out, not that she had much attention for the hand when there were other dangling appendages in close proximity.

'No, really, I'm all right.' Her words rushed out in a flummoxed mess, her sense of propriety returning.

'Don't be stubborn, give me your hand. You don't want to fall again.' He held out his hand, insisting.

'Oh, yes, my hand.' Alixe offered it up as if she'd just discovered it and dragged her eyes a little further up his chest to his face. He was grinning at her with his whole visage: his smile wide and laughing, his eyes bluer than the cerulean of an English summer sky.

He tugged Alixe to her feet, not in the least nonplussed by his lack of clothing. 'Your first naked man, I take it?'

'What?' It took her a moment to follow the question. It was hard enough to train her eyes away from the environs of his thighs, let alone follow a conversation. She opted for sophistication in the hopes of recovering her dignity. 'No, actually. I've seen plenty in...' She faltered here. *Where* would she have seen them?

'Art work?' he supplied helpfully, water droplets sparking like diamonds in the pale flax of his hair.

'I've seen the *David*,' she shot back, sensing the challenge. It was true. She had in pictures, but the *David* of pictures had nothing on this stranger, who stood bold and brash in the sunlight with all his worldly goods plainly displayed. Her eyes darted about the shores of the pond, in a desperate attempt to not look at said worldly goods. It was all his fault. He'd made no move to retrieve any of the garments lying close by. What kind of man stood naked in the presence of a lady? Not the kind of man she was used to meeting in her parents' genteel circles.

The very thought sent a tremor of excitement through her even as she reached for the nearest garment. 'You should cover yourself, sir.' Alixe held out the shirt. It would be too bad, of course, but it was an absolute social necessity. No one stood around conversing without their clothes on.

He took the shirt, his eyes were laughing at her. 'Should I? I was under the impression you were enjoying the view.'

'I think the only one enjoying this is you,' Alixe

countered, mustering all the outrage she ought to feel at this affront to her sensibilities.

He cocked an eyebrow in challenge. 'At least I'll admit to it.'

That comment did stoke her temper. Alixe squared her shoulders. 'You are a most ill-bred man.' *With the body of a god and a face of an angel.* 'I must be going.' She brushed at her skirts to give her hands something to do. 'I can see everyone is all right. I'll be on my way.' This time she managed to exit the clearing without stumbling over any errant logs.

Merrick watched her go with a laugh. He thrust his arms through the sleeves of his shirt in a belated overture to decency. Perhaps he shouldn't have done it—shouldn't have teased her so mercilessly. But it had all been good fun and she'd not shied away from it. He knew when a woman was curious and when she was genuinely mortified. This creature in the drab dress hadn't been nearly as mortified as she claimed. Her lovely sherry eyes had been wide with curiosity satisfied as she looked her fill.

Merrick reached for his trousers and slid them on. To be sure, she'd tried to look away, but healthy inquisitiveness is hard to defeat and she'd lost that battle from the start. Not that he'd been bothered by her frank enquiry into the male anatomy. She wasn't the first woman to see him naked. He'd been naked in front of a lot of them.

Women liked his body, with its lean lines and muscled contours. Lady Mansfield had once, quite publicly, declared it the eighth wonder of the world. Lady Fairworth had spent nights staring at him for hours. She'd made a habit of having him fetch things from around the room so that she could watch him walk across the floor stark naked for her.

He hadn't minded. He understood the needs of those experienced women and, in turn, they understood his. But today had been different. There'd been something unsullied in her gaze. He'd clearly been her first. Even now the knowledge fired a low heat in his groin. She'd been surprised, but she hadn't shrunk from her discoveries. She'd welcomed them. Her response to him had sparked a kind of eroticism he was not familiar with. It had been ages since he'd been anyone's first naked man.

More than that, the very directness of her demeanour had appealed to him. He'd known he could push her sensibilities. For all her clumsiness, he'd known she could handle herself. Helpless misses didn't run through the forest to the rescue of drowning victims. He'd not been disappointed. Her sharp conversation had been every bit as enjoyable as her hot, open gaze. Too bad he didn't know her name. He'd just have to burn on his own.

Alixe's cheeks were still burning when she got back to the summer house. She resolutely settled in with her book, determined to not think about the encounter at the lake. But her mind would have none of it. Her mind preferred instead to recall, in vivid detail, the well-muscled torso with its defined abdomen and lean hips tapering down to that most manly part of him. And that smile. Even now, that wicked, laughing grin sent a curious skittering sensation straight to her stomach. He'd been flirting with her. Those dancing blue eyes knew exactly what they were doing, exactly what kind of havoc they were wreaking on her senses. It had been ages since anyone had flirted with her, even if it had been a little unorthodox.

Well, more than a little. It was the most unorthodox thing that had happened to her to date. Until today, she'd never seen a man without his shirt. Probably, if she thought about it, she hadn't seen a man without a waistcoat since her come-out. A gentleman didn't dare remove even his coat in the presence of a lady, while this man had removed quite a bit more than his coat. It begged the question: what did that make him? Certainly not a gentleman.

The blush started again and Alixe was swamped anew with the sensation. She'd seen a real, live, naked man.

Up close.

Very close.

Extremely close. And it had been gorgeous. Which begged the question: what did that make *her*? Curious? Wanton? Something more? The answer would be worth exploring. She was no prude, genteel rearing and shielding aside. She'd partaken as eagerly in the sights as he'd displayed them. Alixe fought the urge to fan herself like an insipid miss. She had to find her focus and be done with this ridiculous mooning. She'd seen no more today than the gifts God had given mankind in general. Every man had one, which was roughly half the population.

There.

She'd taken the philosophical high ground—and failed miserably to dispel the image from her mind.

It was official: she was definitely unsettled. She would get no reading done at this rate. Alixe tucked her book back into the bag. What she needed was a change of scenery. She might as well head back to the house; if she smiled like an empty-headed fool the whole way back, so be it.

By the time she'd gained the safety of her rooms, Alixe had found perspective. She had indeed smiled the entire walk back to the house. She might even continue to smile her way through the tedious evening that lay ahead. If people wanted to believe she was smiling at them, they could. Only she would know what she was really smiling about. Other than that, she'd come to the realisation there was no harm in her secret. The man from the lake didn't know her; she didn't know him; they would never see each other again, except perhaps in her dreams.

But the knowledge did make her feel undeniably more worldly than she'd felt four hours ago and she dressed with a little more care than she might otherwise have done in celebration of it. She had her maid lay out the pale-blue dinner gown with the chocolate-brown trim and the low-cut bodice. The gown was one of a few exceptions in her otherwise 'sufficient' wardrobe.

She'd always been more interested in her books and

manuscripts than clothes and society; a fact her family was not willing to accept, although she'd achieved the august age of twenty-six and had firmly put herself on the shelf. Despite her most persuasive efforts, not all of the family had despaired of marrying off the controversial, blue-stocking daughter of the Earl of Folkestone just yet. She'd refused to go to London this Season, so her dogged family had brought London to her in the form of a house party peopled with the very best of her brother's acquaintances.

Alixe clipped on her dainty pearl earrings and gave herself a final look-over in the mirror. It was time to go downstairs and pretend she'd never seen a man without clothes. Surely she could do that?

'Alixe, there you are.' Her brother, Jamie, materialised at the foot of the stairs. 'You look pretty tonight; you should wear blue more often.' He tucked her arm through his and for once she was grateful for the assurance of his presence. 'There are some people I want you to meet.'

Alixe stifled a groan. Jamie meant well, but he worried too much about her. As a result, he was always trying to matchmake.

'Alixe, it will be all right. These are friends of mine from university. Now, be nice. Here they are,' he whispered at her ear, whisking her into the drawing room.

A group of gentlemen stood near the doorway. At Jamie's entrance, four pairs of eyes turned her direction. One set she recognised. They belonged to the squire's son. The other six belonged to two dark-haired devils and one angel—one very naughty angel, an angel she'd seen naked.

Alixe froze, her mind racing with all nature of embarrassing scenarios. Perhaps he wouldn't recognise her. In her expensive evening gown she hardly looked like the girl tramping in the woods.

Jamie proudly pulled her forwards. There was nothing to do but brave it out. 'Let me introduce all of you to my sister, Lady Alixe Burke. Alixe dear, these are the old friends from university I was telling you about. Riordan Barrett, Ashe Bedevere and Merrick St Magnus.'

Great, now the angel had a name.

'*Enchanté,* mademoiselle.' Merrick bowed over her hand, his eyes trained on her face the whole while. He'd learned early how to read a woman. Elegant gowns and complicated coiffures often hid a multitude of sins or truths, depending on how you looked at it. To really see a woman's identity, one had to look at her face. In this case, he was not distracted by the fine gown and the sophisticated twist of hair.

It was definitely *her.*

He'd know those long-lashed sherry eyes anywhere. They'd been the most expressive part of her today. They'd been wide with an intriguing mixture of shock and curiosity. If her eyes weren't enough, there was her mouth. Merrick considered himself a great connoisseur of mouths and this one begged to be kissed. Not that he'd be doing any kissing of Jamie Burke's sister. She was the kind of girl who was off limits and he'd already danced fairly near the fire today, even if by accident.

She gave a short incline of her head, greeted the others in a perfunctory manner and made polite excuses to go in search of a girlfriend. But Merrick watched her leave them only to stand with Lady Folkestone and a group of older matrons near the wide fireplace. He didn't sport with those who didn't welcome it. Ordinarily, he'd feel badly about causing a shy young lady discomfort. But in this case, he knew better. Alixe Burke was no retiring miss, no matter her airs to the contrary. She was due for a little provoking. After all, she'd 'provoked' him that afternoon. Turnabout was fair play.

Jamie noticed his distraction. 'Perhaps I could arrange for you to take Alixe in to supper.'

Jamie was one of those rare individuals who could make wishes come true. At Oxford, they'd had only to voice a want and Jamie would see it granted. In the years since then, that ability had not changed and now, even though there were two gentlemen present who technically outranked the second son of a marquis, Merrick found himself conveniently seated beside the somewhat-aloof person of Alixe Burke. That was about to change. He wanted to see her face alive with surprise, or with any emotion. This expression of bland passivity she wore in polite company did not do her features justice.

'Miss Burke, I cannot shake the feeling that we've met before,' he murmured as the first course was set in front of them.

'That would be unlikely. I am not much in London,' came the short ten-word response followed by a curt smile.

He'd thought that would be her gambit. She was pretending she didn't recognise him. Either that or hoping he didn't recognise her. But it was all pretence. Her left hand lay fisted in her lap, a sure sign of tension.

'Then perhaps we've met around here,' Merrick offered amiably, pushing the subject. She'd been a delightful juxtaposition of emotions that afternoon—part of her trying to pretend naked men in ponds was *de rigueur* while the other part of her had been rampantly excited by the titillating disturbance. He wanted that woman back. That woman was intriguing. This woman sitting next to him was a mere shell for that other person.

She set down her spoon with deliberate firmness and fairly rounded on him with all the chagrin allowed at a dinner table. 'Lord St Magnus, I seldom go out even around here. I spend my time with local historians. So unless you are involved in the work of restoring medieval documents from Kent, we most certainly have never met.' That was the shell talking. No woman with a mouth like hers was as proper as she was pretending.

Merrick stifled a grin. He was getting to her. She was past ten words now. 'But surely, Lady Alixe, you must, on occasion, walk through the woods and visit a pond or two. Perhaps we met there.'

'What an outrageous place to meet.' A blush started

up her cheeks. She must realise the game was up or very nearly so.

Merrick gave her a moment to regroup while the servants removed the first course. The second course arrived and Merrick fired his next salvo. 'Of course, it is possible that you simply don't recognise me. If it's the occasion I am thinking of, you were wearing an old olive-green dress and I was wearing my birthday suit.'

To her credit, Lady Alixe choked only mildly on her wine. 'I beg your pardon?'

'My birthday suit, nature's garb, my Altogether.'

She set her wine glass aside and fixed him with a hard stare. 'I knew precisely what you meant the first time. What I cannot fathom is why you want to recall the event at all. A gentleman would never confront a lady with a blatant reminder of such a difficult and accidental encounter.'

'Perhaps you are making faulty assumptions when drawing that conclusion.' Merrick sat back and waited for the next remove.

'You are familiar with syllogisms, Lady Alixe?' he continued easily after the servants had done their work. 'Man is mortal, Socrates is a man, therefore Socrates is mortal. In this case, gentlemen don't discommode ladies, Merrick St Magnus is a gentleman, therefore, he won't bring up the little escapade at the pond this afternoon. Is that how your reasoning went, Lady Alixe?'

'I had no idea the three of you were taking a splash.'

'Ah, so you do remember me?'

Alixe pursed her lips and capitulated. 'Yes, Lord St Magnus, I remember you.'

'Good. I'd hate to be unmemorable. Most ladies find my "Altogether" quite memorable.'

'I'm sure they do.' She took a bite of her beef in a clear tactic to tersely end the conversation.

'Do I hear another syllogism in the making, Lady Alixe? Most ladies like my "Altogether". Lady Alixe is a lady, therefore…'

'No, you do not hear another syllogism in the making. What you hear is an exception.'

Merrick gave her a lingering smile. 'Then I shall endeavour to change your mind.' This was by far the most interesting conversation he'd had in ages, probably because how it would turn out was not a forgone conclusion. He wasn't use to that. With his usual sort of woman, conversation was *always* a prelude to a rather predictable outcome. That wasn't to say the outcome wasn't pleasurable, just predictable.

Too bad it was nearly time to turn the table and engage the partner on his other side. Even if he didn't recognise the signs that the table was about to shift, Lady Alixe's deep sigh of relief would have cued him. He wouldn't let her go that easily.

With a last sortie of mischief, Merrick leaned close to Lady Alixe, close enough to smell the lemon-lavender scent of her *toilette* water, and said in a conspiratorial whisper, 'Don't worry, we can talk later this evening over the tea cart.'

'I wasn't worried.' She managed to smile through clenched teeth.

'Yes, you were.'

Lady Alixe turned to the man on her other side but not before her slipper-clad foot managed a parting kick to his ankle beneath the table. He would have laughed, but it hurt too much.

Chapter Three

Dinner lost some of its lustre after that. The squire's wife on his left was quite willing to engage in light flirtatious banter, but it was far less exciting than sparring with the stoic Lady Alixe. It had been a hard-won battle to wring the slightest smile from Lady Alixe, who'd been trying so desperately to ignore him. The squire's wife smiled rather easily and laughed at everything, a conquest of moments.

After-dinner brandy dragged on with tedium. Merrick spent most of his time attempting to align the pretty but remote Lady Alixe from dinner with the openly curious girl at the pond. There'd been signs of that girl. Lady Alixe's wit was finely honed and quite humorous in a dry sense when she gave it free rein. But she clearly hadn't wanted to be recognised and not surprisingly so. If anyone got wind of their encounter the consequence could be dire for them both.

For the record, he'd have to be clear on that point with Ashe and Riordan. He didn't truly worry they'd match the girl up with Lady Alixe. They'd been too far out in the pond to get a good look at her today and Lady Alixe wasn't the type of girl either of them would look twice at. Most of that was Lady Alixe's own doing, Merrick suspected. She had many excellent features. She simply chose not to maximise them and her sharp tongue would deter anyone from looking more closely at what was on offer. Ordinarily, he'd not have looked more closely either if it hadn't been for the incident at the pond.

But now that he had, he wanted an even closer look at Lady Alixe Burke, who lived in something of a self-imposed social limbo. She had the potential to be pretty, had the propensity for clever conversation and had her father's money. There was no reason she wasn't up in London dazzling the *ton*'s bachelors or at the very least kicking them in the shins. Merrick smiled to himself. Hmmm. A mystery. If there was *no reason*, then by logical extension there was a *very good reason* she wasn't in London. He was eager to get back to the drawing room.

In the drawing room, Merrick spotted Lady Alixe quickly. She was precisely where he thought she'd be, sitting on a sofa with an elderly neighbour, patiently listening to whatever the lady was saying. He filed the information away. Lady Alixe fancied herself a retiring sort, a bookish sort. What was it she'd said at dinner? She worked with local historians? Intriguing.

He approached the sofa and made the appropriate flattering remarks to the older lady, who probably only

heard half of them. 'Lady Alixe, might I steal you away
for a moment or two?'

'What could you possibly have left to say to me?'
she asked as Merrick manoeuvred them over to osten-
sibly take in a painting on the far wall.

'I think we need to agree that our encounter is to
remain a private event between the two of us,' Merrick said in low tones.

'I do not wish to have you blather about it to anyone
any more than you would want me to publicly discover
that the girl in question was you. We both know what
society's answer to such a scandal would be.'

'I do not "blather".'

'Of course not, Lady Alixe. My apologies. I confused blathering with kicking me under the table.'

She ignored the reference. 'And your friends, they
do not blather either, I assume.'

'No, they will not say anything,' Merrick promised.

'Then we have reached an accord and you need not
seek my company out again.'

'Why so unfriendly, Lady Alixe?'

'I know men like you.'

He smiled at that. 'What, precisely, is a "man like
me"?'

'Trouble, with a capital "T".'

'That might be because you're beginning the sentence with it.'

'Or it might be because you charm women into compromising themselves with you. You, sir, are a rake if
ever I've seen one.'

'Have you seen one? A rake? How would you know?

Oh, I forgot, you've seen the *David.* Well, for your information, I know women like you, too. You think you don't have much use for men, but that's because you haven't met the right one.'

That sobered her up. 'You are too bold and you are no gentleman.'

Merrick laughed. 'No, I'm not. You should have known better, Lady Alixe. Don't young misses learn in the schoolroom that you can always tell a gentleman by his clothes?'

Her jaw tightened. 'I must admit, my lord, on that point you have me at a distinct disadvantage.' Lady Alixe turned on her heel and made a smart retreat to the newly arrived tea cart.

In a quiet corner of the room, Archibald Redfield watched the animated exchange between St Magnus and Alixe Burke. It was the second such interaction they'd had that evening. He couldn't hear what was being said, but St Magnus was laughing and Alixe Burke was in a high-coloured huff as she set off for the tea cart. That was nothing new. Alixe Burke was a shrew in his opinion. He didn't have much use for sharp-tongued women unless they were rich or knew how to use their tongues in other ways.

Fortunately Alixe Burke was quite rich and so he tolerated what he classified as her less-attractive qualities. Redfield tapped his fingers idly on the arm of the chair, considering. Things were not getting off to a brilliant start. He'd come to the house party with the specific intention of putting himself into Alixe Burke's good graces. She'd shunned his advances earlier this spring and he was hoping to recoup his losses there. He'd arrived early that afternoon, only to discover she was out somewhere. She hadn't put in an appearance until dinner and then she had been seated too far away from him for conversation. Now, that libertine from London was stealing a march on him.

It was not to be tolerated. He had chosen Alixe Burke as a most specific target. She was the reason he was in this sleepy part of Kent to begin with. He'd done his research in London, looking for 'forgotten' heiresses, or wealthy spinsters on the shelf. In other words, women who might be susceptible to a man's charms, or families desperate to marry them off. That's when he'd heard of Alixe Burke, from a viscount she'd rejected. She hadn't been back in town since. So he'd come to her, pretending to be a gentleman. He'd even gone so far as to buy an old manse in the area to complete the charade. After having done so much, he would not lose his advantage to a golden-haired second son who deserved the title of 'lord' no more than he did himself.

St Magnus—where had he heard that name? Oh, yes, the son of the Marquis of Crewe. Always in the midst of a scandal—most lately it had been something with the Greenfield Twins. Redfield was thoughtful for a moment. Maybe he could use St Magnus and his wild tendencies, after all. He would wait and watch for his opportunity.

Alixe had taken the first opportunity to retire for the night, something she should have done hours ago.

In the privacy of her room, Alixe pulled the pins from her hair and shook the dark mass free, breathing a sigh of relief.

The evening had gone moderately well if she counted the fact that this time she'd managed to stay upright in his presence. Kicking him was probably not the best choice, but, all in all, she had survived mostly intact. Somehow she'd managed to sit through dinner *beside* him and not become entirely witless under the barrage of his clever conversation. While it hadn't gone well, it certainly could have gone worse. If things had gone well, he wouldn't have shown up at all. If things had gone worse…worse hardly bore thinking about. After all, he hadn't shouted their encounter from the rooftops and he'd sworn himself to secrecy.

Her secret was safe with him and depressingly so. If the secret got out, he'd have to marry her and that could hardly be what a man like Merrick St Magnus wanted. He'd want a beautiful, stylish woman who said sophisticated things.

Alixe gave her reflection in the mirror a sultry smile, a smile she'd never dare to use in public. She pulled the bodice of her gown down a bit lower and shrugged a coy shoulder. 'Why, St Magnus, it is you. I hardly recognised you with your clothes on.' She gave a toss of her head and lowered her voice to a purr. 'So you do have clothes. I was beginning to wonder after all this time.' A sophisticated woman would trail a well-manicured nail down his chest, look up at him with smoky eyes and he would know exactly what she wanted. And then he'd give it to her. One had only to look at him to know his body didn't promise pleasure idly. Whereas, she would only be that sophisticated woman in the solitude of her room.

Alixe pulled up the bodice of her gown and rang for her maid. It was time to put the fantasy to bed, among other things. That was precisely what St Magnus was. What he promised was a temporary escape. It wasn't real.

She knew what society said a real marriage was. It was what her handful of lacklustre suitors had seen when they looked at her: a responsible alliance that came with an impeccable lineage, a respectable dowry and a nice bosom. Admittedly, it was a lot to look beyond. No one had made the effort yet. That suited her. She'd seen the reality and decided it was better to hole up in the country with her work than to become trapped in a miserable relationship.

Her maid entered the room and helped her out of the dress and into her nightgown, brushed out her hair and turned down her bedcovers. It was the same routine every night and it would be for the rest of her life. Alixe crawled beneath the covers and shut her eyes, trying to shut out the day. But Merrick St Magnus's face was not easily dismissed. His deep blue eyes danced in her head as her mind chased around the question, 'Shouldn't there be more than this?'

After a restless half-hour, Alixe threw back the covers and snatched up a robe. Sleep was hours away. She could use the time productively, making up for what she'd lost this afternoon at the lake. She'd go to the library and work on her manuscript. Then, she'd try to sleep and when she woke up she would spend the day avoiding St Magnus. A man like him was anathema to a girl like her. Women didn't want to resist St Magnus and she was not arrogant enough to think it would be any different for her. He'd never be more than trouble to any girl. Heaven help the fools who actually fell in love with him.

The routine was somewhat successful in its goal. Over the next few days, she did her best to keep out of St Magnus's way. She was careful to come down only after the men had left for whatever manly excursion had been planned for their mornings while the ladies took care of their correspondence and needlework. At dinner, she managed to avoid being seated next to him. After dinner, she retired as early as courtesy allowed, to her brother's dismay, and spent her evenings in the library.

That was not to say she'd been entirely successful in erasing the presence of Merrick St Magnus. She did sneak a few glances at dinner. It was hard not to. When he was in the room he became its centre, a golden sun around which the rest of the company revolved. She'd hear his voice in the halls, always laughing, always ready with a quip. If she was on the verandah quietly reading, he'd be on the lawns playing bowls with Jamie. If she was taking her turn at the pianoforte in the evenings, he was playing cards near by, charming the old ladies. It quickly became apparent her only real retreat was the library, the one room he had no inclination or purpose to visit. That was all right with her—a girl needed time to herself.

Chapter Four

As house parties went, this one was proving to be exceptionally virtuous. There were guests aplenty of just the right ages and gender to make an excellent population for all the different entertainments Lady Folkestone had meticulously planned. But while the girls were pretty and the widows or other unattached ladies of a certain age happy to flirt lightly with their conversation, they were all respectable. In fact, after three days of taking the party's measure, Merrick concluded the girls in attendance were as notorious for their goodness as the Greenfield Twins were for their badness, a comparison he voiced out loud to the late-night group of gentlemen who'd gathered restlessly in the billiards room after the rest of the company had gone up to bed.

The eight gentlemen laughed heartily at his complaint. It wasn't that Merrick did not appreciate the house party. The affair was brilliant on all accounts. The entertainments were actually entertaining; there had been fishing for the gentlemen just today in the East Stour River at Postling. There'd been cards and billiards with light wagering on the side that had allowed Merrick to add to his stash of pound notes. Certainly not the sums available in London's gaming hells, but something all the same. The food was excellent, Folkestone's easy largesse abundantly displayed on the dining-room sideboards with three meals a day and two teas.

Above all, Merrick was thankful. Whatever was lacking in his usual vices, simply being here offset the loss. Here, he could take double pleasure in having thwarted his father's attempt to rein him in and in having minimised his expenses. For the next two weeks he was free.

All he had to do was please the ladies in attendance. If that pleasing occurred outside the bedroom door, that was a small price to pay. To date, Merrick had done an admirable job of fulfilling his obligations. He'd made himself available to all the ladies present, from elderly Mrs Pottinger to shy young Viola Fleetham. The only lady he'd been unable to charm was the elusive Alixe Burke, whom he had only caught glimpses of since the first evening. It was too bad, really; he enjoyed needling her just to hear what she'd say.

'St Magnus, tell us about some of your scandals in London,' one of the younger fellows present piped up. 'I hear you had quite the curricle race recently.'

'I hear you nearly had carnal knowledge of both Greenfield Twins at the same time,' another rash young pup put in. 'Tell us about that.'

'That's nothing, laddies, compared to his escapade on the way here,' Riordan drawled, swigging heavily from the ever-present flask. Riordan had drunk far too much for Merrick's tastes since they'd arrived, but saying anything about it made him sound like a prude so he'd refrained. 'Tell 'em about the pond.'

Merrick shot Riordan a quelling look. The man was worse than an old biddy. The last thing Merrick wanted to do was talk about the pond. 'That's hardly anything, nothing happened,' Merrick tried to pass it off.

'It's hilarious,' Riordan protested. 'Never mind, if you won't tell it, I will.' He recognised he had the audience hanging on his every word. Riordan leaned forwards hands on thighs. 'We stopped by a pond for a bit of a bathe before we arrived.'

'Which pond?' one asked before another punched him in the shoulder for being a dolt.

'The one on the edge of the property, near Richland's farm.' Riordan said, idly picking up the story again. 'Anyway, *where* the pond is isn't the real tale. It's *what* happened. There we were, stripped down to nothing and splashing away when all of the sudden this girl comes crashing through the woods.' Riordan paused and clapped Merrick on the back in male camaraderie. 'Our man gets out of the pond and startles the poor chit senseless. She's so overwhelmed by the sight of his pizzle she falls over a log and can't get up, so this good chap here offers to help her up. Mind you, he's naked as a newborn babe the whole time and there's more dangling over her than just his hand.'

There was a general uproar of laughter around him,

a few of them slapping him on the back with comments like, 'St Magnus, you're the luckiest devil ever, women literally fall over themselves to get to you.' Merrick tried to laugh good naturedly with them. Normally, he would have laughed the loudest. Riordan was a great storyteller—he'd turned the escapade into the stuff of legends. But knowing the girl in question was Jamie's sister gave the tale a dangerous edge.

Women *did* fall over themselves for him and what he offered, but they were women who could afford the luxury. The Greenfield Twins were courtesans, for heaven's sake. That was the kind of woman he dabbled with. They were like him. He never trifled with women who couldn't afford to play his games, never made them the butt of his wagers. No one suffered for his entertainments. The Greenfield Twins had *wanted* him to take them both. But Alixe Burke had wanted no part of what had happened at the pond. His code of ethics demanded he protect her. That was where he differed from his father. The innocent deserved protection when their paths crossed with those more worldly.

'It's easy to seduce the willing,' came the words from a handsome but sly-eyed fellow lounging on the group's periphery. Redfield was his name. Merrick didn't care for him. He was always watching people. 'Why don't we have you prove your reputation? We'll design a wager for you.'

Merrick raised his eyebrows at that. What in the world could these young rascals design that would actually stump *him*?

'We should all get to wager on it. I'll bet on St Magnus to do just about anything. I'm in.' Ashe withdrew a money clip from a waistcoat pocket and laid its contents on the table. 'Shall we split the winnings, old chap?' Ashe winked at him.

Merrick appreciated the show of support, but not the mounting pressure. Ashe's finances were no more stable than his own. If Ashe was in, there'd be no backing out. He couldn't let his friend down. To be fair, Merrick didn't want to back out. The money accumulating on the table was no small sum. He couldn't win that sum at the genteel wagers made at cards in the next two weeks. Yet, a very small piece of his conscience niggled him to be cautious.

Merrick drew a deep breath and fixed the young cockerel with a confident stare. 'What shall you dare me to do?'

'Well, since the party is so "virtuous" in your own words, I think you should steal a kiss before sunrise.'

'You can kiss me right now, St Magnus, and we'll claim victory before midnight,' Ashe quipped drily from his corner.

'Rule number one, you must steal a kiss from a *lady*,' Redfield qualified. 'That means no going belowstairs to wake the maids, that's too easy.' Redfield looked like the sort who would know; probably spent too much time chasing the maids since he couldn't catch anyone else. Everyone knew the maids were somewhat obliged to endure such advances if they valued their positions. Merrick didn't respect a man like that.

'Other rules?' Merrick enquired coolly. He was already thinking of who'd be most likely to put up with such a dare. The attractive Widow Whitely, perhaps.

'Proof, we must have proof,' one of Redfield's chums put in. The wagering had created a clear division between the young bucks and the 'old regime'.

That was potentially dangerous. 'No, I draw the line there,' Merrick spoke up. 'A token might be recognised, thus incriminating the lady. I won't be a party to that. You'll just have to take my word as a gentleman.' That brought a round of laughter as he expected and Redfield had to relent on that account.

Redfield's eyes gleamed wickedly. 'Since we must keep the game decent, I say St Magnus must confine his efforts to the library. There will be no roaming of the house or sneaking into bedrooms.'

There went the idea of enticing Widow Whitely. Merrick had the distinct impression she didn't read much. But neither did he. 'It's a little past midnight, I doubt there's much feminine traffic in the library at this hour.' Merrick shrugged. 'What happens if I sit there all night and no one suitable for kissing shows up?'

'Then no one wins or loses,' Redfield replied too easily for Merrick's liking. Redfield thought someone would be there. Merrick could see it in the confident tilt of his head. The man was an ass and a pompous one at that. He was a silly man, too, if this wager was the best he could do for excitement. But Redfield clearly had something planned. Did Redfield think whoever would be in the library would be immune to his charms? Merrick was equally as confident. He had stolen far more than kisses for far less than the money lying there on the billiards table and no one had had any complaints. Whatever Redfield had in mind, Merrick wouldn't know what it was if he didn't go and find out. With an exaggerated salute to the crowd, Merrick set out for the library.

The library was dark when Merrick arrived. No surprise there. It was late for reading unless someone was having difficulty sleeping. Merrick took his time, lighting a few of the lamps and giving the room some life. It was a well-appointed room with a long reading table that ran down the centre, a green-veined marble fireplace with a cluster of chairs and sofa about it, a few small tables and chairs scattered near the wide windows for reading and walls lined with carefully selected books.

Merrick scanned the titles with modest interest. He could see Jamie's hand in the selection. Jamie had excelled at history while they were at Oxford and his love for the subject was readily evident in the titles on display. For himself, Merrick hadn't the aptitude for history like Jamie, or Italian music like Ashe or Riordan's love of Renaissance art. He'd discovered his own niche in languages, a field where he could excel in conversation.

Merrick plucked a book from the shelf at random and settled into a chair near the fireplace to wait. He'd managed to get through the first five pages when the door opened. The newcomer was definitely female, dressed in a plain-blue robe with the hem of a white nightrail peeping beneath it. Her back was to him,

showing off a long thick braid of nut-brown hair as
she made great effort to quietly shut the door behind
her. Whoever she was, she wasn't supposed to be here
or at the very least didn't want to be discovered here.
He couldn't help her with that. Any moment now she'd
turn around and be surprised to see him.

But then she did turn and the surprise was all his.
Damn and double damn, the one person who'd come to
the library was the one person he hadn't seen for days:
Alixe Burke. Suspicion flicked across his mind for an
instant. He'd hardly got settled, hardly begun to read
his admittedly boring tome on the history of French
kings, and she'd shown up. If he'd stopped along the
way, he might have missed his chance altogether. Had
Redfield known she'd be here? A simple wager was
becoming suddenly more complex.

Merrick grinned. 'So this is where you've been hiding.'

Alixe clutched the neck of her robe closed at the
throat out of instinct. 'What are *you* doing here?'

'You sound surprised to see me.' Merrick waved
the book he held in one hand. 'I am reading up on the
French kings.'

'I'm surprised to see *anyone* in the library after
midnight,' Alixe retorted.

'And yet *you're* here,' he replied glibly, those blue
eyes of his studying her with a disquieting intensity
that stirred up a warm flurry of butterflies in her stomach. That look made a woman believe he was waiting

just for her. Yet, that was improbable. He hadn't known she'd be here.

'Why aren't you playing billiards with the other men?' She was surprised, disturbed, dismayed. The list of adjectives was quite long. Three days of avoiding him and he'd still managed to turn her thoughts to incoherent mush in a matter of minutes. She needed him to go away.

She'd hoped to make some progress on her latest translation. She'd promised Vicar Daniels she'd have the translation ready for display at the village fair less than two weeks away.

'I haven't seen much of you since the party began. I hope you haven't been avoiding me?' Merrick said casually. He kicked his booted legs, very *long* booted legs, up on the fireplace fender, dispelling any hopes that he might vacate the premises soon. Apparently the French kings were more scintillating than she'd thought.

'Of course not. Why would you think that?' Alixe said, hoping her lie wouldn't show.

Merrick shrugged. 'I'm glad to hear it. I thought perhaps our encounter at the pond had disconcerted you in spite of my assurances.' He opened his book and returned to his reading.

Dratted man. Why did he have to pick tonight to read? Alixe began to debate the options in her head: stay or go? This was absurd. Conventional wisdom suggested she leave the room immediately. Unmarried women didn't entertain men in their nightclothes. Unmarried women didn't entertain naked men at ponds either and she'd already done that. By comparison, this was by far the lesser of those two evils. She should leave.

But her stubborn nature could not tolerate defeat. The thought of departing the field while her work beckoned galled. No man had ever dictated her choices over decisions far bigger than this. She wouldn't give up ground over something so minor. St Magnus had already cost her an afternoon. She would not let him steal a night, too. There was always a chance she could outlast him.

'Are you going to come away from the door? You needn't worry, I've seen ball gowns far more revealing than your nightwear.' He spoke without looking up from his book, but the challenge was clear. He was daring her to stay.

Alixe made a face at the back of his head. She must look like a silly ninny to him, clutching her old robe and hovering at the door. Is that what he saw when he looked at her? A spinster afraid of being in the presence of a dazzlingly handsome man?

Anger flared. That settled it.

She *wasn't* a spinster.

She wasn't afraid.

She also wasn't leaving.

Alixe stalked towards the long table in the centre of the room and pulled out a chair. She sat down and did her best to get to work. It was clear she'd have to try harder to avoid St Magnus. She had not fought her battles for the freedom to live her own life only to give up those victories to a pair of flirting blue eyes. Still, it was better to know the chinks in one's own armour before one's enemy did. She'd recognised that day at the pond St Magnus's potent appeal and how she'd responded most wantonly. It would not do to keep putting such temptation in her path if it could be avoided.

She'd managed the bucks of the *ton*, but they didn't unnerve her the way he did. St Magnus's witty and overly personal conversation at dinner had made her feel unique, made her feel that she was beautiful enough on her own merits to attract the attentions of a handsome man without her dowry to speak for her. But he was a rake. Nothing good could come from an association with St Magnus. She was smart enough to know that from the start.

Her efforts to work lasted all of five minutes.

'What are you working on?'

Alixe looked up from her books and papers. He'd turned his head to watch her. 'I'm translating an old medieval manuscript about the history of Kent.' That should bore him enough to stop asking questions. 'The vicar is putting on an historic display about our area at the upcoming fair and this document is supposed to be part of it.' She put an extra emphasis on 'supposed', to imply that interruptions were not welcome. Usually, such a hint did the trick. Usually there was no need to resort to that second level of defence. Men stopped being interested much earlier. The words 'translating an old medieval manuscript' were typically enough.

In this case, the effect was quite opposite. St Magnus uncrossed his long legs, set aside the French kings and strode towards the table with something akin to interest in his blue eyes. 'How's it going?'

'How's *what* going?' Alixe clutched at the neck of her robe again out of reflex, her tone sharp.

'Your translation? I take it the original isn't in modern English.' St Magnus gestured towards the papers.

It wasn't going well at all. The old French was proving to be difficult, especially in places where the manuscript had worn away or been smudged. But she wasn't going to admit that to this man who played havoc with her senses.

Three days of assiduously avoiding his company had not met with successful results. All her efforts, and he ended up in her—*her*—library anyway, the one room where she thought she'd be alone. Her avoidance strategies certainly hadn't dulled her awareness of him either. Even at midnight, he still looked immaculate. His shoulders were just as broad, his legs just as long, his hips just as lean as she remembered them. She knew for a fact that well-hewn muscle lay beneath the layers of his clothes, providing the necessary infrastructure for that most excellent physique. But all that was merely window-dressing for the arresting blue eyes that had a way of looking at one as if they could see right through a person's exterior, stripping away more than clothes, making one believe she was, for the moment, the centre of his universe.

She had to remind herself that plenty of women had been the centre of his universe. Jamie's quiet caution ran through her head. St Magnus was a fine friend for a gentleman, but not for the sisters of gentlemen. She had no trouble believing it.

'Perhaps I can help?' He settled his long form beside her on the bench.

Alixe's senses vibrated with warning. She could smell the remnants of his evening *toilette* before dinner, the scent of his washing soap mingling with a light cologne, a tantalising mixture of oak and lavender, with something mysterious beneath.

'I doubt it unless you have some familiarity with Old French.' She meant to be rude, meant to drive him off with her high-handed manner. How dare he walk into her life unannounced and stir things up? And not even mean to do it. He was a stranger who knew nothing about her. He had no idea of what his mere presence had done. She'd just reached a point where she was happy with her choices, with devoting her life to her work. The very last thing she needed was to convince herself a man of St Magnus's ilk appreciated her efforts and not her dowry. In the past, that road had been extremely dangerous, not to mention disappointing, to travel.

St Magnus's next words stunned her. 'It just so happens that I have more than a passing acquaintance with Old French.'

This flaxen-haired charmer with azure eyes was conversant in an obscure language? What he did next was even more astonishing. He shrugged out of his jacket and rolled up his sleeves. He slid closer to her, oblivious to their thighs bumping beneath the table.

She wasn't oblivious, however. Every nerve in her body was acutely aware of each move he made.

'The document isn't that exciting.' Alixe tried one last time to turn him away. 'It's just a farmer who writes about his livestock. He's especially obsessed with his pigs.'

Merrick tilted his head and studied her. She shifted uncomfortably in her seat. '*Just* a farmer who writes? In this case, it's not what he writes about that is important, it's that he writes at all.'

The import of it struck her with a shocking clarity. In her hurry to translate the document she'd forgotten to look beyond the words on the page and into the context of the times in which it had been written. 'Of course,' she murmured. 'A farmer who is literate most likely isn't only a farmer or a tenant renting fields, he's probably of some status in the community.'

Merrick smiled. It was a different smile this time, one full of enthusiasm. 'What's the date of the document?'

'My guess is mid-thirteenth century, about 1230.'

'Post-Magna Carta,' Merrick mused more to himself than to her. 'Perhaps he is a self-made man, an early instance of the gentry class, not a noble or beholden directly to a king, but a man who has determined his own worth.' He sounded almost wistful as he voiced his thoughts.

'In pigs.' Alixe smiled. 'Don't forget the pigs.'

Merrick chuckled. 'Show me the pigs. After all your mentions of them, I want to read about them for myself.'

Alixe passed him the pages on the pigs and he fell to reading them with surprising thoroughness, one long finger moving across the lines one word at a time, his eyes following. Within moments, he was completely absorbed in the reading and Alixe turned her thoughts to the pages in front of her, aware in the back of her mind that something astounding had occurred: she was working on her translation with Merrick St Magnus, London's most talked-about male. More than that, he'd shown himself to be more than a handsome face. He'd been interested, intelligent and insightful. Amazing.

Truly, it was nothing short of miraculous. No one would believe her if she told them. She was starting to see why a friendship had sprung up between Merrick and Jamie at school. Like her, Jamie loved history and Merrick understood its sociological aspects.

Merrick laughed suddenly, breaking the compatible silence that had sprung up. 'It's not his pigs he writes about, Alixe.' His eyes were dancing with good humour. 'It's his wife.'

Alixe furrowed her brow. 'I don't believe you.' She reached across him without thinking for the page. 'There…' She pointed to a line. 'That is very clearly the word for pig. More specifically, "sow".'

Merrick nodded. 'It is. But you're forgetting the use of "like". It's a simile. I think you were reading it as "she is a big sow". But we should be reading it as "she's as big as the sow".' Merrick reached around her. 'Show me the later pages. I want to bear out my hypothesis that his wife is expecting a child in the very near future.'

'Yes!' Merrick crowed a few moments later. 'He's writing about his wife. Have a look, Alixe.' He pushed the page towards her and leaned close, one arm on the other side of her to brace himself as they studied the page together.

'You're right.' Alixe enthused, her excitement evident. Her mind rushed forwards. 'I wonder if there would be parish records. I wonder if we could find him. If we could, we might be able to determine where his land was. We could find out how the story ends, if his baby is born safely.' Alixe bit her lip, realising what she'd done. She'd said 'we'. 'I'm sorry, I'm getting carried away. We'll probably never know what happened to him.'

Merrick smiled. 'Maybe *we* will. I'll be here for two weeks. Surely that's enough time to puzzle out how your farmer's story ends.' For all purposes, he looked as if he was genuinely enjoying himself. He looked as if he wanted to be here with her instead of downstairs playing billiards.

Alixe looked down at her hands, regretting some of her earlier thoughts about him. 'I must apologise. I didn't think it could be like this.'

He covered her hands with one of his own where they lay on the table. It was a gentle gesture and his hands were warm and firm. She didn't think it was meant to be a seductive gesture, but that didn't stop a *frisson* of warm heat from shooting through her arm at the contact.

'It or me? You didn't think *it* could be like this or

that *I* couldn't be like this?' Merrick spoke in low tones, his gaze holding hers.

'You,' Alixe replied honestly, meeting his gaze. 'I didn't think you could be like this. I misjudged you.'

'I'm glad to have surprised you,' Merrick said softly, his voice igniting the tiny space between them with a sharp awareness of one another. Their eyes held and in the cocoon of the moment the briefest of thoughts occurred to Alixe: he's going to kiss me.

That was exactly the same idea voiced seconds later when Archibald Redfield burst into the library with an angry, newly awoken Earl of Folkestone in his wake, still belting his robe and all but bellowing the traditional words of horrified fathers everywhere when discovering their daughters in compromising situations. 'What is the meaning of this?'

To which Alixe managed the most unoriginal of answers, 'It's not what it looks like.' But she knew what it looked like—Merrick sitting so very close to her, his sleeves rolled up, and she in her nightclothes.

To which Archibald Redfield countered unhelpfully with an arrogant smirk, 'It's precisely what it looks like. St Magnus wagered several gentlemen in the billiards room not an hour ago that he'd steal a kiss from a lady before the night was out', then went on to add as if it would improve matters, 'I have witnesses.'

Alixe groaned. He'd bet on stealing a kiss. She should have left the room when common sense had demanded it.

'No, no witnesses, please.' Her father held up the hand of authority. He had his robe belted now and was in full command of the situation. 'We are all men of honour here,' He looked pointedly at St Magnus as he said it. 'We can sort this out and do what must be done in a quiet manner. There is no need to make an unnecessary fuss.'

Alixe had never seen her father so angry. No one else would guess the depths of his anger. He was one of those men whose voice became more controlled when angered. Then he spared a glance for her, taking in her completely inappropriate attire. There was more than anger in his gaze. There was disappointment, which was worse. She'd seen it before when he looked at her. It seemed she'd spent an inordinate amount of her life disappointing him. But this time would be the last time. She could see in his face he'd decided it would be so and that frightened her very much.

Her father jerked his head at her with a dismissing nod. 'Go to your room and stay there. We'll speak in the morning. As for you, St Magnus, I'll settle with you right now. Put your jacket on and make yourself presentable.'

Alixe shot a parting glance at St Magnus, although what help she thought she'd find there she didn't know. He'd never been truly interested in her or her work. She'd merely been his most convenient target. He would have kissed whoever walked into the library. He had no reason to help her and, right now, he'd be more worried about trying to help himself.

St Magnus had risen, arms folded, eyes narrowed and burning like hot blue coals. He was a formida-

ble sight, but he spared not a glance for her departing form, she noted. All his attention was directed at
Archibald Redfield.

Chapter Five

Who would have thought the road to nowhere in particular led straight to the Earl of Folkestone's library? Granted the journey had taken the better part of ten years, but right now that only served to make matters worse.

Merrick shifted ever so slightly in his chair. It was one thing to be called on the proverbial carpet by a stuffy peer when one was a young buck about town. It was another when one was nearly thirty and an established rogue. Rogues didn't get caught engaged in minor infractions. One could be caught *in flagrante delicto* with a lovely widow and live it down. But one could absolutely not be caught stealing kisses from an earl's daughter. Yet it seemed he had been and it seemed he was going to pay. The terrible irony was that he hadn't done anything. This time, everything was innocent. Admittedly it looked bad: her apparel, his shirt sleeves, the time of night, their close proximity at the table. Most of all the looming reality of the damning wager with Redfield. All the signs pointed to disaster. In another five minutes it might even have escalated to a real disaster; he might actually have claimed the kiss he was accused of stealing.

'You were attempting to kiss my daughter,' Folkestone spoke, his face a mask of icy contemplation.

'Yes, the key word here is attempting. I had not yet achieved that goal.' Merrick pointed out. Folkestone frowned, not appreciating the clarification.

'I do not care if you were attempting to turn metal into gold. It does not change the fact that you were alone with her at midnight.'

'In the library, sir,' Merrick protested. He'd been about to say the library was the least amorous room in a house, but then he remembered what he'd got up to in the library at the Rowlands' ball a few weeks ago with the lovely Mrs Dennable and thought better of it.

'Thank goodness Redfield is the soul of discretion,' Folkestone commented.

Assuming he has a soul. Merrick let a raised eyebrow convey his question of the assumption. Redfield had set it up, he was sure of that, if not the man's motives. But saying as much would appear petty and it hardly sounded better to say 'any girl would have done as well; it just so happened your daughter walked in first'.

'You've compromised my daughter, but that does not make her an innocent in this. She could have walked out of the room once you made your presence known,' Folkestone mused. His sharp dark eyes, the colour of Alixe's, never left Merrick's face.

'Alixe has always been unconventional. A husband and family would go far, I suspect, in settling her and giving her life some stability.' Merrick sensed Alixe would disagree with her father's assessment, but discreetly kept it to himself.

Folkestone continued. 'Alixe needs a husband.'

It took all of Merrick's willpower to not cringe. He waited for the inevitable. After this evening, Folkestone would expect him to do the right thing and offer for her, a girl he hardly knew.

Folkestone leaned back in his chair and steepled his fingers. 'I am sure you are aware that in most situations of this nature, the gentleman would be expected to marry the lady in question. However, to be blunt, you are not precisely "husband material", no matter who your father is. You have a reputation ten miles' long for licentiousness and general mayhem. Here's what I propose: make my daughter the Toast of the Season.'

Merrick sat a little straighter in his chair, not certain he'd heard correctly or that he'd been reprieved. This option might be worse. 'Sir, it's already June. There will only be six weeks left. I hardly think…'

'Or marry her yourself at Season's end as penance for your failure,' Folkestone cut in. 'You're not the only gambling man in the room, St Magnus. I know all about your reputation. You have no desire to be legshackled. I'm willing to bet you love your freedom enough to see the job done. Goodness knows I'd prefer almost anyone else than you as a son-in-law. I think that's one thing you and I just might agree upon. You no more want to be my son-in-law than I want to have you, no matter what Jamie thinks of you as a friend.'

Valiantly ignoring the insult, Merrick tried a different approach. 'Sir, the people I know are not the best, I'm not sure…'

This too was easily dismissed. 'You're here, aren't you?' Yes, dammit, he hadn't meant to insult the earl's sterling reputation.

'You do have connections when you choose to exert them, St Magnus. Exert them now or accept the consequences.' Folkestone rose, signalling the end of the interview. 'There's really nothing else to discuss. This is not your decision to make. You made your choice when you engaged my daughter in the library for your silly wager. You have a little under two weeks here in the country to get her up to snuff and the rest of the Season to make her attractive to gentlemen or else align yourself with the fact that you will be taking a September bride.'

The study door opened, admitting Lady Folkestone, hastily dressed and followed by Redfield. 'I've brought your wife,' he said with a tragic flourish. 'Sometimes a woman's view can soften these things.' Yes, definitely a tragic flourish. Surely a man as astute as Folkestone could see through Redfield's façade of helpfulness.

Lady Folkestone was no shrinking violet. She sailed to her husband's side and demanded an explanation, which Folkestone promptly gave. Afterwards, Lady Folkestone turned her thoughtful gaze in Merrick's direction. 'So, you're to marry our daughter?'

'Not necessarily, my lady.' Merrick replied smoothly. 'I hope to help her find a more suitable match.'

Lady Folkestone laughed. 'There is no such thing as a suitable match for Alixe. We've tried for years now. When I say "we", I mean London society collectively, not just her family. She'll have none of the young men on offer.' The bitterness surprised him. It wasn't the attitude he expected a mother to have.

Lady Folkestone waved a dismissive hand. 'She has no regard for the family's wishes. After the last business with Viscount Mandley, all she wants is her manuscripts and her peace.'

Then why don't you let her have it? Was that so much to ask? Folkestone had enough money to support one spinster daughter. The vehemence of his thoughts shocked Merrick.

'Ah, Mandley. That was an unfortunate business indeed. She'll not see a better offer,' Redfield commiserated from the doorway where he hovered as some post-facto guard to their privacy.

'Hardly,' Merrick scoffed. 'Mandley didn't want a wife, he wanted a governess for his three daughters whom he didn't have to pay.' The man might be handsome for a fellow over forty and have plenty of blunt, but he was legendary in London's clubs for his unnecessary penny-pinching. He'd once asked if his subscription to White's could be reduced for the months he spent in the country.

'There's nothing wrong with frugality,' Redfield retorted.

Ah, that reminded him. There was one score he

could settle tonight. Merrick turned and shot Redfield a hard stare. He couldn't do anything more for his own situation at present, but he could still salvage Ashe's. He rose and approached Lady Folkestone. 'I deeply apologise for the untoward actions which have taken place here tonight. I will do my utmost to see that Lady Alixe's reputation emerges from this thoughtless escapade unscathed.' With that, he bent over her hand with all the charm he possessed and kissed her knuckles. 'If you will excuse me? I will look forward to meeting with Lady Alixe in the morning.'

Merrick brushed past Redfield on his way to the door, stopping long enough to murmur, 'I believe you owe me. I'll be waiting outside and expecting payment.'

Merrick found Ashe and Riordan alone in the deserted billiards room, each of them slumped in their chairs. Crisis always had a way of thinning out the crowd. He tossed down a substantial roll of pound notes on the billiards table. 'There's your portion of the winnings.'

Ashe sat up a bit straighter. 'How did you manage this? Were you faster than Redfield?'

Merrick grinned. Besting Redfield was about the only good thing to have happened tonight. 'I kissed Lady Folkestone's hand right in front of him. He had to be the witness to his own dare.'

Ashe visibly relaxed and reached for the winnings. 'Redfield had it planned all along. After you left, he was bragging he knew a certain lady had been visiting the library the last few nights.'

Merrick stiffened at that. 'Was he careless enough to share her name?' Folkestone was counting on discretion, on the fact that no one but he and Redfield knew Alixe had been caught with him in the library.

Ashe shook his head. 'No, no names, just that he knew.'

Merrick nodded. Good. But it didn't make sense he'd deliberately set up a wager he'd lose. Unless he thought Alixe wouldn't succumb.

'But I can surmise from the presence of Lady Folkestone at the interview that the lady in question was Lady Alixe. Jamie will not be pleased,' Ashe said quietly.

'Jamie is not to know.'

'Are wedding bells in your future?' Riordan slurred, offering Merrick his flask.

Merrick waved it a way with a rueful smile. 'Sort of.' He explained the agreement to hush up the indiscretion if he 'helped' Lady Alixe become the Toast of London.

'Then you have truly become a *cicisbeo*, a man whose status and welfare in society rests on his ability to please a lady,' Riordan slurred, unmistakably well into his cups. 'You know, in Italy it works this way, too. Usually it's the husband who picks a *cicisbeo* for his wife, but in this case, her father has picked you to bring her out into society.'

'I don't think it's an apt comparison at all,' Merrick snapped, eager to cut off Riordan's rambling. He was showing all the characteristic signs of launching into a full-blown lecture on Italian culture.

Ashe idly twirled the stem of an empty snifter. 'Do you remember that night at Oxford when we formed the *cicisbei* club?'

Merrick nodded, losing himself for a moment in the reminiscences of a long-ago time. They'd been fool-hardy and a bit naïve. It had seemed a wicked thrill to commit themselves to a lifestyle of 'love', to devote themselves to the pursuit of beauty in all its feminine forms.

'I suppose I've been a *cicisbeo* long before tonight,' Merrick sighed in response to Riordan's comment. He'd made a large part of his living based on charm and ro-mance. He might not be a 'kept' man who was obvi-ously dependent on a woman's gifts to him, but if he looked closely enough at his life, he was dependent in other ways, not that the honesty made him proud to admit it.

A 'life of love' wasn't as glamorous as they'd imag-ined it all those years ago sitting in a student-populated tavern. Then, the road to the future had been long and untravelled—anything was possible. They'd toasted the fact that they were second sons with no expectations placed upon them. There was nothing to inherit but a future they'd carve for themselves. They'd make great reputations as London's finest lovers. It had seemed like jolly good fun at the time.

'Don't worry about it,' Ashe said rather suddenly, his eyes serious and sober in contrast to Riordan's. 'We've all sold ourselves in some way or another. It's impossible not to.'

Merrick stood, adopting a posture of humour, not

wanting to be sucked into Ashe's maudlin philosophy. 'There's no time to worry about it. I've got a bride to transform and a bridegroom to find.'

Heaven forbid that bridegroom end up being him, Merrick mused, taking himself out into the darkened hallway and finding the way to his room. He wasn't a marrying man. His father had made sure of that ages ago and, in the intervening years, he hadn't done much to improve the notion. He was well aware there were too many rumours surrounding him and his profligate behaviours. While the rumours inspired curiosity they also inspired distrust.

An image of Alixe's face, alight with excitement over the translation, came to mind. Tonight had been an unlooked-for surprise. He'd not expected to enjoy the work so much. In fact, there'd been a point where he'd forgotten about the stupid wager altogether. For Alixe's sake, he couldn't forget himself like that again. To a woman of her standards, it wouldn't matter that while many of the rumours were true, a few of the most damaging were false.

Alone in his room, Archibald Redfield drank a silent toast. St Magnus would be gone by sunrise. A man like him had no particular code of honour. With the matrimonial noose dangling over his head, St Magnus would run as fast as he could, leaving the path to Alixe open. Archibald would be on that path, ready to approach Folkestone with an offer to rescue Alixe. Who knew what kind of rumours St Magnus would spread? It had been an expensive victory, but worth it. In one move, he'd managed to eliminate St Magnus from the house party and he'd put Alixe Burke in a corner from which he would gallantly offer to rescue her.

Archibald took another swallow of brandy. An engagement would scotch any blemish to Alixe's reputation. Archibald was certain after this last *débâcle*, Folkestone would be eager to marry Alixe off to the first man who asked, even if he was a mere mister, and Archibald would be there, only too ready to comply. Folkestone would be grateful and that could be useful, too, in perpetuity. Everything was working out brilliantly at last. He couldn't make Alixe marry him, but Folkestone could.

'You cannot make me marry anyone,' Alixe said evenly, matching her father glare for glare across the expanse of his polished mahogany desk. So, this was his plan, the plan she'd waited all night to hear. Merrick St Magnus was to marry her or find someone else to do the deed for him. It was implicitly understood that was the only reason for being made over into the Toast of London.

'I can and I will. We've tolerated your foibles long enough,' came the reply.

Her foibles? Alixe's temper rose. 'My work is important. I am restoring history about our region. This is as much the history of Kent as it is the history of our family.' Her family knew that. 'You think it's important as long as Jamie's the one doing it.'

'It's not appropriate for a woman. No man wants a woman who is more interested in ancient manuscripts

than she is in him.' Her father stood up and strode
around the desk. 'I know what you're thinking, miss.
You're thinking somehow you'll get out of this, that
you'll reject every suitor St Magnus finds and you'll
find a way to run him off at the very last. If you do
that, I'll cut you off without a penny and you can see
exactly how it is for a woman on her own in this world
without the protection of a man's good name.'

That was precisely what she was thinking: the driv-
ing-the-suitors-away part anyway. The last bit worried her. Her father would do it, too. He was furious
this time. If it was possible, he was even more furious
over this than he had been about her rejection of Viscount Mandley.

She had to throw him a proverbial bone if she meant
to renegotiate this. 'I'll go to London after the house
party and finish out the rest of the Season, *without* St
Magnus.' That should appease him.

'No. You've had a chance, *more* than one chance,
to turn London to your favour.' Her father sighed, but
she did not mistake it for a sign that he might be relenting. 'The arrangement isn't all bad. St Magnus has a
certain *savoir-faire* to him; he's stylish and charming
and he's risky without being a full-fledged black rake,
although he skates pretty close to the edge. Being with
him will bring you a cachet of your own, it will help
others see you in a different, in a *better* light. There's
no real chance of actually marrying him, thank goodness. Use him and drop him, Alixe, if he's so distaste-
ful to you. Everyone has a place in this world. It's time
you learned yours.'

So much for her father's version of sympathy.

Alixe cast a beseeching glance her mother's direction, only to receive a slow shake of the head. 'Your father and I are together on this, Alixe.' No help from that quarter. Perhaps she could cajole Jamie into pleading her case. There were any number of stories he could likely tell that would persuade her father to keep her as far from St Magnus as possible.

'One more thing,' her father added. 'We are to say nothing of this to Jamie. It would create a grievous rift in his friendship. We've all agreed to keep this incident quiet.' There went her last hope. Now all that was left was to appeal directly to St Magnus. Surely he was no more enamoured of the tangle they found themselves in than she was.

Chapter Six

It was over. Her bid for freedom was truly over this time. Alixe sank down on a stone bench in the flower garden, setting her empty basket beside her. She was in no mood to pick flowers for the vases in the house, but it gave her a useful excuse to be away from the gaiety of the party. Most of the guests were still lingering over breakfast before preparing to ride out on a jaunt to the Roman ruins.

Her father had meant it this time. There would be no reprieve. In all honesty, he'd been generous in the past. He'd tolerated—she couldn't say forgiven—*tolerated* her rejection of Mandley and, before that, her rejection of the ridiculous Baron Addleborough. He'd tolerated—she couldn't say supported—what he viewed as her oddities: her preference for books and meaningful academic work. She knew it had all been done in the hope that she'd come around and eventually embrace a more traditional, accepted life.

Only it hadn't worked out that way. Instead of deciding to embrace society on her own after realising the supposed error of her ways, she'd retreated. The retreat had started simply. At first, it had been enough to stay in the country and devote her efforts to her history. Then it had become easier and easier to not go back at all. Or perhaps it had become harder to go back. Here, she was less bound by the conventions of fashion and rules under the censorious eyes of society. Here she could avoid the realities of an empty, miserable society marriage. Here, she was happy.

Mostly.

The truth was, for all the solace the country offered, she'd been restless even before St Magnus's foolish wager. She'd spent the summer roaming the countryside, looking for...something. Restlessness and loneliness were the apparent going prices for the relative freedoms afforded by the isolation of the countryside. Now, all of that was about to change and not for the better. She should be more careful what she wished for.

'There you are.'

Ah, her unlikely fairy godmother had come to make a silk purse out of sow's ear. She met St Magnus's easy demeanour with a hard stare. In that moment she hated him, truly hated him. After a night that had upended whatever future he had imagined for himself, he looked refreshed and well dressed, a rather striking contrast to the picture she knew she presented with her dark circles and plain brown gown.

She hadn't slept at all and she hadn't taken any pains this morning to disguise the fact. But St Magnus was impeccably attired for riding in buff breeches, polished boots and deep forest-green jacket. The morning sun glinted off his hair, turning it platinum in the bright light. It was the first time that she had noticed his hair was almost longer than convention dictated, hanging in loose waves to his shoulders, but not nearly long enough to club back. Or was it? Hmmm.

'Is something wrong with my face?' St Magnus enquired, lifting a hand tentatively to his cheek.

'No.' Alixe hastily dragged her thoughts to the present. Wondering about his hair would serve no purpose, no *useful* purpose anyway.

'Good. I've come to discuss our predicament.' St Magnus set her empty basket on the ground and sat down uninvited beside her on the little bench. She was acutely aware of his nearness in the small space and of the other time they'd been so close.

'Do you think this is a good idea?' She tried to slide apart, but there was no place left to slide.

'Discussing our situation?'

'No, sitting so close. The last time was a disaster.'

He eyed her with a wry look. 'I think that's the least of your worries, Alixe. It's certainly the least of mine.'

Alixe. The sound of her name on his lips, so very casual as if they were friends, as if working together last night had meant something instead of being contrived to steal a kiss, sent a small thrill through her until she remembered why he was there. She folded her hands in her lap. 'I imagine you're quite concerned about the little matter of your wager.'

'I am and you should be, too.' He stretched his long legs out in front of him and crossed his booted ankles.

'If I fail, your father will see us married. Neither of us wants that, so tell me who you want to marry and I'll see to it that you have him.'

Alixe snorted. This was like a bad fairy tale. 'How do you propose to do that? You can't wave a magic wand and conjure a husband out of thin air.'

'No, but you can. I can teach you what you need to entice your man of preference. So, name your man. Who do you want?'

Alixe stood and paced the path. 'Let me think… He should be moderately good-looking, moderately young. I don't want anyone too terribly old. He should be intelligent. I would want to have decent conversation over a lifetime of dinners. He should be respectful and he should appreciate me for who I am—'

'No,' St Magnus interrupted.

'No? He shouldn't be respectful or able to make decent conversation at meal time?'

His blue eyes flashed with irritation at her recital of characteristics. 'No, as in I don't want a list of qualities. I want a name. For example, Viscount Hargrove or Baron Hesselton.'

'Then we are at cross purposes,' Alixe snapped. 'I don't want a name. I want a man, a real person.'

St Magnus rose to meet her, arms crossed. 'Listen, Lady Alixe, you can play stubborn all summer, but that won't change the outcome, it will only change the husband.'

'And that would be intolerable since it would be you. Don't stand there and make it seem as if all your plans are for my benefit. You're only interested in saving your own precious hide,' Alixe said angrily. 'You're not concerned about me. This is all about you getting what you want, just like it was last night. You didn't care about the translation. You cared about the wager and I was fool enough to believe otherwise.'

Merrick's eyes narrowed to dangerous blue slits. Good. He was angry. She'd managed to shake his attitude of casual insouciance. It was about time he was appalled by what faced them. Goodness knew she was.

His voice was cold when he spoke. 'We are most unfortunately in this mess together. You can either take my help and take charge of how this ends, or you can be saddled with me for a husband. I assure you, such a result will only bring you grief.'

She saw the truth in it. Marriage to a man like St Magnus was perhaps worse than the reality of a traditional society alliance. At least then there would be no illusions like there had been momentarily last night.

'Are you threatening me?' Alixe tipped her chin high. Women who married the fantasy were inevitably betrayed when their husbands created the fantasy with other lovers.

'That's your father's threat, my dear, not mine.' Mischief twinkled in his eyes. 'I think you might enjoy certain aspects of being married to me. It's not as though it's a case of *caveat emptor*. You know exactly what you're getting. There won't be any surprises when the clothes come off on our wedding night, after all.'

Alixe felt the hot blush creep up her neck. This man was impossible. 'Really, you must stop mentioning it.'

St Magnus laughed. 'I probably will when it ceases

to make you blush. Now, we must get you back to the house and get you changed for the excursion out to the Roman ruins.'

This was too much. 'You do not have the ordering of me.'

'I thought we'd established that I do until you choose another husbandly candidate.' There was almost a chill to his tone, cautioning that she'd better be careful about pushing this man too far. His easy manners hid a deeper, angrier soul. It was a surprise to discover it. Nothing in his behaviour to date had suggested such a facet to his personality existed. The glimpse was gone as quickly as it had come.

'I hadn't planned to go on the excursion.' She picked up the flower basket.

'I hadn't planned to get caught in the library with you.'

She turned to face him with hands on hips. 'Look, I'm sorry you lost your wager, but that doesn't give you leave to make my life any more miserable than it has to be under the circumstances.'

'I think you'd better get used to calling me Merrick, and you're wrong about the wager. I won, after all.' He gave her a cocky grin. 'I kissed your mother.'

She knew the look on her face was one of pure astonishment. She couldn't help it. The most incredible statements kept coming out of this man's mouth. 'You kissed my mother?'

St Magnus—no, *Merrick*, chuckled and sauntered down the path back towards the house. 'On the hand, my dear girl,' he called over his shoulder. 'I'll see you in half an hour at the carriages. Don't even think about being late.'

Alixe humphed and stomped her foot. He was infuriating. She had no doubts he'd come looking for her if she wasn't there. She'd tried to avoid him this morning and he'd found her anyway. Well, he could demand she be at the carriages, but he couldn't tell her what to wear. Alixe smiled to herself. He'd soon see what a Herculean labour her father had set before him. When her father realised there was no way Merrick could free himself from marrying her, her father would relent. Her father didn't want Merrick for a son-in-law.

Alixe hummed her way back to the house. For the first time since midnight, she had a plan and it *would* work. Then she'd be right back where she'd begun the summer. Never mind that the two words 'restless' and 'lonely' hovered on the periphery of her thoughts. She'd worry about that later. At present, she had a husband to lose.

She was prompt, Merrick would give her that. At precisely eleven o'clock, Alixe Burke presented herself on the front steps with the other milling guests, ready for the outing to the ruins. It was something of a surprise that she was on time given she looked a fright. Mastering such an unattractive, nay, *invisible* look took time.

If he'd been wearing a hat, he would have tipped it to her in temporary recognition of victory. She wasn't going to concede quietly. Lucky for him, he liked a challenge. Just as long as he won in the end.

Merrick excused himself from the group he chatted with and made his way to Miss Burke's side. '*Touché*, Lady Alixe,' he said in low tones for her ear alone. 'You will have to do much better than that.'

Her eyes flashed, but her chance for a rejoinder was cut short by the arrival of carriages and horses. There were a few moments of organised pandemonium while Lady Folkestone sorted everyone into vehicles and those who wished to ride.

Alixe chose to ride. Merrick watched Alixe mount the roan mare, taking in the leaping head on the pommel of her side saddle. She was something of a serious horsewoman, then. No one would consider jumping without it. That she considered jumping at all said something about the quality of her riding. She reached down to adjust the balance strap on her stirrup, further testimony to her competence. That was when he looked more closely at the hideous habit. Its lines weren't ugly. In fact, the outfit was efficiently cut. It was merely the colour. Where other women wore traditional blue and greens, she'd chosen a mousy grey that did nothing to enhance the amber sherry of her eyes or the chocolate lustre of her hair.

'You don't fool me for a moment, Alixe,' he said casually once the crowd had separated into groups along the road. The road was only wide enough for two to ride abreast and the riders had neatly paired off with the partner of their choice. Merrick would remember what a formidable hostess Lady Folkestone was. No doubt, this outing was designed with matchmaking in mind, the road chosen for this exact purpose. There'd be plenty of chances for the young couples to exchange semi-private conversations while in plain sight of others along the road to the ruins. It was a stroke of brilliance on his hostess's part.

'What fooling would you be referring to?' She kept her eyes straight ahead, her tone cool.

'This attempt to be invisible, not to mention unattractive. It will take more than that to get me to beg your father to reconsider, or to send me running back to London, refusing to honour my agreement.'

'Perhaps I like this habit. Perhaps you err by insulting a lady's dress.'

Merrick laughed out loud. 'You forget I saw your evening gown a few nights back. At least one item in your wardrobe suggests you have some sense of fashion. As for your "liking" the habit, I *do* think you like that riding habit. I think you like being invisible. It gives you permission to sail through life without being noticed and that makes you unaccountable. People can only talk about things they see.'

That made her head swivel in his direction. 'How dare you?' Now she was angry. The earlier cool hauteur had melted under the rising heat of her temper.

'How dare I do what?' Merrick stoked the coals a little more. He liked her better this way—she was real when she was angry.

'You know what I mean.'

'I do and I want to be sure *you* know what I mean. I want you to say it.' The real Lady Alixe didn't think about what she was going to say or do, she just did it, like kicking him under the table. Such a quality would make her unique, set her apart from the pattern-card women of the *ton*. Well, maybe not the kicking part, but there was a certain appeal in her freshness. The real Lady Alixe had a natural wit and a sharp understanding of human nature. The masked Lady Alixe was prim and invisible and quite the stick-in-the-mud. That Lady Alixe thought too much and acted upon too little, tried too hard to be something she wasn't—a woman devoid of any feeling.

Merrick took in the smooth profile of her jaw, the firm set of her mouth. There was plenty of feeling in Lady Alixe. She'd simply chosen to stifle it. It would certainly help his cause if he could work out why. Then he could coax it back to life.

She wasn't going to answer his question. 'It's not in your best interest to ignore me, Alixe,' he prodded.

'I know. Don't remind me. If I ignore you now, I'll spend the rest of my life ignoring you as my husband.' She rolled her eyes in exasperation. If the road had allowed room for it, Merrick was sure she'd like to have trotted on ahead. But she couldn't keep running from this; surely she knew it.

Just when he thought he'd made her squirm a bit mentally, forced her to face the reality of her situation, she startled him. 'You are quite the hypocrite, St Magnus. How dare you accuse me of being invisible for the sake of *unaccountability* when you've made yourself flagrantly *visible* for the same reason. Don't look so surprised, St Magnus. I warned you I knew men like yourself.'

'I warned you I knew women like you.'

'So you did. I suppose that gives us something in common.'

Merrick gave her the space of silence. He wasn't impervious to her feelings. He understood she was angry and he was the only available outlet for that anger. He also understood he was the only one with a chance of truly emerging victorious from this snare. He could turn her into London's Toast and walk away. He'd still be free to go about his usual ambling through society. But Lady Alixe's days of freedom would be over whether he succeeded or not. He did feel sorry for her, but he could not say it or show it. She would not want pity, least of all his. Honestly, though, she had to help him a bit with this or they would end up legshackled and her chance to choose her fate would be sealed. She was too intelligent to be blind to that most obvious outcome.

Alixe kept her eyes fixed on the road ahead. St Magnus's silence was far worse than the light humour of his conversation. His silence left her plenty of time to be embarrassed. She wanted to take back her hot words. They'd been mean and cruel and entirely presumptuous. She still could not believe they'd tumbled out of her mouth. She wasn't even sure she truly thought them, believed them. She'd known St Magnus for a handful of hours, far too little time to make such a damning judgement. It might have been the unkindest thing she'd ever said.

She snuck a sideways look at him in the periphery of her vision. Thankfully, he did not *look* affected by her harsh words. Instead, he looked confident and at ease. He'd chosen to ride without a hat and now the sun played through his hair, turning it a lovely white-blonde shade aspiring debutantes would envy. Buttermilk. That was it. His hair reminded her of fresh buttermilk.

'Yes?'

Oh, dear. He'd caught her staring—gawking, really—like a schoolroom miss. But his remarkable blue eyes were friendly, warm even. 'I'm terribly sorry. I spoke out of turn. It wasn't well done of me,' Alixe managed to stammer. It wasn't the most elegant of apologies; needless to say she had had very little practise apologising to extraordinarily handsome men with buttermilk hair and sharp blue eyes that could look right through her if they so chose.

He gave her a half-grin. 'Don't apologise, Lady Alixe. I know what I am.' That only made her feel worse.

Now she'd really have to make it up to him—as if someone like her could ever make anything up to someone like him. But her conscience demanded she try.

She started by giving him a tour of the ruins. The ruins were in two parts. There was an old Roman fort and the villa. Since the fort was closer to the space the group had appropriated as the picnic grounds, she started with that. Afterwards, they joined the other guests on blankets strewn on the ground, where she promptly began a polite but boring conversation about the state of food being served.

'Why is it, Lady Alixe, that people talk about food or the weather when they really want to talk about something else,' St Magnus murmured when she stopped speaking long enough to take a bite of strawberry tart.

'I'm sure I don't know what you mean,' Alixe said after she swallowed. She *did* know what he meant. People had the most ridiculous conversations about absolutely nothing because saying what one honestly felt was impolite. But she'd quickly discovered that when conversing with St Magnus, the conversation grew more interesting when he expounded.

St Magnus had finished eating and taken the opportunity to stretch his long form out on the blanket, propping himself up on one arm, a casual vision of indolence and sin in the early summer sun. He lowered his voice slightly above a whisper just loud enough for her to hear. 'Do you truly believe everyone here *wants* to talk about the ham sandwiches and jugs of lemonade? Yet everyone's conversations are the same if you listen.'

'The ham *is* rather fine and the lemonade is especially cold,' Alixe dared to tease.

St Magnus laughed. 'I'd wager William Barrington over there with Miss Julianne Wood isn't thinking about the ham and tarts.'

'What is he thinking about?' The words were entirely spontaneous and entirely too curious, hardly the right sort of conversational banter for a proper miss. A proper young lady would never encourage what was likely to be an improper avenue of discussion. But St Magnus had a way of encouraging precisely that. She was under the impression that no conversation with him would ever be completely proper.

St Magnus gave a wicked smile. 'He's probably thinking how he'd like to lick that smear of strawberry off her lips.' He gave his eyebrows a meaningful arch. 'Shocked? Don't be. They're all thinking roughly the same thing. Perhaps the place they want to lick varies.'

She was indeed shocked. No one had ever said anything quite so outrageous to her. Ever. But she would not retreat from it. She was fast discovering that being shocked did not have to be the same as being appalled. Since she'd met St Magnus, shock had only increased her curiosity. What else was out there to discover? She'd always thought there was more to life than the veneer society put on its surface. Now, she was starting to discover it, one shocking conversation at a time. Shocking, yes, but intoxicating, too. And, yes, even a little bit empowering, a boost of courage to be the woman in her mind who said witty things, who made challenging statements of her own.

She met his blue eyes squarely, a little smile hovering on her lips. 'I don't know what shocks me more: what you said or how you said it with such nonchalance as if you were indeed discussing something as mundane as the weather.'

'Why not treat it with nonchalance?' St Magnus gave an elegant lift of his shoulder and reached for a last berry. 'It shouldn't be a secret that all men really think about is sex.'

Had he just said 'sex'? In the presence of an un-married female?

'Oh, yes, Lady Alixe. Males are not complex crea-tures when you get right down to it. Why not be honest about it? Consider this your first lesson in becoming London's Toast. The sooner you embrace the fact as common knowledge, the sooner you can successfully cater to it.'

'How ironic that you've used a food-related term. We're right back to where we started. Food, the subject people talk about when they're really thinking about licking people's lips for them.' Oh my, oh my. Now was the time to be appalled. She ought to be horrifi-cally shocked by what had come out of her mouth, but she wasn't. It seemed the natural response to St Mag-nus's comment.

'You can be a rare treat when you decide to employ that tongue of yours for good and not evil, Lady Alixe.' St Magnus was laughing outright now.

'People are starting to look,' Alixe said through the gritted teeth of a forced smile. She was not so given over to the levity of their conversation that she was oblivious to the conditions of their surroundings.

'We want them to look, don't we? We want them to wonder what Lady Alixe has said that has St Magnus so captivated. They're conversational voyeurs. They're only looking because we're having more fun than they are.' He winked a blue eye. 'And do you know why?'

'Because we're not talking about food,' Alixe re-plied smartly, thoroughly enjoying herself.

'Precisely, Lady Alixe. We're talking about what we want to talk about.'

'Are you always like this?' she asked before she lost her courage, before 'sophisticated woman with witty things to say' retreated. She'd never let that part of her out to play before. She had no idea how long it would last before she stumbled or ran out of things to say.

Something like solemnity settled between them; a little of the hilarity of the previous conversation receded. His eyes were serious now. 'I am always myself, Lady Alixe. It's the one thing I can't run away from.'

She sensed a reprimand in there somewhere, whether for himself or for her she could not tell. Perhaps she'd crossed an invisible line in her heady excitement. She seemed to be an expert at doing that today. 'I'm sorry, I've been too forward. I don't know what's wrong with my mouth today.'

'Nothing's wrong with your mouth except maybe a smudge of strawberry tart, just here.' He gestured to a corner on his own mouth. Alixe's pulse ratcheted up a notch. *He was going to do it.* Merrick St Magnus was going to lick her lips. Perhaps the most irrational and wicked thought she'd ever had, but it was a day for all those types of firsts. She took a deep breath, her lips parting ever so slightly in anticipation, her stomach fluttering with curiosity.

He leaned forwards, closing the gap between them... and most disappointingly reached for a napkin.

He dabbed it against her lips, gently wiping away the stain. She knew it was bold. No man had ever touched her mouth before, not even with a napkin. Yet she couldn't help but feel it wasn't bold enough. After all their talk of mouths and food and what men were really thinking, a napkin seemed far too tame.

There could only be one awful truth. He hadn't wanted to. She'd let herself get carried away. In the end, he was Merrick St Magnus, man about town who could have any woman he wanted any time he wanted her, and she was plain Alixe Burke, with an emphasis on the plain. He didn't want to lick her lips any more than he wanted to marry her, which, of course, was why he was trying so hard so he wouldn't have to.

Alixe let out a deep breath and stood up. 'You should see the villa before we go. It's a bit of a walk, so we'd best start now or there won't be time before we leave.'

Chapter Seven

'The villa probably housed military officers, although the larger Roman defences were built at Dover. The lack of a deep-water harbour made Folkestone an unlikely place of attack from the sea. Folkestone was used only as a look-out point.'

She was seeking refuge in her history again. Merrick didn't think she'd stopped chattering since they'd left the blanket. She'd talked about the local fauna on the walk to the ruin and she'd been a veritable fountain of knowledge once they'd actually reached the ruin. It was undeniably interesting. She was well informed, but he was more interested in what had brought on the change, the reversion. She'd been a lively match for him on the blanket, one that he'd enjoyed far beyond his expectation.

'This main room here was a banquet hall. We know this because shards of pottery have been found…' Merrick moved away from her recitation, his eye caught by a short crumbling stair. He went up, thankful for the traction of his boots on the rubble of the remaining steps. But the short climb was worth it. The upper chamber afforded a spectacular view of the sea and of the current Folkestone harbour in the distance. Merrick let the breeze flow over him for a moment as he took in the panorama. He'd discovered that most things looked peaceful from a distance. Distance was useful that way.

'St Magnus, you shouldn't be up there,' she called. But he ignored her. '*Merrick*, it's dangerous. The steps aren't stable and goodness knows how treacherous the ground up there is.' She was looking up at him, shielding her eyes from the sun's glare.

'The view is spectacular and not to be missed,' he called down. He moved towards the steps and offered her a hand. 'Come up, Alixe. The ground is dry and firm. I don't think we're in any danger of sliding down the cliff side today.'

Alixe gave him a look as if to say 'oh, very well' and took her skirt in both hands for the climb. She tripped on the third step, giving him another look. This one saying 'It's dangerous, I told you so'.

'Don't be stubborn, Alixe. Take my hand.' He came down a few steps to meet her, forcing her to acknowledge his offer. Her hand slid into his, warm and firm, and he tightened his grip, ready to haul her up if necessary. But there were no further mishaps.

At the top, Alixe was transformed. 'Oh, look at this!' she gasped. 'This would have been a splendid look-out. They could see all the way down the coast. Perhaps they could even have sent signals from here. A tower in Dover or Hythe would be able to pick them up.' She turned to him, her enjoyment evident on her face. 'I've never been up here, you know. In all the years I've lived here, I've been to the ruins several times, but I've never come up the stair.'

She turned back to the view spread before them. 'To think it's been here all the time and I've missed it.' The last was said more to herself than to him. The breeze took that moment to be slightly more forceful, toying with her hat. She reached up, hesitated for an instant, then took it off. 'That's better,' she said to no one in particular. Then she closed her eyes and gave her face over to the wind and the sun.

Realisation hit him all at once.

Alixe Burke was a beautiful woman. It was objectively true. He could see it in the fine line of her jaw, the elegant column of her neck, visible only because her head was tilted upwards to the sun. She had a perfect nose, narrow and faintly sloped at the end to give it character. It fit the delicate boning of her face, the slightly raised cheekbones one could only fully appreciate in profile, the generous mouth. Cosmetics could not manufacture a bone structure like that. The grey habit she wore might distract from those finer points of beauty, but a discerning man would see the narrow waist and long legs beneath the bulky skirt. A man wouldn't have to be that discerning at all to note the high thrust of her breasts beneath the jacket, tempting a man to wonder whether or not that was the doing of nature's bounty or the assistance of a corset.

It would be simple work to see her gowned according to her attributes, her beauty fully displayed to the gentlemen of the *ton*. He doubted her earlier debutante wardrobes had done her beauty complete justice. No whites or pale pastels for this lovely creature. She belonged in rich earthy tones, deep russets and golds to show off the walnut sheen of her hair.

Merrick moved behind her, his hands finding a comfortable place at her shoulders. He was used to touching women. He hardly thought anything of the gesture. It was casual and easy. But she tensed at the contact. They would have to work on that. She would want to be comfortable with a casual touch now and then, perhaps even doling out a few touches herself, light gestures on a gentleman's arm. Men liked to be touched as much as women. Touch had enormous effects to the positive; it made a person memorable, it created a sense of closeness and trust even when a relationship was new.

Well, now he might be going too far. She wasn't going to seduce anyone. She didn't need to know *all* of the tricks he could teach her, just enough to be pleasant, to draw London's attention and thus the eye of the right kind of gentleman.

'The view is intoxicating,' Merrick murmured at her ear and was rewarded with a small sigh of wistfulness.

'The sea goes on and on. It makes me realise how little of the world I know. I wonder if the Roman who sat here watching wondered the same thing—what's out there? How much more of the world is there beyond what we've already discovered?'

With one of his experienced lovers he'd have drawn her back against him at this moment and wrapped his arms about her, but he knew better than to dare such a thing with Alixe. 'I wasn't talking about *that* view,' he whispered. 'I was talking about this one.' He tucked an errant curl behind her ear. 'You're a beautiful woman, Alixe Burke.'

She stiffened. 'You shouldn't say things you don't mean.'

'Do you doubt me? Or do you doubt yourself? Don't you think you're beautiful? Surely you're not naïve enough to overlook your natural charms.'

She turned to face him, forcing him to relinquish his hold. 'I'm not naïve. I'm a realist.'

Merrick shrugged a shoulder as if to say he didn't think much of realism. 'What has realism taught you, Alixe?' He folded his arms, waiting to see what she would say next.

'It has taught me that I'm an end to male means. I'm a dowry, a stepping stone for some ambitious man. It's not very flattering.'

He could not refute her arguments. There *were* men who saw women that way. But he could refute the hardness in her sherry eyes, eyes that should have been warm. For all her protestations of realism, she was too untried by the world for the measure of cynicism she showed. 'What of romance and love? What has realism taught you about those things?'

'If those things exist, they don't exist for me.' Alixe's chin went up a fraction in defiance of his probe.

'Is that a dare, Alixe? If it is, I'll take it.' Merrick took advantage of their privacy, closing the short distance between them with a touch; the back of his hand reaching out to stroke the curve of her cheek. 'A world without romance is a bland world indeed, Alixe. One for which I think you are ill suited.' He saw the pulse at the base of her neck leap at the words, the hardness in her eyes soften, curiosity replacing the doubt whether she willed it or not. He let his eyes catch hers, then drop to linger on the fullness of her mouth before he drew her to him, whispering, 'Let me show you the possibilities', a most seductive invitation to sin.

Alixe knew she was going to accept. He was going to kiss her and she was going to let him. She could no more stop herself than she could hold back the tides on the beach below them. There was only a moment to acknowledge the act before she was in his arms, his mouth covering hers, warm and insistent that she join him in this. He would not tolerate false resistance and, frankly, she did not want to give it. His tongue brushed her lips. She opened, instinctively parting her lips, giving him access to her mouth, kissing him back with all the enthusiasm her limited skill in this area permitted.

She felt his hand at her nape, his fingers in her hair, guiding her ever so gently into the kiss, his other hand at her back, guiding her not into him precisely, but against him. The planes and ridges of him were evident beneath his clothes: the structured hardness of his chest, the muscled pressure of his thighs. She had seen all this at the pond, of course, but to feel it, ah, to *feel* a man was heady indeed.

It ended all too soon. Merrick drew back, murmuring, 'My dear, I fear you tempt me to indiscretion.' He stepped backwards, putting a subtle distance between them, his eyes soft with a look that warmed her to the toes of her half-boots and made her feel bold beyond her usual measure of cautious restraint.

'Surely a *little* temptation is tolerable? It is just a kiss, after all,' Alixe flirted, stepping forwards—perhaps this time *she'd* kiss *him*. Her intentions must have been obvious.

Merrick side-stepped her efforts. 'Careful, minx. There are those who would take advantage of your enthusiasm for the art. With the gentlemen of London, you'd do best to let them do the pursuing and to be discriminate in bestowing your favours. The rarer a treasure is, the more sought after it becomes.'

Alixe turned sharply, presenting Merrick with her back. She flushed, furious and embarrassed. She'd let herself get carried away. She'd let herself believe they were two people caught up in the beauty of the moment, the kiss a celebration of having shared the stunning vista together. It was no use. No matter how she tried to rationalise it, it sounded like nonsense even in her head. The point was, she'd got carried away and pretended the kiss was something more than it was, which obviously it wasn't. He was unperturbed by what had transpired while she was all too worked up.

She wasn't ready to turn around and face him yet, but she could see him in her mind's eye leaning with easy grace against the rock wall of the ruins, letting the breeze ruffle through his hair. At least he could be angry.

'Alixe, look at me.'

'Don't you dare be nice and say something pithy.'

'I wasn't going to.'

She could hear him pushing off the wall and crossing the villa floor, pebbles crunching beneath his boots. She blew out a breath. She wanted to vanish, wanted the cliff to swallow her up, embarrassment and all.

'What I was going to say, Alixe, is that if you want to kiss a man, you need to know how.'

Oh. *That* made it better. 'Just for the record, you're not boosting my confidence.' The best kiss she'd ever had and it was entirely juvenile to him, probably no better than the sloppy work of a three year old.

He was standing behind her. She could feel the heat of his body. She couldn't put off facing him any longer. She turned, trying very hard to look irritated instead of mortified. Her eyes darted everywhere in an attempt to avoid looking at him directly. He would have none of it. After a few futile seconds of looking past his shoulder, he gently imprisoned her chin with his thumb and forefinger.

'Look at me, Alixe. There's nothing wrong with your kiss, just your approach. You need finesse. Your suitors will want to feel this was all their doing. You can initiate the kiss as long as they think it was their idea. Here, let me show you.'

That was a dangerous phrase. Alixe made to move backwards, but he captured her hand and continued smoothly with his instructions. 'Touch your gentleman on the sleeve. Make it look like a natural act during conversation. Lean forwards and laugh a little at something he says when you do it. That way it looks spontaneous and sincere. Then, flirt with your eyes.

Give him a little smile and look down as if you hadn't meant to get caught staring. Later, when you're walking in the garden, let your gaze linger on his lips a bit. Make sure he catches you at it. You can shyly bite your lip and look away quickly. If he's any sort of man at all, he'll stop within the next ten feet and steal a kiss. When he does stop, you can close the deal by parting your lips, a sure sign that his affections will be welcomed.

'I should have brought paper for notes,' Alixe mumbled. 'I was not expecting a treatise.'

'Now that's a fine idea. Perhaps I should write a book on kissing as a noble art.' Merrick laughed.

Unfazed by her reticence, he pushed on. 'Now you try it. I already know it works. Sit there and I'll pretend I've brought you some punch.' Merrick gestured to a rounded boulder.

'This is silly,' Alixe protested, but she did it any way.

'I've heard the very best bit of news while I was at the refreshment table,' Merrick began their *faux* conversation.

'Oh, you have?' Alixe widened her eyes in simulated interest.

'Yes. I heard that the Cow is about to run away with the Spoon,' Merrick said in his best conspiratorial whisper.

'Isn't the *Dish* supposed to run away with the spoon?' Alixe corrected.

Merrick didn't so much as blink over his error. He leaned closer, a wicked grin taking his elegant mouth. 'I do believe it is. That's why my "news" is so astonishing. It's entirely unexpected.'

Uncontainable laughter surged up inside her. Before she knew it, she was leaning forwards, her hand on his forearm in gentle camaraderie. 'Oh, do tell,' she managed in gasps between bouts of laughing.

'Well, I heard it from the Cat who heard it from the Fiddle…' Merrick was struggling against losing his composure entirely. It was a fascinating battle to watch on his expressive face—mock seriousness warring futilely with the hilarity of their conversation. In that moment it was all too easy to forget who he was, who she was, as they had in the library.

Alixe's eyes dropped to his mouth with its aristocratically thin upper lip. Merrick's eyes followed her down, his head tilting to capture her lips in a gentle buss. He sucked lightly at her lower lip, sending a pool of warm heat to her belly. This slow, lingering kiss carried an entirely different thrill. There was sweetness in its tender qualities. She wanted to fall into it, wanted to feel it turn into something more passionate. She'd never guessed kissing could be such a lovely pastime.

'That's how you know you did it right. The proof is in the pudding. Top marks,' he whispered playfully. 'You're an apt pupil. Keep this up and we'll have London at your feet in no time.'

The words were said in jest and perhaps reassurance, but Alixe could not take them that way. How had it become this easy to forget what this man was? He was a flirt. No, he was more than a flirt. He was a consummate seducer of women. She'd been warned by her own brother. She knew precisely what his role was in this farce to see her married. And yet that knowledge had not been able to prevent *it*; when he kissed her, it felt real. It didn't feel like a lesson. It was positively mortifying to forget herself so entirely.

Alixe stood up and brushed at her skirts, summoning anger to be her shield. 'Let me make one thing clear. I do not need love lessons. Most especially, I do not need them from you.'

Merrick laughed softly at her indignation, having the audacity to smile. 'Yes, you do, Alixe Burke. And you most definitely need them from me.'

Love lessons, indeed! Alixe fumed. She could barely sit still long enough to let Meg dress her hair for dinner that night. The man was insufferable. He treated the whole shambles as if it were a lark. More than that, he treated *her* as if she were a lark.

He'd merely laughed at her riding habit. If he thought he could laugh away her ugly gowns or cajole her into better looks, he would soon learn she wouldn't give up her strategy easily. Her excessively plain wardrobe had been an excellent defence against unwanted suitors up until now. He was very much the exception. She would remind him of that this evening.

Meg had laid out her second-best dinner gown, but Alixe had opted for an austere beige gown trimmed in unassuming lace of the same colour. Meg had clearly disagreed with her choice. Her maid tugged a braid up into the coronet she was fashioning.

'I don't know why you want to wear that old thing. Lord St Magnus seemed plenty interested in you this morning. He's a handsome fellow. I would have thought you'd want to wear something pretty tonight.'

'He was just being polite.' Alixe sat up straighter and squared her shoulders. Polite enough to trade banter at the picnic, polite enough to show her how to kiss. Polite enough to make her forget he had a job to do and that job was her. But she couldn't confess that to Meg.

Her father had truly humbled her this time, blackmailing St Magnus into this ludicrous proposition. No. She had to stop thinking that way. She had to stop thinking of St Magnus as a victim. *She* was the victim. St Magnus was on her father's side. Perhaps not by consent, but he was on the side that wanted to see her married off and that meant her father's side.

'Would you like a little rouge for your cheeks?' Meg suggested hopefully, holding a little pot.

'No.' Alixe shook her head.

'But the beige, miss, it washes you out so.'

Alixe smiled at the pale image she presented in the mirror. 'Yes, it does do that beautifully.' She was ready to go down to supper. St Magnus would see that she meant business. No matter what kind of love lessons he offered, she did mean to scare him off by revealing to him the futility of his task.

Chapter Eight

In the drawing room, Merrick discreetly checked his watch. Alixe was late and he worried that he'd overstepped himself today with his offer of love lessons. There was some irony in that offer. What did he know about love? He knew about sex and every game that went with it. But love? Love was beyond him. It had not existed in his home. His father did not love his mother. His father did not love him. He was merely another means to an end—a loose end in this particular case. Growing up, he'd loved his mother, a beautiful, delicate woman, but that had turned out poorly. His father had used that devotion with merciless regularity in order to obtain what he wanted until Merrick had finally decided to put as much distance between himself and his family as he could. That had been seven years ago. No, Merrick knew nothing about love and he'd prefer to keep it that way.

There was a rustling at the door and Merrick spied Alixe immediately. He'd been hoping she would not meekly accept defeat. Part of him was intrigued about what she would do next, and he was certain there would be a 'next'. He understood his situation was precarious for a bachelor wishing to avoid matrimony. But regardless of the peril, he'd been intrigued by Alixe Burke again today, proving that his earlier fascination hadn't been a one-day novelty.

She was a beautiful, spirited woman attempting to hide in dismal clothing. He suspected she was hiding not only from the world, but from herself. It had been difficult for her to acknowledge the passionate side of her nature today. The responses he'd drawn from her had surprised her greatly. Watching her let go and simply be herself for even a few moments had pleased him immensely.

Alixe made her much-anticipated entrance and Merrick smiled. She had not disappointed. The beige gown was even 'better' than the grey riding habit because there was less one could technically take issue with. The gown was cut in the latest fashion. She wore very proper pearls around her neck and her hair was done up neatly. But she looked invisible. Everything about her ensemble was completely unassuming, from the colour to the sparse trimmings. She was almost convincing. *Almost.*

Her head was held too high for the kind of woman who would wear that gown and her eyes were too sharp. Her natural disposition betrayed her in ways the gown could not hide. Merrick would be damned if he'd tell her.

Merrick made his way to where she stood surveying the room and probably wondering where best to put herself out of notice.

'You look beautiful tonight.'

'I do not.' She responded proudly. 'I'm the plainest woman in the room.'

He took her arm and tucked it through his own. It was a lovely proprietary act, one that everyone in the drawing room noticed while they were trying hard not to. He was well aware every woman's eyes in the room had discreetly watched him cross the floor to Alixe's side.

'Beauty is often found in the eyes of the beholder,' Merrick replied smoothly, strolling them around the perimeter of the drawing room.

'A very useful cliché.'

'A very *true* cliché. You'll see.' Merrick winked slyly. She was not nearly as seasoned at the games of flirtation as he was. She only knew how to avoid them. He knew how to play them. She didn't quite understand what he was doing. But he did.

A man's undivided attentions were a potent lure for other males. Once other men saw his attentions they would swarm: some out of curiosity, wanting to see what he saw, others out of fear that something of merit might slip beyond their grasp and still others because men were by nature competitive creatures and could not stand to be bested. And the women in the room would make sure the men noticed. Already, a few of them whispered to companions behind their fans.

Ah, yes, Merrick thought. He would pretend the

beige gown was beautiful and by the end of the evening the other men would think so, too.

Merrick was up to something. The knowledge that the 'game was afoot' had Alixe on edge throughout dinner. But she could detect nothing. Merrick sat beside her, solicitous and charming, his manners without fault. She heartily wished she knew more about the games men and women played with one another. She was starting to see the large flaw in her strategies. Her tactics had all been focused on avoiding the game. As a result, she hadn't the faintest idea how to play the game or even what the rules might be.

The 'rules of engagement' was taking on a vastly differently meaning. Before Merrick, Alixe had thought of the term solely in its military capacity, part of the historic vocabulary of war. But now she was starting to see it in a different light, unless one wanted to speculate that love and war were fought on similar fields of battle.

Rules, like the ones Merrick had introduced, were *not* the rules she'd learned from her governesses. Governesses taught a person how to walk, how to sit and how to make polite conversation; all of which were apparently useless skills in spite of society's argument to the contrary. What a girl really needed in her arsenal was the ability to coax a kiss. A man, too, for that matter.

Merrick hadn't said as much, but Alixe suspected the converse was indeed true. Merrick had demonstrated that quite aptly this afternoon at the villa. His allure most definitely did not stem from his ability to make polite conversation or from his talent for sitting ramrod straight. In fact, he was proving it right now across the drawing room while they waited for the games to begin. It was the first time all evening that he'd left her side.

Merrick *lounged* where other men stiffly posed against the mantelpiece. Merrick *said* what he thought while others searched for careful phrasing.

And it was working. The pretty Widow Whitely tilted her blonde head to one side, giving Merrick a considering look, a coy half-smile on her lips, her eyes dropping to his mouth and then to an unmentionable spot just below his waist.

Oh. Alixe felt a blush start to rise on Mrs Whitely's behalf. Had Mrs Whitely really done that? It had happened so quickly, Alixe couldn't be entirely sure of what she'd seen. Merrick was leaning forwards and smiling, a behaviour that sent an unlooked-for surge of jealously through Alixe. He had smiled at her in a similar manner up at the villa today. Jamie had warned her Merrick liked women. But a warning wasn't quite as effective as seeing the evidence first-hand.

Watching him with Widow Whitely was a gentle reminder that these were the tools of his trade. It was also a reminder that he wasn't hers to command. He was merely her unconventional and secret tutor at the moment. If he wanted to flirt with Mrs Whitely, she had no right to countermand him.

As if drawn by her thoughts, Merrick looked up

from his tête-à-tête with the engaging widow, his eyes discreetly finding hers.

Five minutes later, he materialised at her side. 'Did you learn anything, *ma chère*?'

Other than that Mrs Whitely might have a fascination with certain parts of yours? That could absolutely *not* be said out loud. Alixe elected to say nothing. She shook her head.

'I did,' Merrick continued, his voice low at her ear. 'We were noticed at the picnic today and again in the drawing room. I've been approached by no less than three ladies who have commented on it.'

'In a good way, I hope.' Alixe could imagine the ways they might have been noticed. She was not used to deliberately drawing attention to herself. 'The last thing I need before going to London is too much attention.' She would prefer no one had spied them up at the villa or actually heard what they were laughing over at the picnic.

Merrick gave one of his easy smiles. 'There is no such thing as too much attention. Don't be confusing attention with scandal. They are two different animals entirely. One is good and the other is to be avoided at all costs.'

Alixe raised an eyebrow in quizzing disbelief. 'And you're a prime example of avoiding scandal?'

'Scandal is to be avoided at all costs, if you're a woman,' Merrick amended.

'Quite the double standard since it's pretty hard to fall into scandal without us,' Alixe said drily.

'Still, there are ways.' Merrick laughed, then sobered. Alixe followed his narrowing gaze to the arrival of a newcomer to the drawing room. Archibald Redfield entered with Lady Folkestone on his arm, his golden head bent with a smile to catch a comment.

'Your mother seems quite taken with our Mr Redfield.'

'My father, too. They dote on him.'

'Whatever for? He's a sly sort. Surely they can see that.'

'They only see his manners, his standard-bred good looks. He's solid, not the sort to stir up trouble. He's exactly what this sleepy part of England is looking for in a landowner. He took over the old Tailsby Manse last year. It was the most exciting thing to happen in Folkestone for ages. Everyone with a daughter under thirty was thrilled.'

'Do you include your mother in that grouping?' Merrick's eyes followed Redfield about the room in a manner reminiscent of a wolf stalking prey.

'Of course.' Alixe shrugged, hoping to fob off any further inquisition.

'But to no avail?' Merrick probed. This was uncomfortable ground.

'To no avail on my end. I was not interested in Mr Redfield's attentions.'

'But he was?'

'Yes. Yes, he was interested,' Alixe replied tersely. She'd retreated from London to avoid men like Archibald Redfield. Merrick looked ready to ask another question. 'This is not a seemly topic of conversation for a drawing room,' Alixe said quickly. She had no desire to delve further into just how interested Mr Redfield had been or how naively she'd been taken in for a short time.

'Then perhaps you'll do me the honour of continuing the conversation later in the garden after the games. I believe I am to join old Mrs Pottinger and her cronies at whist shortly.' Merrick was all obliging affability at the thought of an evening spent at cards with old ladies.

'I hadn't planned on staying for the games,' Alixe admitted. 'I am behind on my manuscript. I'd hoped to sneak off and get some work done tonight.' She'd lost so much time since the house party had begun and the manuscript was still giving her fits.

'Oh, no, that will not do,' Merrick scolded. 'You can't be noticed if you're not here. You need to stay *and* you need to enjoy yourself. Go over and join Miss Georgia Downing and the young ladies by the sofa. I promise they'll be delighted to make your acquaintance. With luck, you can all make plans to call on one another in London.'

It would be fun to spend an evening in the company of people her age—well, roughly her age. She knew she was a bit older. Still, Jane Atwood was in that group and she was twenty-two. 'But the manuscript…' Alixe protested weakly.

'I'll help you with it in the morning,' Merrick promised.

That coaxed a smile. Alixe could feel it creeping across her mouth. 'So you really do understand Old French?'

'Did you think I didn't?' Merrick feigned hurt. He touched a hand to her wrist. 'You doubted me?'

'Well, I did suppose rumours of your abilities might have been greatly exaggerated in that regard.' Alixe found herself flirting in response to the light pressure of his hand at her gloved wrist. It was impossible to hate him; his charm proved irresistible even when she knew precisely what he was.

'Bravo, that was nicely done, quite the perfect rejoinder—definitely witty and perhaps even a bit of naughty innuendo thrown in. Why, Lady Alixe, I do think you might have the makings of a master yet.'

Alixe let herself be drawn into the fun of conversing with Merrick. She dropped a little curtsy. 'Thank you, that's quite a compliment.'

'Then I shall depart on a good note and take up my chair at the whist table.'

'Do take care. Mrs Pottinger is sharper than she looks.'

Merrick gave her a short bow. 'I appreciate your concern. But I assure you, I can hold my own against county champions of Mrs Pottinger's skill.'

Alixe laughed. 'I wouldn't be so certain of that. She counts cards like an inveterate gambler.'

Damn, but if Alixe wasn't right. He shouldn't have played his heart. He'd suspected Mrs Pottinger was out of them and would trump his jack, but he'd lost count. Apparently there were only two hearts left against his jack and not three. From under her lace cap, the elderly dame gave him a smug look of triumph and led her ace of spades.

Merrick gathered his wandering attentions and focused on the game. If he wasn't careful, he and his partner would lose this rubber. There'd be no living it down in London if word got back he'd lost at cards to a group of old country biddies.

Mrs Pottinger let out a sigh and tossed her last card. 'You're a wily fox, after all, St Magnus. For all my finessing I can't wheedle the eight of spades out of you and it will be my undoing. My poor seven will fall to it and the game is yours.'

'But your skill is not in doubt, Mrs Pottinger,' Merrick said gallantly, tossing his eight of spades on to the trick. 'You are a most impressive player. I was rightfully warned about you.' Merrick rose from the table and helped each of the ladies rise after their long sit. 'Thank you for the game, ladies. It's been a delightful evening.'

He'd done his duty for Lady Folkestone. Now it was time to give his full attention to the interesting situation with Archibald Redfield. He'd meant to confront Redfield about the questionable nature of the wager. 'Rigging' a wager was not honourable conduct among those who gambled and Merrick, as one who wagered rather often, knew it. He was not going to let Redfield slip by on this one. Redfield's attempt at rigging the wager had nearly jeopardised a lady's reputation. It had most definitely jeopardised the lady's future.

Not all of his attentions had been diverted to the 'Redfield situation'. The lady in question had done her share of distracting, too. Many of his thoughts had, in fact, been diverted to the 'Alixe conundrum'. On more than one occasion, his eye had been drawn to her across the room where she'd taken his advice and joined a group of young ladies. Why had she refused Redfield's attentions? Her past association with Redfield put an entirely different cast upon the wager, one that suggested the wager hadn't been about himself, but about Alixe and quite possibly retaliation.

Revenge seemed a long way to go merely because a lady rejected the man's attentions. But perhaps there was more to it. Alixe had seemed loathe to discuss the situation in detail. Originally, he'd attributed her reticence to their circumstances. A drawing room full of people was hardly conducive to divulging secrets. Now, he was starting to wonder if the reticence didn't come from something more.

Merrick strolled towards the wide bay of French doors leading out to the spectacular Folkestone gardens. Games were breaking up and people were starting to mill as they waited for the end-of-evening tea cart. Once he caught Alixe's eye, it would be easy to slip outside unnoticed and wait for her.

Waiting was the harder part. He'd been about ready to go inside and detach her from the group when she finally came out. 'This is dangerous.' She scolded. 'What if someone sees us?'

'I hope they do. There's nothing to hide. I'd have to be completely foolish to try to steal a kiss with the entire house party looking on.' Merrick scowled, toss-

ing a hand to indicate the long bank of French doors.
'I thought you were never coming out.'

'I didn't think we had anything urgent to discuss.'

'I disagree. We aren't done talking about Redfield.'

He recognised defiance. Her chin went up a slight
fraction, just as it had at the villa.

'I'm starting to think he made the wager on purpose,
that perhaps he wanted revenge. The wager was meant
to land you in the suds. I was merely a tool.' Merrick
laid out his hypothesis, noticing that she didn't rush
to deny the claim. 'Is there merit to that? What might
have transpired between you that would cause him to
take such drastic measures?'

Alixe smoothed her skirts, another gesture he was
coming to associate with her when she was not certain
what to say. 'I don't think it has any bearing on our
current circumstances,' she replied coolly.

'I do.' Merrick crossed his arms over his chest,
studying her in the light thrown from the drawing
room. He wished he could see her eyes more clearly.
They would tell him if she was as cool as she sounded.
'Redfield tried to fix the bet and not for his benefit.
He knew you'd be there; if I succeeded, he would lose
money, not to mention the money his friends would
lose. Have you thought about why a man would set
himself up for a likely failure?'

'Perhaps he thought I'd resist your attempts.' She
squirmed a little at that. 'For that matter, how do you
know he knew I'd be there?'

'He brought your father, hardly someone who'd be
interested in who I was kissing unless it was his own

daughter. Your father wouldn't care two figs if I was in there kissing Widow Whitely. Besides, Ashe told me Redfield was boasting he knew someone would be there.'

'Oh.' It came out as a small sigh and her shoulders sagged just the tiniest bit, the only acknowledgement she'd make that he was quite possibly right. 'I refused him when he put the question to me. Needless to say, he was stunned. He should not have been. The daughter of an earl is quite a reach for a man of his modest antecedents. We did not discuss it, but I had reason to believe his intentions were not as true as he represented them to be.'

Merrick believed that. It was how polite society conducted its business. Redfield would never know the reasons she'd refused him. He would have hidden his disappointment just as she'd hidden her true reasons. It did not take great imagination to envision them sitting properly in the Folkestone receiving rooms, voicing polite platitudes of having been honoured by the other's attentions and regretful the outcome could not be otherwise. Then they'd gone about the business of being courteous neighbours because there was no other choice. Neighbours must first and foremost always maintain a veneer of politeness, which often precluded being able to speak the truth.

The situation with Archibald Redfield was untidy beneath the placid surface. It made her anxious to speak of it. Even now, her gaze was drawn towards the doors, looking for distraction. She found it in the tea cart's arrival. 'We should return inside.'

'You go in first and I'll follow after a decent interval.'

He'd wait five minutes before returning and then he'd stay at her side for what was left of the evening. He counted off the minutes, letting his mind wander, mulling over what Alixe had revealed and even what she hadn't.

Redfield's former relationship with Alixe put an entirely different cast on his motives for the dangerous wager he'd made. Redfield had been taken aback by her refusal—so stunned, in fact, that he wanted revenge enough to plan a compromising situation, to see Alixe Burke ruined. But to want revenge seemed an uncharacteristically harsh action.

More questions followed. Alixe had hinted she'd discovered something unsavoury about Redfield's intentions. Did Redfield suspect she'd made such a discovery and did he fear she might expose it? What would Redfield have to hide?

All of it was supposition. But if any of it were true, Alixe Burke might be in danger from more than an unwanted marriage. Whether she realised it or not, she was in need of a champion.

Ashe would be the first to point out the hero did not have to be him. Merrick was not required to champion Alixe Burke against jilted suitors. Yet he could not help but feel a need to champion this woman who had dared to carve out a life contrary to society's preferences. Her daring had left her alone. Perhaps that was the kinship he felt with her. In spite of his notorious popularity, Merrick St Magnus knew what it meant to be alone.

* * *

Archibald Redfield considered himself a man who was rarely surprised. Human nature held little mystery for him. Yet St Magnus had managed to surprise him. He had not expected to see the devil-may-care libertine that morning. St Magnus had stayed. Not only had he stayed, he'd played his role to the hilt at the picnic, never once leaving Alixe Burke's side. It was not what he had expected and that made him nervous.

What made him even more nervous was the sight of Alixe Burke slipping back in to the party, trying hard not to be noticed. No doubt she'd been sneaking out to see St Magnus. He didn't like that in the least. The last thing he needed was for Alixe to decide she actually liked the rogue or for St Magnus to do the deciding for her. It would be death to his plans if anyone caught St Magnus and Alixe being indiscreet.

Redfield knew rogues. He feared that the reason St Magnus hadn't left was that St Magnus wanted to woo Alixe for himself, compromise her if need be and the dratted man was now perfectly positioned to do that, having been given *carte blanche* to act the role of an interested suitor. This was a most unlooked-for complication. Redfield would have to keep his eye on the situation most carefully.

Fortunately for the present, no one else had noticed Alixe's return. She wasn't the 'noticeable' type, not dressed like that anyway, in a beige gown that matched the wallpaper. He was astute enough to know the Earl of Folkestone's well-dowered daughter could afford better, but he simply didn't care what she wore or why.

He didn't care if she'd rather live in the country with her books. He only cared that she came with a great deal of money. Plain women, ugly women, beautiful women—he'd had them all when it served his purposes. In the dark they were all the same. Except that Alixe Burke was the richest prize he'd ever gone after. She'd be the last, too, if he was successful.

Scratch that. There could be no 'ifs' about it. He had to win her. He'd sunk his funds into the Tailsby Manse, the first step in his bid to be a respectable gentleman. The manor was definitely a gentleman's home, but that also meant it was in a certain state of disrepair. The roof leaked, the chimneys smoked and it took servants to run the place. All those things required money. Alixe Burke had money and prestige. Marriage to her would solidify his claim to a genteel life.

But she had turned him down. He had not expected it. A woman on the shelf didn't turn down offers of marriage, earl's daughter or not. It was a setback he could not easily afford. She would find she could not afford it either. He would push the choosy Miss Burke into a corner until she had no choice but to accept his twelfth-hour offer and this time she'd be all too glad to accept.

As long as St Magnus played by the rules and did not compromise her for himself, all would be well. Not even St Magnus could turn her into an interesting woman, the kind of woman who could be labelled a Toast. Yes, there'd be fortune hunters like himself who wouldn't care what she looked like, but she was to be made a Toast precisely to avoid those men and draw the right kind of man to her side. Folkestone would know the difference. Redfield was confident the right man would not emerge.

He was even more confident Folkestone would not want to see his daughter married to St Magnus, a man with his own social ghosts and demons to contend with. That would be when he made his generous offer to marry Alixe, saving the family from the scandal of attaching themselves permanently to St Magnus. It would all be wrapped up neatly by Season's end and there'd be time to have his roof patched before winter set in.

Chapter Nine

Alixe was dressed hideously again in a shapeless work dress when she met Merrick in the library the following morning, her hair left to hang loose in her hurry to make up for oversleeping. There was no one to notice this grooming oversight on her part. The house party had taken themselves off to the village for a day of shopping and touring the local church. But one would have thought the king was coming to call the way St Magnus was turned out in sartorial perfection for the simple and isolated task of working in the library with her.

He was waiting for her, attired in fawn breeches, crisp white linen shirt and a sky-blue waistcoat in a paisley pattern that managed to deepen the hue of his already impossibly blue eyes. He'd been freshly shaved and his hair was brushed to the pale sheen of cream. His morning elan was perhaps a not-so-subtle commentary about her own choice of clothing. But if she'd meant to get a more obvious rise out of Merrick over her clothes, she was to be disappointed.

His comment extended merely to a raised eyebrow. Instead, he turned his attentions to the project at hand and after a few minutes of study to familiarise himself with the text, he said 'I think you're taking the translation too literally again. The sentence makes more sense if *profiter* means taking advantage of. You're using it to mean making money, the way one would use the word today.'

Merrick slid the document back across the long library table to let her look at the section in question, the understated scent of his morning *toilette* teasing her nostrils as he leaned forwards slightly to push the document towards her. He smelled clean, the very idea of freshness personified. Then he pulled his arm back and the delightful scent retreated. She wanted more. Alixe wondered what he would do if she acted on the impulse to lean across the table and sniff him, a great big healthy sniff. A giggle escaped her at the very thought of acting on the notion.

'Is there something humorous?' Merrick was all stern seriousness.

'Um, no.' Alixe blushed and feigned a throat-clearing cough. 'A tickle in my throat, I think.' *I was just thinking about sniffing you.* Alixe hastily shifted her gaze to the manuscript and pretended to read, using the pretence to gather her scattered thoughts. She'd worked on this manuscript for weeks without distraction until St Magnus's arrival. Now, her focus fled at the smallest provocation from him. The isolation of the country must be getting to her. She took a deep breath.

'Better?' St Magnus enquired, needing only a pair

of eye glasses to look the consummate college professor, albeit a very handsome one.

'Yes, much better, thank you.' What was wrong with her? She did not usually think in such terms. Then again, she wasn't in the habit of taking kissing lessons from men she hardly knew either.

Alixe scanned the document. It didn't take long to see his interpretation was correct. 'It seems so obvious now that you've pointed it out. The rest of the document should translate easily from this point.' His translation made perfect sense. Really, it was a marvel she'd missed it.

Too bad swallowing her pride wasn't as simple. She was a historian, even if she had been self-trained. She'd had the benefit of tutors and a fine education up until Jamie had left for Oxford. How was it that a well-educated person like herself had not seen what Merrick had noted immediately? She scribbled some notes on a tablet and then looked up, considering. Morning sunlight streamed through the long windows of the library, turning his buttermilk hair to the pale flax of corn silk. 'How is it that you know so much about French?' It seemed patently unfair this gorgeous male should also be in possession of an intellect. He'd demonstrated on two separate occasions that intellect was quite well developed.

'It's the language of love, *ma chère*.' Merrick flashed her one of his teasing grins. 'I didn't have to be a genius to see all the uses I could find for it.'

Alixe wasn't satisfied. He knew far more than a passing phrase for impressing the ladies. 'Don't trivialise your skill.' The vehemence of her defence startled them both. 'You don't have to pretend you don't have a brain. Not with me anyway.'

An awkward silence followed in the wake of her outburst. It was one of those moments when they stepped outside their prescribed roles of rake and blue stocking and the revelation that had followed was nothing short of surprising. It was difficult to think of her and Merrick having something so significant in common.

'You studied French at Oxford. I hardly think the curriculum there was limited to a few *bon mots*.' Alixe cast about for a way to restore equilibrium to the conversation, not entirely comfortable with what she'd learned.

'Have you ever considered that Oxford might be overrated?' Merrick leaned back in his chair, propping it up on its hind legs, his hands tucked behind his head, an entirely masculine habit. He tried for evasion. 'Rich men send their sons to Oxford to get an education when they know full well we spend most of our days and nights carousing in the taverns and getting up to all nature of mischief. It's a different sort of education than the ones the dons intend for us. Our fathers don't care as long as we don't get sent down in disgrace.' There was a bitterness that underlay the levity of his tone.

'Jamie mentioned there was time for a few larks.' Alixe got up from the table and absently strode to one of the long windows to take in the morning sun. 'But I don't believe you picked languages entirely on whim.' She wouldn't let him get away with skirting the question. Evasion was an unexpected strategy from a man who'd stood on the edge of the pond unabash-edly naked.

'I like to talk and languages are another way to talk. At the time it seemed like a kind of rebellion. I liked the idea of being able to say something that can't quite be said in English.'

'Such as…?' Alixe faced him, her back to the window. She'd not have guessed a discussion of his personal life would send this extroverted man into full retreat, discreet as the retreat was. It touched her in dangerous ways that he would be vulnerable. It made him far more human than she'd like.

Merrick gave a lift of his shoulders. 'Like *esprit de l'escalier.* It means thinking of a retort after the moment has passed. Diderot introduced the phrase in one of his works.'

'The spirit of the staircase?' Alixe quizzed, absently lifting her hair off her neck and then letting it spill through her hands in a careless gesture as she pondered the phrase. 'I'm afraid I don't understand.'

Merrick was studying her with his blue eyes. She shifted uncomfortable with his scrutiny. Something had changed in the moments since her comments. The air had become charged with a sweet tension that implied impending action.

'Do that again,' Merrick ordered, a low-voiced demand edged in sensuality. 'Pull up your hair and let it sift through your fingers.'

She did as he commanded. He'd risen from his chair. He was stalking her now, with his eyes and his body, coming towards her in slow strides, his eyes locked on hers. She did it again, raising her hands to gather up the thick length of her hair, her teeth delicately worrying her bottom lip subconsciously. She wasn't aware she'd even done it.

'Ah, yes, Alixe, very good. Every man likes the innocent wanton,' Merrick whispered, lifting his arms to take her hair in his own hands. She trembled at the feel of his warm hands skimming her shoulders as he dropped her hair. Her stomach tightened in anticipation. He was going to seduce her again as he had the day before. She ought to resist. There was nothing here but another lesson.

'My Alixe, your body is so much more eager than you know.' He leaned in, feathering a light kiss against her neck in the hollow beneath her ear.

A moan escaped her lips and she swayed towards him, all thoughts of resisting vanished in the wake of the curious warmth that spread through her, conjured there by his touch, his kiss, his words. Her face was between his hands and her mouth was open beneath his. With her eyes shut, it seemed all her senses were heightened. She was acutely aware of the feel of his hips pressed ever so gently against hers. The clean smell of him enveloped her—she could make it out now, a light *fougère* layered with oak and moss, a hint of lavender and something else that called to mind grass on a summer day—and the taste of him was in her mouth, the sweetly pungent remnants of morning coffee.

With the morning to guard her, Alixe had thought she'd be safe from him and the wickedness he awoke in her. She had imagined such seduction could not occur in the bright light of day. She should have known better. The afternoon had not served her well yesterday.

Her hands needed somewhere to go and it only seemed right that they should anchor in the buttermilk depths of his hair. The move pulled her closer to him, her breasts pressed against the masculine planes of his chest. This was most wicked of her and in the light of the window, too...

'Oh!' The realisation was enough to make her jump, a hand hastily covering her mouth. 'The window! Anyone might see us.' She knew she was clumsy in her panicked retreat past him to the relative safety of the table.

Merrick only laughed, in no hurry to back away from the window. Why had she thought he'd react differently? It was all a game to him, one of the many games he played.

'Oh, hush!' she scolded.

'I do believe you are a hypocrite, Alixe Burke.' Merrick returned to the table and resumed his seat, eyes full of mischief.

'I don't know what you're talking about.' Alixe seethed. She'd been caught out again by that scoundrel.

'Yes, you do, you little fool.' Merrick gave a warm chuckle. 'Look at you, sitting there with your straight back and folded hands like a genteel angel all worried about propriety when moments ago you were the very devil in my arms and propriety be damned.'

Alixe's face burned. She could not gainsay the truth. He was right. She'd been all hot abandon and it was positively disgraceful. She could not argue otherwise.

'Come now,' Merrick coaxed, 'there's no need to be ashamed. Why not admit you enjoy our lessons?'

'There can be no more lessons, as you call them.' Alixe made an attempt to return her attentions to the manuscript. He'd shown her his vulnerable side and she'd shown him hers. She was certain it was far more than either had intended.

Merrick was letting her stew. She didn't dare look up, but she could hear him rifling through book pages and shuffling papers. She pretended to read and scribble some illegible notes in the margins and waited.

'You do realise you're in an enviable position to combine business with pleasure. You should make the most of it,' Merrick said casually at last, not bothering to look away from his papers.

'I'm afraid you'll have to explain that,' Alixe replied with the aloofness that had staved off most of male London.

It didn't freeze Merrick in the least. If anything, it had the opposite effect, encouraging him to indecently honest conversation.

'Most young women would like to be in your position, privy to the secrets I can teach you.' He leaned back again in his chair, his feet hooked about the front legs. 'Perhaps your father has accidentally started a new fad: coaching one's daughter in the ways of Eve.'

Alixe slammed down her notebook. She was angry at herself for having proved so gullible as to allow herself to be seduced. She was angry at her father for forcing her into this situation and most of all she was angry at Merrick, who refused to be anything but outrageous. 'My father may have blackmailed you into this, but he did not expect you to take such liberties. You were only assigned to raise interest in me. I dare say that can be done without the "lessons" you've apparently designed for my edification.'

Merrick was thoughtful for a moment. 'All right. No more lessons unless you ask for them. However, I do need to raise interest in you and you must allow me to do my duty—'

'Without kissing, without excessive touching beyond what is expected in polite society,' Alixe interrupted.

'Agreed,' Merrick said without hesitation.

'Agreed,' Alixe answered with equal swiftness. But deep down, her confidence faltered. She'd got her terms. There'd be no more moments like the one at the villa, like the one in front of the window. But she was going to pay—she just couldn't determine how.

Or when.

Chapter Ten

Four days into their agreement, Alixe was regretting it. Merrick had kept his word. He'd not kissed her, not tempted her to wanton passions, at least not in any way she could take issue with. He'd kept his part of the agreement, holding to the letter of the proverbial law, if not the spirit of it.

Even the slightest of his touches at her elbow managed to send *frissons* of anticipation through her, reminding her of other, less-decent touches, and of possibilities that existed if she would only ask for them. Mostly those touches reminded her that this was all her fault. The frustration that plagued her late at night alone in bed was of her own doing.

He was doing it on purpose, but she couldn't prove it, just as she couldn't substantiate the niggling feeling that the other shoe still hadn't dropped.

And then it did with a resounding clatter bright and early one morning when she'd least expected it. Of

course, that was how it always happened. She should
have known.

Alixe awoke to a sun-soaked room, well aware that
today held both excitement and danger. Today was the
day she was to take her completed translation to Vicar
Daniels and help set up the historical society's display
for tomorrow's fair in the village. That was the exciting part. The danger was what the fair stood for—a
day closer to the departure to London and the fate that
awaited her there.

She was keenly aware the house party had reached
its zenith and was careening towards its conclusion:
the fair in the village followed two days later by her
mother's much-anticipated midsummer ball. And she
had failed to stop it—not the ball, but her imminent
departure.

It wasn't all she'd failed at. She'd failed to shake
Merrick from her side and where she'd failed, he'd succeeded magnificently. She might not be the Toast of
London yet, but she'd become the Toast of the house
party. Merrick's presence at her side ensured a heightened interest in her that not even her plain, unobtrusive
garb could counteract. Being in his company made her
visible to others.

She had not noticed until it was too late that he'd
orchestrated their days into an easy pattern—mornings spent in the quiet seclusion of the library working
on the manuscript where they were joined at times by
Jamie or Ashe pursuing their own projects. During the
afternoons, she and Merrick were taken up with various groups until no one even considered inviting Mer-

rick without her. They played lawn bowls with Riordan and the young bucks he'd gathered whom he felt met his standard of debauchery. There was croquet and a badminton match against Ashe and Mrs Whitely. Merrick cheered from the sidelines for her at an impromptu archery contest among the young ladies and he saw to it that she stood beside him while he and Ashe engaged a pair of bragging riflemen in a friendly competition of marksmanship.

She had never lived like this before. She'd never allowed herself to as part of her self-imposed exile from society. She was discovering it was fun to be the centre of a group, to play and to laugh. Most of all it was fun to be with Merrick and it was easy to forget why he was with her.

Such forgetfulness was her biggest failure. He was luring her to London and then he'd disappear when his job was done. It had to stop. Today would be a day to start afresh in her campaign of resistance. The first thing to do was get dressed. She had a dress in mind, a sallow-yellow muslin that did nothing for her complexion.

With renewed determination, Alixe threw open the doors to her wardrobe, expecting to be met with the usual chaos that lay inside, stockings and ribbons peeking out of drawers where she'd haphazardly stuffed them. But there was nothing. It took a moment to digest the vision. Her wardrobe was entirely empty.

She had no clothes.

The olive dress she'd worn to the summer house was gone. The grey riding habit was gone. The pale-blue dinner gown she'd worn the first night was gone. There wasn't even a dressing robe she could throw over her nightrail. Alixe reached for the bell pull and yanked. There was something odd about all this. Wardrobes didn't simply disappear and Meg was far too experienced of a maid to do all the laundry at once.

Meg arrived in record time, having trouble hiding a smile. Alixe eyed her suspiciously. 'You seem happy today.'

'Yes, I suppose it's the prospect of the fair tomorrow.' Meg nearly giggled. 'Lord St Magnus's man, Fillmore, has asked if he could walk down with me.' Wonderful—now Merrick had got his well-manicured claws into her maid.

'I'm looking forward to the fair, too, only I'm afraid I won't be able to go since I haven't anything to wear.' Alixe gave a dramatic sigh. Meg had the good sense to look slightly sheepish.

'My wardrobe is empty, Meg. Do you know anything about that?'

Meg's sunny smile returned in full force. 'That's because you have all new clothes, my lady. Isn't it exciting?'

Alixe sat down hard on the bed. 'How is that possible? I haven't ordered anything.'

Meg opened the door and gestured out into the hallway. Her room began to fill with a procession of maids carrying box after box in all assorted shapes and sizes. 'It's all Lord St Magnus's doing, although I helped him a bit since he couldn't very well go rummaging around a lady's bedroom.'

Alixe listened, stunned. With Meg's help it hadn't been difficult to determine sizes. Nor had it been difficult to spirit her old gowns away, which had apparently been done last night while she was down at dinner.

Meg held up a white-muslin walking dress sprigged with pink flowers. 'This will be perfect for today, my lady. There's a light shawl in pink and a matching parasol to go with it.'

The gown was lovely in its simplicity, but it was not drab. She wanted her gowns back. She felt comfortable in them. She knew her limits in them. She needed them. Without them, her plans would fall apart. How could she convince St Magnus she was hopeless if she showed up wearing that pretty creation?

Yet what choice did she have? If she didn't put it on, there was nothing else to wear. She'd spend the day in her room, an unpalatable option. She'd miss the fair, miss seeing her manuscript on display and she'd have to explain why. The explanation sounded petty even to her. She couldn't very well argue she wasn't going downstairs because she had nothing to wear when there were boxes piled up in her room full of new clothes.

This all assumed Merrick would allow her to remain in her room. She fully expected he wouldn't. If she failed to appear for the departure to the fair, he'd come charging up here to demand the reason why. There she'd sit in her nightclothes without a robe to cover herself. Those blue eyes of his would run over her body and he would say something provocative that would make her blush, then something that would make her laugh and forget his insolence. At which point, she'd give up being angry. She would dress because she had no good reason not to that didn't sound childish and they would go about their day.

'My lady, should we dress?' Meg was still standing there, holding out the pretty muslin.

'Yes,' Alixe decided. She would not wait for the fight to come to her. The only way to stop Merrick would be to best him. 'Where is Lord St Magnus, Meg? I want to thank him, personally.'

'I believe Fillmore mentioned he was already at breakfast with Mr Bedevere on the verandah.'

Alixe grinned. Perfect. She knew exactly what to do. A stop by Merrick's rooms was in order. She was about to redefine sartorial elegance for him and return the 'favour'.

Ashe and Merrick sat at a small table on the verandah, enjoying a leisurely breakfast. Most of the ladies had opted for trays in their rooms. Other male guests ate in the breakfast room or at small tables nearby, taking in the coolness of the summer morning before the heat of the day.

'Riordan's not up yet?' Merrick enquired.

Ashe shrugged. 'We won't see him until noon and when we do, he'll be as growly as a bear. Celibacy and hangovers don't mix well for him.'

'It's barely been a week and a half.' Merrick laughed. 'Surely Riordan can manage that long.'

Ashe slid him a sly look. 'We haven't all had the

company of Lady Alixe to keep us occupied. Billiards and fishing lose their ability to keep a man fulfilled after a while. It'll be good to get back to London in a few days and the bountiful supply of willing women. This house party is a bit too chaste for me.' Ashe nudged Merrick with an elbow. 'Perhaps you and I should throw a house party, males only, at my hunting box after the Season. We can have Madame Antoinette send over her French girls. We can have a little competition, lay some wagers while we're laying the girls. How many are you up to, by the way? Have you hit two hundred yet?'

This was an old score. He and Ashe had long competed for who could claim the most conquests. Actresses, willing ladies of the *ton* and skilled courtesans of the *demi-monde* peopled the list of past lovers. But this morning, the claim was somewhat awkward. The lustre of the brag had become tarnished. It didn't seem to be a point of pride. What would Alixe think? She would not respect such behaviour. What others thought had never bothered him before, but this morning it did, especially when it came to a particular someone. 'What about you, Ashe? Up to fifty yet?'

'You're surly, Merrick.' Ashe laughed. 'Is the parson's mousetrap getting a bit dangerous? You've been spending a lot of time with Lady Alixe. Is there any hope of getting her up to snuff?'

Merrick tensed at Ashe's tone, wanting to defend Alixe. 'She's quite decent once you get to know her. You have to understand how difficult her predicament is. She's being forced to marry. None of this is of her choosing. I find I've come to admire her fortitude in the face of adversity.'

Ashe leaned forwards in deadly earnest. 'Listen to yourself, Merrick. You make it sound like a Drury Lane drama. *She's* being forced to marry? We're all forced to marry when it comes down to it. It's the price for being born noble. You and I are the lucky ones. We're second sons. We might escape that particular fate as long as our brothers don't see fit to die too soon. But Lady Alixe was fated for the altar the moment she was born. If you're not careful, you'll end up as her "predicament".' He paused and added a considering look. 'Unless that doesn't bother you? There are certain benefits to marrying her. She would solve your cash-flow issues.'

'I don't have a cash-flow problem.'

'Yes, I suppose that requires the possession of money to start with.' Ashe laughed. 'You are the slyest old fox, Merrick. I think you will marry her, after all, with just the right amount of remorse to convince old Folkestone you hadn't planned it this way all along.'

'That is hardly my intention,' Merrick ground out, fighting a rising urge to take a shot at Ashe's perfect jaw. He didn't like thinking of Alixe in those terms. She was more than someone to be bartered away. She was full of passion and life, intelligence and spirit. He didn't want to see that quashed by a heartless marriage to him or to anyone not of her choosing.

'You're not really her protector, you know,' Ashe drawled. Merrick recognised that drawl. Ashe was about to make some profound statement. 'Don't fool yourself into thinking you're a knight in shining armour awakening her to her true self, that whatever you've been doing with her these past days is in her best interest. You're not on her side. You're leading her away from everything she professes to want in order to save your own freedom. If she's as smart as you say she is, she'll work that out eventually. Be ready for it. Don't kid yourself into thinking otherwise.'

Because she'll hate you for it. Merrick heard the unspoken message. He pulled out his pocket watch and flipped it open. She was probably upstairs hating him right now. By his calculations, Meg should have presented the new wardrobe already. It would be enough to get Alixe started in London. The other half would be waiting for her once she arrived. After the debacle with the riding habit, he'd sent measurements and style notes to a dressmaker in London for evening wear and ball gowns. The other gowns had been supplied by a local draper. It had been rather enjoyable spending someone else's money and the earl had been all too glad to pay the bill.

Alixe would look stunning in her no-expense-spared wardrobe. But Ashe's comment gouged. He wasn't Alixe's protector. More honestly, he was her betrayer. Thanks to his efforts, she was well garbed and, with her funds, she'd have the choice of the right kind of husband this go-round, a choice she couldn't refuse for a third time. He didn't want to betray her. He was not a malicious man by nature, but if he didn't help her find a decent husband, it would be far worse to be married to him and his family full of secrets.

'Look at that,' Ashe murmured appreciatively, nodding at a point over Merrick's shoulder. 'Exactly what have you been doing with Lady Alixe? You might just be free of the parson's mouse trap yet.'

Merrick turned. Alixe stood on the verandah, wearing the sprigged muslin he'd told Meg to lay out. She looked exquisite. The pink-ribbon trim beneath her breasts drew the eye ever so subtly upwards to the high, firm quality of those breasts while the tiny lace trim on the low-scooped neckline of the bodice reminded the looker those breasts belonged to a lady. Her hair had been simply styled into a soft chignon at the base of her neck. Everything about her was cameo perfect. Alixe did look beautiful. She also looked angry.

Chapter Eleven

'May I have a word with you?' Alixe approached the table, her colour high and flushing her cheeks delightfully.

'You must know it is highly unorthodox for a young lady to approach a gentleman,' Merrick began in low teasing tones, noting with a surreptitious sweep of the verandah the amount of eyes turned in their direction.

'*You* must know it is highly unorthodox to take a lady's clothes,' Alixe hissed.

'Oh, my, Merrick, whatever have you done now?' Ashe stifled a chuckle.

Alixe shot Ashe a quelling look. 'Well? Might I have that word?' She trained her gaze on Merrick, her foot tapping. 'I must speak to you right away.'

Merrick scanned the verandah. He didn't want a scene. His best option for privacy was the gardens that lay at the foot of the shallow verandah stairs. 'Perhaps a walk in the garden would settle my breakfast. Would you care to join me?'

'I want my clothes back,' Alixe began the moment they reached the bottom of the wide stairs.

'Why? You look perfectly lovely in this ensemble. You cannot argue that this outfit is less fetching than that olive sack you tramp around the countryside in.'

'Because they're mine and you had no right to take them!'

Tears threatened in her eyes, a reaction that made Merrick feel decisively uncomfortable. This was one area of the female mystery he'd not yet solved with any great success.

'You couldn't go to London looking like a farmer's daughter,' Merrick offered. No woman he'd ever known would balk at the size of the wardrobe he'd had delivered to Alixe's room. He'd counted on that assumption to overcome any opposition.

'That's just it. I don't want to go to London at all.' Merrick heard the frustration welling up in her voice. She'd all but stamped her foot. This wasn't about clothes. This was about all the things that had been taken from her in the last two weeks. The urge to protect surged strong and hard within him. Alixe Burke was getting to him in the most unexpected ways. He'd not expected to care so deeply about what happened to her. He'd always thought of himself as a selfish creature. It was surprising to realise otherwise.

'Alixe…' he began, looking for a way to apologise. But Alixe was too impatient.

'No, don't say anything. There's nothing you can

say. There's nothing you can do. This is all your fault, you and your stupid wager with Redfield. You never should have taken it.'

'If not me, then it would have been someone else.' Merrick stopped strolling and turned her to face him. 'Don't you see? Redfield was out to get you. Someone that night would have taken the wager.' He had yet to gather up any substantial proof of that. Redfield had spent the house party dutifully charming the matrons and putting on a well-mannered performance that suggested he was all he purported to be. But Merrick's instincts were seldom wrong.

'So it is inevitable. I am to accept my fate and go meekly to London.'

'Quite possibly, my dear, although it gives me no pleasure to say it. However, no one says you have to hate it.'

Alixe's brow made a small furrow. 'Isn't the expression "no one says you have to *like* it"?'

'That's what *everyone* says. It's not what *I* say. Why not enjoy the experience? Enjoy the beautiful clothes, enjoy the glittering parties. Enjoy each day, Alixe. Don't fret too much about the future, it spoils the present.' Merrick looked around the garden. 'Here's a perfect example. We have this glorious day spread before us and no plans. Let's drive down to the village and help with your historical society. Fillmore and your Meg can come to make it decent. We can pack a picnic to enjoy on the way home.' He didn't wait for an argument. 'Go get your things and meet me on the drive in twenty minutes.'

* * *

The fair itself was to be held on the green, a wide
space atop the west cliffs. The cliff end of the green
was edged by a promenade overlooking the sea and
Alixe couldn't imagine a more striking setting. With
the blue sky overhead and the bustling excitement of
friends and neighbours on the green, it was hard to
stay angry at Merrick for spiriting away her clothes,
especially when she felt wonderful in the new sprigged
muslin. She'd dressed in her plain gowns for so long
she'd forgotten how much fun it was to dress up.

Merrick helped her down from the gig and a group
of workers waved them over to the booth being assem-
bled by the historical society. It was a heady moment
to be swept up into the group, everyone exclaiming
over her translation. Headier still were the hours that
followed. Alixe put an apron on over her gown and
threw herself into organising the displays with the other
women while Merrick joined the men in constructing
the wooden frame for the booth and hanging bunting.

His willingness to join in came as a surprise. He
was always immaculately turned out and building fair
booths was not the immaculate work of a gentleman.
But Merrick had not hesitated. His coat had come off
and his shirt sleeves had gone up. She caught sight of
him with a hammer in one hand and nails clenched between his teeth. She could not help but stare.

It was hard to imagine London's premier rake engaged in such work. Then again, it was hard to con-
ceive of London's premier rake doing most of what
he'd done in the past two weeks. He had not balked at

playing cards with Mrs Pottinger's group or cringed at donating himself to the cause of charming wallflowers at the house party. Neither had he shied away from his pledge to her father. In their own ways, these were the actions of a man who was more honourable than he might first appear.

'Your fellow's a handsome man,' Letty Goodright commented beside her, sorting through a pile of sixteenth-century bonnets someone had donated to the display.

'He's not my fellow.' Alixe quickly returned her gaze to the items in front of her where her eyes should have been all along.

'Isn't he?' Letty reached for another pile of miscellaneous clothing. 'A man doesn't spend the day sweating in the sun for no good reason. Other than you, I can't see what reason he has for helping out. He's not from around here. This village fair is nothing to him. I know men, my dear, and this one is interested in you.'

'Well, maybe.' What else could she say? She couldn't very well explain the arrangement between her and Merrick. At least it wasn't an outright lie. Merrick was interested in her, just for different reasons than the ones Letty presumed. Letty did know men. She was one of those lush-figured, earthy women that managed to be pretty while possessing a rather robust figure. She'd had her pick of men in the village at sixteen, had married a local farmer of good standing in their little community and now, ten years later, trailed a string of seven rambunctious children behind her whenever she went to market.

'There's no maybe about it. He's smitten with you. Look at him.'

Alixe looked up to see Merrick flash her a smile, nails and all. It was a ridiculous grin and she couldn't help but laugh.

'He's a charmer.' Letty clucked. 'Let me give you some advice. Don't give in too soon. The charmers all like a challenge whether they know it or not.'

'I don't mean to give in at all,' Alixe retorted. But the idea was secretly tempting. He played his role so convincingly, it would be easy to believe Merrick was falling in love with her.

Letty tossed her a coy look. 'Giving in is all the fun. Of course, you'll give in, just don't do it too soon.'

'I'm leaving for London when Mother's house party is done. I expect I'll meet some other, more suitable men,' Alixe said with a touch of primness.

'Unsuitable men are more fun and they make the best husbands once they've reformed. Take my Bertram, for example, a scalawag if there ever was one. Why, before he met me, he was in the public house every night, drinking and playing cards. His father had despaired of him ever becoming a serious landowner. But then he met me...'

Alixe smiled politely. She'd heard the stories about Bertram and Letty before. Her thoughts could safely meander from the conversation. There was soundness in Letty's counsel. There was no one more unsuitable than Merrick and he was extraordinary amounts of fun. Her life had been considerably more entertaining since he'd entered it. But she mustn't forget the price. She must *never* forget the price. He was going to entertain her all the way to the altar where he'd leave her to another man. For which she should be thankful. There was no amount of reform that would make him into an exemplary husband who did not stray from his wife. Jamie had said as much when he'd warned her. Based on what she'd seen of Merrick, she was inclined to believe her brother.

Merrick came striding towards them, his shirt splotched with sweat and his hair tousled. He'd never looked more handsome or more real than he did at that moment. The realness of him was far more intoxicating than any sartorial manufacturing could create. His grin was easy. 'The booth is complete, if you would like to start bringing your displays over.'

A half-hour later, the displays were arranged to satisfaction, her translation in pride of place at the front in a glass case Vicar Daniels had taken from the church.

'I hope *that's* not the church.' Merrick pointed to a large ruin on the edge of the Leas and everyone laughed.

'No, that's the church of St Mary and St Eanswythe,' Vicar Daniels explained. 'What you're looking at are the ruins of the original Abbey. It was destroyed around 1095. But there's a priory now and monks still live there, although I suspect they will be moved in the near future to a less-ancient home.'

'We are hoping to do some restoring of the Abbey. The project will be extensive. We've been raising money for quite some time,' Alixe put in. This was a project dear to her. St Eanswythe was not only a local saint, but a woman who had challenged a king for the right to found and rule an abbey in a man's world. 'We're nearly there. We're hoping this display will help generate the last few donations.'

'I don't think I've ever heard of St Eanswythe,' Merrick admitted with a grin.

'Our Alixe can tell you all about her. She's made the saint a special point of study.' Letty smiled mischievously. Alixe would have pinched her if she'd been standing closer. 'You should show Lord St Magnus the ruins and tell him the stories of Eanswythe's miracles.'

Merrick complied, immediately understanding Letty's game. 'I would love to see the ruins. Perhaps you and I might find a place to picnic in the shade while we tour your landmarks.'

'We can't abandon everyone when there's work to be done,' Alixe protested. The last time she'd picnicked with Merrick had been disastrous for her. He'd kissed her at the Roman villa.

'Off with you.' Letty made a shooing gesture with her hands. 'There's hardly anything left to be done and you've worked through lunch.' The group agreed, making short work of Alixe's last line of defence.

'Resistance is useless, my dear,' Merrick said smugly, tucking her arm through his and leading her away from the safety of the group. 'Relax, it's just lunch, Alixe. We're going to talk about ham sandwiches and lemonade. What could happen?'

'Plenty happened the last time we picnicked,' Alixe reminded him sharply. Being in a group of her mother's house guests had not protected her from her flight of fancy at the villa.

'Yes, but now you have your agreement in place. What could possibly happen with your friends a mere shout away and Fillmore and Meg to hand? Really, Alixe, you make me out to be a wolf.'

Merrick-logic was all too persuasive. He made it sound safe and reasonable. What could happen indeed? Regardless of the facts, she knew better. Even the most usual of events turned into adventures when Merrick was around. A naughty, rebellious part of her could hardly wait to find out—the part that wanted to take his advice and not worry about the future, the part that wanted to appreciate the present. Perhaps Merrick was right. If she couldn't change the inevitable, she might as well enjoy the journey. Why shouldn't she enjoy the fact that she was wearing a new dress, the weather was fine and a handsome man wanted her attentions? Why shouldn't she dice with the devil just a little, just once?

'You shouldn't have done it,' Merrick said between bites of cheese. 'You should have followed your instincts and resisted. You have very fine instincts about people, Alixe.'

They'd found a place under the shade of a leafy maple in the corner of the ruined churchyard. Their picnic lay spread out before them: a cheese wheel of cheddar, a loaf of brown bread and a basket of pears. Merrick had stretched his long limbs and lay back, hands behind his head. Alixe wished she could afford the luxury of doing the same. It would be heaven to lie back on the blanket and look up at the sky through the leafy canopy of trees. But a lady did not indulge, especially not when it would mean lying next to a man.

'Why do you say that? Especially since it's far too late for me to go back now.'

'Because I am a wolf, contrary to my protests otherwise.' Merrick took a savage bite from a pear to illustrate his point.

Alixe took a more delicate bite of her food. 'You may be a wolf, but you are not a ravenous wolf. You are in complete control of yourself and for that reason, I have nothing to fear from you.'

Merrick rolled to his side, propping himself up on one arm, his eyes alight with his special brand of mischief. 'I have been coaxing women off the paths at Vauxhall since I was sixteen. Coaxing a well-bred lady into a churchyard is child's play by comparison.'

He was teasing her, but there was a hard truth lurking around his humour. 'Why do you think that is?' she queried.

'Women know what can happen in the dark shadows at Vauxhall. They're warned about the possibilities. But well-bred virgins never believe anything untoward could happen in a churchyard.' Merrick took another crisp bite of his pear and chuckled. 'As if God pays more attention to what is happening in his churchyards than he does to the dim paths of Vauxhall.'

Really, he'd gone too far there. A scold was in order, but she barely got the words out before her own laughter bubbled up at the image his words created. 'Merrick, you shouldn't say things like that.'

'No more than you should laugh about them and yet here we are doing both.' Merrick finished off his pear and tossed the core towards the base of a tree trunk for the birds to find later.

'Now, tell me about St Eanswythe in the hopes that we can redeem ourselves with a more suitable subject for our surroundings.'

The request took her by surprise. No one had ever asked her to tell them about St Eanswythe. She'd delivered a talk about the local saint to a few clubs and the historical society, but no one socially in the course of polite conversation had ever asked her about her favourite topic. She began tentatively at first, giving Merrick a chance to interrupt, to show any sign of uninterest. But no sign came. Instead, his blue eyes remained attentively fixed on her, his head nodding in attention.

'She performed three miracles and won the king's approval to establish the first convent in England,' Alixe concluded.

'You sound impressed with her,' Merrick commented.

'I am. She fought for what she wanted. She turned down marriage to a king.'

'Ah, correction.' Merrick wagged his finger, throwing his recently acquired knowledge back at her. 'She offered the king a chance to win her. She wagered and she would have had to pay if she'd lost.' He reached for another pear. 'Not unlike yourself.'

'I did not wager.'

Merrick shrugged a shoulder. 'A slight discrepancy, I should think. Like her, you have also given up the complications of life for a simple one and, like her, you have devoted yourself to thwarting suitors for your hand.'

'She did it on purpose,' Alixe said to be contrary.

'So have you,' Merrick countered readily enough. 'You're pretty, you're smart, you're titled and you're rich. You've merely taken pains to hide all that and make yourself difficult to obtain.'

Merrick inched closer to her on the blanket and reached out a hand to tug at her chignon, his hand softly sweeping the gentle curve of her jaw. 'Do you think it worth the sacrifice, pretty one? The world of man is not as bad as you think.'

Alixe's breath caught at the sound of his voice, low and personal in the quiet of the afternoon. Meg and Fillmore had taken themselves off a while ago to see if they could spot France from the cliff-walk promenade.

Her hair came loose with another tug and spilled down her back. 'Would you die as your Eanswythe did? Without knowing the touch of a man? Without knowing the secret pleasures she was made for?' His hand tangled gently in her hair, pressing her forwards to him, his mouth taking hers in a kiss. She thought fleetingly of their agreement, but those words seemed to provide inadequate protection at the present. Instead, she gave herself up to the kiss, a small moan escaping her. She was all heady compliance.

She would never remember quite how it progressed from there. Had she drawn him down to her, or had he pressed her back on to the blanket? Somehow she was beneath him, her hips moving in rhythm against his, his sex heavy against her thigh where trousers met skirts and neither of them thinking much beyond the moment. His hand was at her breast, tracing teasing circles through the cloth. She arched against him, intuitively looking for release from the frantic heat pulsing through her, knowing he possessed the answer, the ability to assuage her. Her hands were at his shoulders, kneading the muscles beneath his shirt, wanting to do more. Then her fingers were working his buttons, pushing the halves of his shirt back, finding the muscled expanse of bare skin underneath. Her palms skimmed the planes of his chest, her thumbs running over his nipples much as he'd done for her. He groaned his delight, his hips pressing harder against hers in response. His mouth was devouring her now, his hands shoving up her skirts so that she would be bare to him and it was still not enough. She was hungry, so very hungry for this, for his touch.

She was aware of his hand at her most private place, of his hand unerringly parting her damp curls and stroking the secret nub until the sensations he ignited drowned out any thought of reality, of recognition over what they were doing. Then he took her beyond all thought where she bucked hard against his hand and he lay beside her, crooning soft words of encouragement until she gave herself over entirely to the pleasures that swamped her.

She was a long time recovering. Alixe wanted nothing more than to lay beneath the maples in a well-sated stupor for ever. Merrick seemed content to lay there, too, propped on an elbow, looking down at her face, an idle hand stroking back an errant strand of hair.

'What was that?' Alixe said, her voice coming out slightly hoarse.

Merrick smiled. 'The pleasures of the world of man, my dear. Did you like it?'

'You know I did.' It was an embarrassing admission. From what she'd been told, a lady didn't like such things.

'You should. There's nothing wrong with liking it. You were made for it, I was made for it,' Merrick said softly.

'Is this what happens to virgins in churchyards?' Alixe quipped, her wits coming back to her as the haze of sated desire receded.

Merrick chuckled. 'Yes, except your Eanswythe.'

A wave of sadness and reality swept over Alixe. She turned to face Merrick, acutely aware they lay side by side in such close proximity. It would be entirely shocking if anyone found them this way. 'Is that why you did it? To show me what she missed?'

Alixe didn't want it to be the truth, that this most incredible experience, most intimate experience, had been another of his lessons.

'No, pretty one, it's not.'

Chapter Twelve

Merrick cut through the water, cleaving it with powerful strokes in the hopes that if he swam hard enough, long enough, he could exorcise the heat *she* raised in his body, the turmoil she raised in his mind. Alixe Burke had become dangerous to his sense of well-being.

He had not meant for things to progress as they had that afternoon. He had not risen in the morning with any thought of showing Alixe pleasure on a picnic blanket beneath a summer sky. Merrick flipped on to his back and began a long, methodical stroke that took him across the lake. If it had been an instructive interlude or a love-game of the type he played with his myriad women, he would have a proper perspective for understanding what had transpired—the generating of physical pleasure. But that had not been what had happened.

She had roused to him with a natural passion devoid of coy artifice. Those sherry eyes of hers had widened in awe and amazement, her untutored hips had sought release against his with no concept of what they were asking of him; the artlessness of her wanting had been a heady aphrodisiac to his jaded sense of sexual conquest. And it had fired him beyond reason, driven him to answer the calls of her body in ways she wanted, but could not imagine without him.

His body remembered every moment of her pleasure, of her body arching into his, her hips bucking against his hand. Even now, hours later, the memory of it was burned into his body, the simple recalling of it enough to bring to life a hard-suppressed erection. He had told her the truth. Touching her had nothing to do with lessons. He had touched her because he'd wanted to, because he was enchanted with her storytelling. Her face had come alive as she'd spun her tales of Eanswythe. He could have lain on the blanket and listened to her all afternoon. His London cronies would have laughed to see the sophisticated Merrick St Magnus captivated by the simple tales of country saints. For that matter, they would have laughed to see him with hammer in hand building fair booths.

But it had seemed right. He'd spun a fantasy for himself today with Alixe at the centre of it. It had been a lovely escape to imagine himself a country squire working with his neighbours, casting a glance every now and then to where his pretty wife chatted with other women. It was a perfect image, free of the entanglements of his debauched ways. The man in his fantasy didn't wager on how many women he could bed in a year. The man in his fantasy needed only one woman and had the ability to remain constant. That man would not grow bored in the country as Merrick most certainly would.

Merrick floated on his back, his body exhausted, his mind still restless. It was an escape, nothing more. London waited and with it his regular life, his social rounds, his endless search for wagers and women that would keep his pockets lined. And his father waited. Reality waited. Alixe Burke would see him for what he was behind the clothes and easy words. In London there would be no hiding from the rumours. Even if he did nothing outrageous for the next six weeks of the Season, there were rumours enough from his past to convince her most thoroughly of his unsuitability.

That would be for the best. He'd not been the only one caught up in his little fantasy today. He'd caught her watching him in the same manner he'd been watching her. For all her protestations, Alixe was not immune to him. He'd initiated her into the pleasures of physical intimacy. That would count for something with a woman like Alixe Burke.

Merrick snorted up at the dusking sky. It was laughable really, the idea of he and Alixe together. Rakes didn't marry good women who wanted to rebuild churches and translate old documents. And yet Merrick could not dismiss the idea that Alixe would be a perfect lover, that hard-to-find mix between untutored honesty and a curiosity in her own sensuality that overrode any annoying pretence towards modesty and embarrassment. He had no use for any woman who was too shy to admit to her own longings.

Merrick gave up on the pond. The heat of the afternoon had faded to the pleasant warmth of a summer evening. He would be missed and Lady Folkestone had entertainments planned for the evening—an alfresco dinner on the lawn and fireworks. Merrick towelled himself dry with his shirt and reached for the clean change of clothes he'd stopped by the house to get before setting out. He thrust his hand through the sleeve, tugging at the shoulder, and stopped, the sleeve coming off in his hand. What the hell...?

Merrick slid the ruined shirt off his body and studied the seams. They'd been ripped out so that only the basting remained. No wonder the sleeve had torn so effortlessly. He'd have to speak to Fillmore. He'd also have to walk home shirtless. Not that he cared. The evening was warm and he knew enough back paths to avoid encountering anyone.

He reached for his trousers and pulled them on. He bent to collect his boots and heard an ominous rip. Merrick straightened and laughed into the evening sky. It wasn't Fillmore he needed to speak with. It was an amber-eyed minx who'd wanted a little bit of revenge for his having stolen her clothes.

The west lawn looked like a fairyland with coloured lanterns strung from poles and candles under glass shields lighting the tables. Around Alixe, guests exclaimed over the summer magic her mother had created for the alfresco dinner. The meal would be the talk of London when the guests returned to town in a few days. But Alixe had little time to appreciate the summer splendour. Her eyes were busily quartering the guests for any sign of Merrick. He'd returned her to the house and abruptly left again. To her knowledge he had not returned yet. When she'd asked Fillmore where he might be, Fillmore had merely said he'd taken a change of clothes and left for a swim.

Now she was worried. And she was feeling a little bit guilty. What if he had picked up the clothes she had altered that morning? She had meant for him to discover her little prank in the privacy of his room. If he'd taken those clothes to a swimming hole… The image of a naked Merrick striding through the forest like a primordial god, tattered clothes in hand, brought a hot flush to her cheeks. He would act as if it didn't matter, as if roaming around in his 'altogether' was a perfectly natural experience. She had not meant to embarrass him, just to show him that she would not submit easily.

It seemed a poor prank after what had happened that afternoon. The simple pleasures of the outing had become complicated in the wake of what had occurred on the picnic blanket. He said he hadn't done it to teach her a lesson and she had found comfort in those words as long as she didn't examine them too closely.

If it hadn't been a lesson, what had it been? She knew without doubt that she was harbouring a perilous fascination with him. The interest she held in his life, the attraction she felt, the frantic wildness he raised in her when he touched her could no longer be explained away as general curiosity. There had been suitors before, but none with whom she'd felt this level of allure.

None of them had inclined her to even a kiss, let alone risk the temptations he'd presented her with today.

Those temptations went beyond the intimacy of what he'd done for her, although that had been exquisite and extraordinary in the sense that nothing had prepared her for the possibilities of such pleasure. She was still awash with the sensations. But there had been other temptations, too. He had listened to her tell the tales of Eanswythe with a sincerity that could not be faulted.

Today, she had been the centre of his attentions, not just during the stories, but throughout the entire afternoon. He'd built those booths for her, helped with the historical society for her. She could not recall the last time anyone had been so entirely devoted to her and she hadn't even asked. The greatest temptation of all was to fall for the fantasy he'd created: a fantasy where she wasn't being carted off and paraded on the marriage mart, a fantasy where he was not the greatest lover of women in all of London and had likely pleasured countless women the way he'd pleasured her. In this fantasy, he was hers alone.

And for all that, she'd ripped the seams on his clothes so that they wouldn't hold when he put them on. She wished she hadn't.

Couples were pairing up at the round dinner tables set out across the lawn. The house party had been a success. Several matches would come of these two weeks. Alixe's gaze darted through the groupings, searching for Jamie. She was feeling distinctly *de trop* without a partner. She had not realised how implicitly she'd come to rely on Merrick's presence at her side throughout the week. If he was absent, walking around naked out there in the summer night, she had only herself to blame.

Gentle hands skimmed her bare shoulders and a familiar scent enveloped her. 'Missing me yet?' came Merrick's voice at her ear.

'Please tell me you're wearing clothes,' Alixe whispered back.

Merrick's warm chuckle was all the reassurance she needed, bringing with it a sense that rightness had been restored to her world. 'I am, no thanks to you, minx.' It was a playful reproach. He was not angry.

'I am sorry.'

'Don't be, I rather enjoyed the joke.' He leaned in, the delightful smell of his cologne wrapping around her. 'You could have enjoyed it, too, if you'd been there. I did have to walk back half-naked.'

'I am sorry, truly.'

'To have missed it? Of course you are. Most would be.' His voice was a naughty whisper against her neck. 'But you are already familiar with my altogether, so perhaps you feel the loss more keenly.'

Alixe laughed. 'If I had a fan, I'd smack you for that.'

Merrick made a small bow and pulled something from his inner pocket. 'But you do.'

He presented her with a small ivory-boned fan done in lace on the points and the fabric of the body painted with delicate multi-coloured flowers. 'Oh, there are even sequins sewn on the petals,' Alixe exclaimed over the little details, delighting in how the sequins caught the play of the candlelight. 'Merrick, it's lovely. It might be quite the loveliest thing anyone has ever given me.' She looped the ribbon strap about her wrist and let it dangle experimentally. 'Thank you.'

'I am glad you like it. Now, shall we find a table?'

Merrick's hand was warm at the small of her back and she could feel the fantasy rushing back. 'I see Ashe and Mrs Whitely over there. We could join them and seal everyone's suspicions.'

It would be the smart thing to do. Her mother had most adroitly allowed her guests to sit where they'd like. It allowed the gentlemen to declare their preferences most subtly, a very fitting gesture as the party came to a close.

Merrick guided her through the maze of tables, his hand a constant light pressure at her back. She was well aware of people watching them. She was sure many had seen him give her the fan and many more were watching to see if he'd 'declare' himself the way others had tonight with their seating preference.

Merrick held out the chair for her and helped her arrange her skirts before sitting beside her. Riordan and Jamie joined them, Jamie bringing over a distant cousin who'd come for a few days to take in the ball before going on to London.

They made a merry group. Wine flowed freely, but carefully, and the gentlemen indulged them by telling stories from their college days that Alixe was certain were heavily edited for public consumption. This was a side of Merrick rarely seen, although she had glimpsed it on brief occasions, a Merrick who was at ease the way he'd been earlier today. This was not the cynical Merrick with his jaded innuendos, nor was it the Merrick whose proper behaviour was almost so perfect among society it seemed to subtly mock that same society.

Merrick was the life of the table, engaging the quiet cousin, and ribbing Riordan when his manners flagged. *My word, he is truly the sun they all revolve around,* Alixe thought. He really was remarkable.

After cheese and summer fruit had been served, Jamie rose and took his leave. Fireworks would be starting and he had hosting duties that required him to circulate among the tables. Soon, candles would be doused to make the most of the summer darkness. In anticipation of that, couples were making their way to viewing locations around the lawn.

'Come with me,' Merrick said in hushed tones. 'I have it on good authority from Jamie that the best viewing will be on the rise over there.'

Discreetly, he led her apart from the larger group. He'd planned well. A blanket awaited them, already laid out, pinned to the ground with a small woven basket. The location was indeed ideal. It put them at the back of the crowd. Everyone else would be facing away from them when the fireworks went off and it was just dark enough to not be noticed.

Alixe seated herself on the blanket and opened her fan, still touched by the unexpected gift. 'It is very pretty.'

'Not nearly as pretty as the one who holds it.' Merrick smiled. 'How do you like your wardrobe now that you've had time to become accustomed to it? You've chosen well tonight—the gold silk de Chine is deeper than a yellow, it sets off your hair wonderfully.'

'It's magnificent. You chose well.'

'I chose for *you*. Enjoy it even if you cannot bring yourself to enjoy the reasons for it. I liked thinking of all the money your father was spending. It served him right for putting you in this position,' Merrick said slyly with a wink that made her laugh. He reached over and captured her hand where it held the fan, his voice dropping. 'But this was not something your father paid for.'

A true souvenir, then. More complications. What did it mean that he'd chosen this token of his own accord? Jamie had insinuated Merrick's pockets were thinly lined and yet he'd spent his limited funds on a trinket for her. Was it merely his custom to give ladies presents? Did it mean anything? She wanted it to mean everything, that he'd fallen for the fantasy, too. A dangerous truth began to take root in her mind: after fighting it for so long, she might be falling in love.

A hushed pop and the soft hiss of liquid being poured into a glass called her back to reality. 'Champagne, Alixe?' Merrick passed her a flute.

'So that's what was in the basket!' Alixe took the glass. 'This is a rare treat indeed.'

Merrick clinked his glass against hers, his eyes on her, burning with their intensity. 'A toast, Alixe, to all a man can ask for: a beautiful woman to himself on a lovely summer night.'

Alixe sipped the cool liquid to dissipate the lump

that welled in her throat. If the afternoon had been magical, the evening had quickly become astonishing. She had not missed the import of the fan, and now the champagne and—oh, my, was that a bowl of strawberries he was laying out? All for her. He was making it so easy to believe.

'Open, Alixe,' he commanded huskily, popping a juicy berry in her mouth. She could feel the berry dribble on her lip and flicked out her tongue to catch the droplets.

'Allow me.' Merrick leaned forwards, taking her mouth in a kiss.

'No, allow me,' Alixe said, seized with a sudden daring. She offered him a strawberry and he took it in his mouth, teeth bared, and bit, his eyes never leaving hers. She drew a sharp breath, struck by the sensuality of it.

'I could do that to you, too, Alixe.' He gave a wicked smile. 'My mouth at your breast, suckling and perhaps the tiniest of nips to heighten the sensation.'

The mere suggestion sent a thrumming heat to the core of her and she felt herself rouse as she had that afternoon. Madness surged.

'And you? What could I do for you? Can I pleasure you the way you have pleasured me?' A dangerous wildness edged her voice. He was holding her with his eyes and she could not look away. The future could be damned in exchange for this moment, this adventure.

'You can, if you're willing. You could take me in your hand.'

His hand covered hers, guiding it to where his length

pressed against the fall of his trousers. He was fully aroused beneath the fabric and Alixe knew to touch him this way was not enough.

'I want to feel *you* against my hand, not the cloth,' she murmured. She could be astonished by her own audacity later, but not now. She did not want to think here in the summer night. She fumbled with the buttons and sought him in the darkness. Her hand closed over the length of him, hot and hard within the circle of her fist.

Merrick gave a small moan as her hand clasped him and began to move over the thick extent of him. Above them the first fireworks fractured the sky with their colours. She experimentally stroked the wide tender head of his manhood, eliciting a gratified exhalation from Merrick. This was glorious power indeed to know she could excite him so thoroughly. Merrick wrapped his hand about hers once more, settling her into a rhythm as her hand moved up and down his shaft. Then he leaned back, giving himself over to her ministrations while fireworks sprayed their colours across the night's dark canvas.

Alixe felt him surge once more against her hand, spending himself in warm release, and she knew she would not forget this, no matter what happened in London, no matter what happened for the rest of her life. She would not forget the evening she pleasured *him* beneath a summer sky with champagne and fireworks.

She could not expect to hold him beyond the few days that remained, but she could make the most of what time she had. There would be plenty of time later to sort through the foolishness of falling for Merrick St Magnus.

Chapter Thirteen

'What the hell do you think you're doing?' Ashe threw back the curtains, letting sunlight splinter mercilessly against Merrick's eyes.

Merrick threw up a hand to ward off the bright glare with a groan. 'More to the point, what the hell do you think you're doing?' Merrick opened one eye a crack. Ashe was dressed for riding, a fact worth noting given Ashe's penchant for late nights and later mornings. By the look of things from the one eye he'd managed to open, the morning was not far advanced.

'*I* am leaving, something I'd advise you to consider as well. Toss your necessities into a valise and we can be on the road before breakfast.' Ashe was already tearing through the wardrobe on the hunt for his travelling valise.

'Whatever are you talking about?' Merrick groused.

'I'm talking about last night. You're damned lucky I was the only one who saw you up on the hill last night with your champagne seduction and Lady Alixe's hand on your cock.'

Merrick sat up, instantly awake. It was funny how shocking news could do that to a body. Merrick's mind raced even as his words fumbled. His first instinct was to protect Alixe. 'I can explain.' The words sounded ridiculous. He couldn't come up with a plausible alternative for Alixe's hand between his legs.

Ashe laughed outright at his poor effort. 'Explain? I assure you, I don't need an explanation for what I saw. There was no mistaking it.'

Another panicked thought swept him. 'Did anyone else?' He'd been fairly sure the location would not draw attention.

'No, I told you already I was the only one out that way. You weren't the only one with seduction on your mind.' Ashe was impatient. 'Now, let's get you packed and be off.'

'I can't leave. I've got to take Alixe to the fair and there's the masquerade ball tomorrow night—'

Ashe cut him off in mid-list, disgusted. 'All of which are reasons you should be leaving today. Listen to yourself, Merrick.'

'Why are you leaving?' Merrick opted for a different tack. 'There's only two days to go and there's entertainment aplenty.' He eyed Ashe with a speculative gaze. 'Is it Mrs Whitely?'

Ashe was not forthcoming. 'I prefer to leave before things sour,' he offered, purposely obtuse. 'You ought to prefer it, too. You've done your job for Folkestone. The party is winding down, no one has exposed Alixe for being discovered in the library with you and she's ready to lay siege to London. You can meet up with her there, dance a few times and call it square with Folkestone. Whatever you still need to do for her relies on being in town. There's nothing more that requires you here. Tell Folkestone you want to go on ahead and prepare the way with a well-placed comment here and there.' Ashe paused, carefully considering his next words. 'Leaving now will make it clear your time with Alixe is nothing more than discharging a gentleman's agreement. Even I can see things are starting to get "confused" if last night was any indicator.'

Merrick shook his head. 'Alixe is counting on me today.' Alixe would be devastated to wake and find him gone. She would think his departure had to do with last night. He could not bear for her to think he'd fled because of *that*.

'Dear lord, I have a fool in love on my hands.' Ashe faced him, hands on hips, a challenge to deny his claim. 'You've gone and fallen for your own creation.' Ashe shook his head. 'It's impossible, you know. For one thing, Jamie will kill you. For another, his father will kill you. Either way, you'll end up dead. You weren't meant for her.'

Ashe gave a scornful laugh. 'Men like you and me aren't supposed to marry the virgin daughters of earls. There's only marriage if you continue down this road, Merrick. Surely you know that? You cannot expect to dally with her and play at love simply to walk away when you get tired of this little fantasy. You will get tired. You're not made for monogamy and you know it.'

Merrick shoved back the bedcovers and rolled out of

bed. 'Thank you for the sermon, Vicar.' He was cross with Ashe and with himself. He hardly knew what the truth was any more when it came to his feelings for Alixe Burke. He had gone far beyond being sympathetic for her. Sympathy had long ago morphed into admiration and admiration had turned into something much more powerful. He had only a few days left with Alixe and it would be a hardship to say goodbye. He would prolong it if he could.

'You're upset because I speak of reality,' Ashe said from the bank of windows. 'A gentleman knows when to make his exit.'

Merrick snorted at that. 'You and I have never pretended to be gentlemen.'

Ashe relented, his tone softening. 'Stay if you must, but see things as they are, not as you wish them to be. I am off and I am taking Riordan with me.'

Merrick gave a rueful smile at the notion of Ashe playing nursemaid to Riordan. Ashe was hardly the tolerant nurturing sort. 'Try to sober him up. He's been drinking too much.'

'I will. London has its distractions, if nothing else.' Ashe was all seriousness. His tone provoked Merrick's curiosity, but there was no time for that conversation at present.

'Godspeed, then, Ashe.' For a moment Merrick prevaricated. Perhaps he should go. If Riordan was in true need, he should be there for him. But Alixe needed him, too. There were things that needed sorting out between them for his own peace of mind and Riordan might simply be being Riordan.

'I will see you in London.' Ashe saluted with the riding crop and exited the room, leaving Merrick with the chaos of his thoughts.

Merrick dressed himself with care, gingerly testing the seams of his second-best day shirt in case Alixe had tampered with more than one set of clothes. He let out a sigh of relief when the sleeves held.

Ashe was right. Things had gone far off course where Alixe was concerned. He was no longer a social tutor to her. In all honesty, that role hadn't lasted much beyond the outing to the Roman ruins. He'd kissed her that day for himself because beautiful things should be kissed. She'd been uncertain and trusting in his arms, but not naïve. Even then, she'd questioned his motives as he should have done. It had been too easy to explain his actions to himself as an act of good will, part of some secret curriculum to turn Alixe Burke into a social sensation.

He knew now that she didn't need to be turned into anything. Ashe had called her his creation. But he had not created Alixe Burke, he had not even refashioned her. All she'd become had already been there. He'd merely uncovered what she'd chosen to hide and now he was about to turn all that over to another man.

The very thought made him sick.

He did not want to turn Alixe Burke over to another. But any other answer was impossible as Ashe had so adroitly argued. To not turn her over to London's fine young men meant marrying her himself, a prospect he was not fit to fulfil. He had secrets. She didn't really know who he truly was. If she did, she would despise him. She would demand faithfulness, something he wasn't sure he was equipped to give. Even if he could give her that, he had no means of supporting her.

He'd be completely reliant on her dowry and whatever her father saw fit to endow them with. Those were invisible chains that would chafe him every day. He would have become a kept man in every sense of the concept. There would be no wagers to hide behind, all disguises for what he was would be stripped away. Society would whisper behind their hands that he was Alixe Burke's pet. He would not bear the brunt of society's scorn alone. Alixe would share it. Society would say Folkestone had bought his daughter a husband. He and Alixe would live in a kind of cruel exile without ever leaving town.

Merrick reached inside the wardrobe for his boots. The travelling valise Ashe had sought tumbled out. He could still follow Ashe and Riordan. No. That was the coward's way and it would serve no purpose. His feelings, his confusion, would still exist. It was best to stay here and wait them out. If this was infatuation, it would pass. He never stayed infatuated for long. If it was something more, that would have to be sorted out, too. Better to do it without the rosy glasses of distance to diffuse it.

Alixe was waiting for him downstairs in the main hall among the other guests taking carriages over to the Leas. Merrick halted for a moment on the stairs to

study her. The apple-green muslin walking dress she
wore gave her the appearance of a summer goddess, the
white-ribbon trim at the bodice adding a hint of virtue
to the lush charms on display. A bonnet of matching
green moire fashioned in the new French shape dangled by its ribbons from her hand. She looked up and
her face lit with pleasure at the sight of him. It was a
kind of genuine pleasure he was not used to seeing on
a woman's face. It had nothing to do with coy calcula-
tion about how to get him in to bed and how to exact
the thrills he could coax once there.

Yet he felt his arousal stir at the sight of her wanting him. He thought of her touch on his phallus, the
otherworldly expression on her face when she'd come
against his hand. And the burning started all over
again. He highly suspected there wasn't enough swimming in the world that would quench that particular
fire. And yet he could not have her, not completely.
That was one thing he could not take from her. He was
not a rake who trifled with virgins.

Merrick made his way to her side and swept her
hand into the crook of his arm. She felt natural beside
him, being with her an easy sort of companionship.
It would take some getting used to being without her
when the time came. But that day wasn't today. He
must not let the future ruin the present. She was his
for today, and for tomorrow and a little time beyond,
that was all that mattered. 'What shall we do first?'
Merrick asked.

'Let's see the animals. The animal pens smell better in the morning.' Alixe laughed and let him lead her to a waiting gig. He helped her up and they set out on the road to the Leas.

The fairgrounds were bursting with people who'd come to enjoy the June treat. Excitement trembled on the light breeze and Merrick felt himself get caught up with it. Today was not a day to worry about what might come. Alixe felt it, too. Her smile was contagious and she squeezed his arm as they strode towards the animal pens to see who had the biggest pig or the fattest calf.

He bought her a pasty and ducked her behind a tree to lick a juicy droplet off her lips with his tongue. She laughed and sank into him. 'How is it that you always smell so good?' she murmured, her eyes dancing up at him with mischief. 'You smell like lavender and oak and something else I can never quite name.'

Merrick chuckled. 'It's the coumarin. I have a perfumer on Bond Street make it especially for me. It's supposed to simulate hay after it has been cut.' The cologne was one expense he hadn't been able to force himself to forgo. It reminded him of innocent summer days before his life had become corrupted with all its various vices.

'What's it called?' Alixe made a show of burrowing her nose into the collar of his shirt and breathing deeply.

'The scent is *fougère*. Many perfumers can mix a *fougère*, but I have a place I prefer.' Merrick winked. 'Perhaps the *fougère* is part of my charm.'

'I think your charm is more than that.' Her eyes

turned misty. 'What are we doing, Merrick?' Her arms were settled about his neck, his own hands were settled at her hips, resting as if they belonged there.

'We're doing the best we can, all we can.' There was no sense pretending he didn't understand what she was asking. It was the very same thing he'd been grappling with himself. He moved to kiss her again. She turned her head and evaded the gesture.

'What sort of answer is that supposed to be?' she challenged softly.

'The only answer we can make. What do you want me to say, Alixe? Do you think I can save you?' He dropped his voice to a husky growl. 'Or do you think you can save me? I'll tell you neither is possible. We have shared time. We have found pleasure together. We have come to care for one another beyond what we expected when we began this association. We are caught in the throes of those feelings, but that doesn't mean we should marry.' Merrick stroked the curve of her jaw with the back of his hand. 'Marriage to me will not save you and it certainly won't save me, my dear, although I do appreciate the thought.'

Alixe shook her head and laughed up at him. 'Are you really as bad as you make out?'

'I'm probably worse.'

'Not at all. There's a streak of honour in you whether you admit it or not.'

Merrick cocked an eyebrow. 'There are many who'd disagree with you. I am not the heir, so I am not learning to run the family holdings. I am not the current marquis, so I am not taking up a seat in Parliament.

I am not a military man, so I am not considering my next post in some godforsaken region of the empire. I am not a man of the cloth contemplating the philosophies of religion or how to best bore my parish from the pulpit on Sunday. In fact, I follow none of the pursuits that make a man honourable.'

His speech made her uncomfortable. He could see the slight furrowing of her brow. 'You're right to be uncomfortable, Alixe. The truth often is. Better to know it now than before you delude yourself into thinking I'm something I not. Here's another truth. I'm a bounder. I follow the money, I live from one wager to the next.'

'Then why didn't you leave? The man you describe wouldn't have stayed under the conditions my father laid out. That man would have been out of Folkestone as fast as he could saddle a horse,' Alixe countered.

Merrick favoured her with a fond smile. Apparently, she was not willing to be swayed just yet. 'It's nice to think someone still believes I can be redeemed.' That it was Alixe Burke, a woman who had little to gain from an association with him, touched him beyond measure. This was dangerous ground for them both. Her feelings did not go unreciprocated. For the first time with a woman, he wished it could be different, that *he* could be different. That was when he knew it. Alixe Burke was in love with him. The realisation was overwhelming. He had to protect her from that before it went any further. He had no business encouraging sentiments he could not return, no matter how he felt.

'Alixe, you don't want to get bound up with me.' He groped for words to make her see that his failings were far too big for her to solve. 'My family doesn't know how to love.' He voiced his worst fear. 'Why would I be any different?' He'd never said it out loud, this nagging concern that he would only create an empty, cruel marriage like his father had. But now that he'd started, the words poured out.

'My father married my mother for her money.' He put up a hand to stop any questions. 'I know a lot of people marry for money, but many times it's mutual and people understand what they're getting into. They have rules about how to deal with their "arrangement". But not my mother. She loved my father and I think she thought he'd love her, too, eventually.' Merrick shook his head. 'She died still hoping, still believing. Perhaps she even died of a broken heart. She never got over her illusions.' He drew a deep breath. 'When I look at you, I fear the same will happen. Don't love me, Alixe. I'm not worth it.'

Alixe wouldn't budge from her position. 'If there is no hope, why didn't you leave with Ashe this morning?'

'I wasn't ready to leave you yet. I can't have you beyond a few days, but I will take what I can if you will have me.' He could see her debating the options in her mind. He pressed on, his groin tightening at the prospect that she hadn't refused yet. 'It's hardly a fair proposition.'

Alixe held his gaze with all seriousness. 'It's the only proposition, though, isn't it, Merrick?' Then she gave a smile that took him entirely by surprise. 'Well, now that's settled, we can get back to having a good time today.'

'Alixe Burke, you astonish me.' Merrick grinned. 'I'll make it worth your while.'

She nudged him with her elbow. 'You had certainly better. I have expectations.'

It was better this way. They knew where they stood with one another. Merrick's disclosure had put the fantasy into perspective and now she could enjoy it for what it was. There would be no gallant offer of marriage for which she would eventually be thankful. She had not really expected one. He wasn't the marrying type and he'd gone to great lengths to explain why. She could not bear the idea that he might have offered out of pity or a sense of misguided honour to save Jamie's sister from her unwanted fate. She was in love with him and there was nothing worse than unrequited love. That kind of love had the power to enslave. He understood that and wanted to protect her from falling victim to it. What he could offer her was the pleasure of his company and the pleasure of his body for a limited time. If that was all, so be it. She would reach out and take it with both hands, then she would set him free. It would be her gift to him. She would accept the first decent offer she received in London and set him loose from any further obligations. Merrick St Magnus was a wild creature and wild things were meant to be free.

But that was for later. For now he was hers and she was his by mutual consent.

They returned to the fairgrounds and strolled the

booths. He bought her pretty ribbons to match her dress and she laughingly tied them to her bonnet. They stopped at the historical booth where she accepted praise over her work on the medieval document. They wandered over to see the games. Targets were being set up for a knife-throwing contest and the men were coaxing Merrick into joining the line of contenders.

'All right, all right.' Merrick gave in and laid aside his coat. He began rolling up his sleeves while the instructions were announced. Three knives per thrower. The top scores would move on to a final round.

Alixe stood on the sidelines with the other spectators. She recognised several of the contestants, but she held her breath when Merrick stepped up to the line, hefting the first knife in his hand. Archibald Redfield sidled in beside her, finished with his own throws. 'Don't worry, St Magnus is supposed to be a dab hand with throwing knives.' His tone was jovial, but Alixe sensed something smug lurking beneath. Merrick's first throw landed in the ring that preceded the bullseye and she straightened her shoulders with pride.

'I have it on good authority he was involved in a knife-throwing wager at a high-class bordello in London. The winner won a certain lady's favours for the evening,' he said in quiet tones for her alone.

Alixe's skin crawled. 'I cannot believe you thought such a rumour fit for my hearing.' Merrick's second knife found the bullseye. The crowd applauded.

Redfield was not subdued. 'I cannot believe you wouldn't want to know such a thing about someone with whom you've spent so much time recently.'

'If I have, that's your fault,' Alixe dared to reference the odious wager. 'You've put him in my path.'

'And I regret it,' Redfield said. 'I had hoped he'd play his end of the wager with honour, although your father is more to blame than myself for those particular conditions.'

Merrick's last knife found the bullseye, making him an easy candidate for the final round. 'A fair opponent for me,' Redfield said cockily. 'I'll enjoy facing him in the finals. He owes me for last time.' He leaned close. 'Surely you know he woos you for himself. He doesn't care if you succeed in London. He'll gladly marry you. Your father misjudged him there. He's a whore of the highest order. If the price is right, he'll sell himself in marriage. You would solve a lot of problems for him and after you have, he'll leave you alone and carry on with his usual debaucheries.'

Alixe blanched at Redfield's coarse warning. It wasn't true. She and Merrick had just discussed the improbability of marriage. Surely Merrick couldn't ensure her failure in London—only she could do that. If she chose, she would dazzle every last bachelor in town. Redfield was wrong. A horrible suspicion came to her: unless Merrick had lied. No. It wasn't possible. She simply wouldn't believe it.

Archibald Redfield stepped up to the line and waited his turn while St Magnus threw. A rough childhood on the docksides of London had served him well today. His own throws had been excellent and the competition was down to him and St Magnus now, the other finalists having been eliminated. He'd sown his seed of doubt well. He'd been pleased with how the conversation with Alixe had gone.

She was a smart woman and smart women usually had a healthy streak of cynicism, always overthinking things. Just when she'd started to believe in the bounder, he'd come along and punctured that fragile bubble of hers. Oh, he knew she wanted to believe St Magnus—what woman wouldn't want to believe him? But she hadn't completely allowed herself to give up all logic yet and he'd played havoc with the small piece that remained. She'd not said as much, but he'd seen it in her face.

Best of all, he'd done it without really telling any lies. If she asked around, she'd find the story of the bordello readily confirmed and probably much more he'd not yet uncovered.

Those kinds of rumours would lead her to the conclusion he'd already put before her. St Magnus needed her money. He had nothing of his own and enjoyed an estranged relationship with his father. She would easily put all the pieces together and conclude St Magnus was using her for his own ends. That was when he'd be there to make his offer of marriage for the second time. This time, he would deal through her father. Folkestone would see that he was the only way out of facing St Magnus at the altar.

The crowd applauded. St Magnus had struck two more bullseyes, beating his own single and two near-misses. The bastard was as lucky as they came. St Magnus strode to the sidelines and swept Alixe Burke into his arms and kissing her full on the mouth in a victor's kiss. Too bad, Redfield thought, he couldn't bury those knives in St Magnus's heart instead of hay targets. But he could beat St Magnus to the prize and he would do that tonight.

Chapter Fourteen

A subdued tension underlay the rest of the afternoon like the heavy stillness that precedes a thunderstorm until Alixe was ready to burst from the anticipation. He'd kissed her in public. Word of it would reach her father and there would be the devil to pay for Merrick's indiscretion. One could kiss country lasses like that, but one could not kiss the Earl of Folkestone's daughter. Archibald Redfield's warning rang through her head. Perhaps Merrick had kissed her on purpose, knowing full well her father would not be able to let it pass.

While her mind cared a great deal about being manipulated by Merrick's flirtations, her body cared not at all, only that it was aroused with an adventurous curiosity. Her body wanted again the pleasures he'd shown her. With every look, every smile, every touch, her body was drawn taut with wanting until she thought she couldn't stand it a moment longer.

Merrick was not oblivious to the presence of mounting tensions as they finished touring the booths late in the afternoon. Alixe noted a growing tightness about his mouth when he smiled, an agitated distraction to his gestures. They had promised each other to enjoy the time they had left, but that had changed since the knife throwing. They were both avoiding something, although Alixe doubted it was the same thing. Merrick had been nearly giddy with the win and the small purse that came with it. She had been more restrained, her enjoyment of Merrick's victory tainted by Redfield's accusations.

Their amblings took them to the place Merrick had left the gig and he helped her up, both of them implicitly finished with the fair. The gig gave under his weight as Merrick took his seat next to her and grabbed up the reins. Alixe was extraordinarily sensitive to the nearness of him, of every brush of his thigh against hers. There was nothing for it. She knew the tight proximity of the bench seat demanded such touching be permissible.

'What did Redfield say to you?' Merrick asked once the fairgrounds were behind them. The grimness of his tone caught her unawares. She'd become accustomed to his usual laughing tones, or his low, sensual murmur. This grimness was a not something she'd come to associate with Merrick.

'Nothing of merit.' Alixe shrugged. But she was not convincing in her nonchalance. Merrick eyed her speculatively with a raised eyebrow and a sideways glance that said he didn't believe it.

'Clearly it was something of note. It has upset you.' He paused. 'Unless it was my kissing that upset you?'

'No, it was not your kissing,' Alixe confessed. She looked down at her hands, searching for the right words. 'You do know my father will hear of it, though.' Alixe gathered her courage. 'Is that what you intended? Do you mean to force my father's hand to see you as an acceptable suitor?'

Merrick gave a sharp bark of laughter. 'You know it's not. Did I not assure you of that very thing this morning?'

She felt his eyes on her, his gaze strong and probing. 'Ah, I see. That's what Redfield told you while he was over there, whispering his poison in your ear.' He had nothing but disdain in his tone now and not all of it was for Redfield. A healthy dose of it was reserved for her. 'You believed him. You believed him over me.'

Alixe felt her cheeks burning. She had not seen it from his point of view, of how it would appear to Merrick.

'For shame, Alixe—only this morning you thought I might still be redeemable. How fickle is a woman.' Merrick clucked to the horses and that was the last sound either of them made until they arrived home.

Alixe was in tears by the time she reached the sanctuary of her room. Meg wouldn't be back until evening to help her dress for dinner and Alixe was glad for the privacy. She wanted to be alone with her misery. She had behaved shabbily towards Merrick. For all his reputation to the contrary, he'd not treated her poorly. Nothing had happened without her consent and he'd shown her a sincerity no suitor before him had.

Yet, at the first hint of chicanery, she'd been influenced by a man whom she'd previously turned down, who might possibly be bent on taking revenge for that rejection. Archibald Redfield might not be a scandalous rake with an obvious history of womanising and wagering, but neither was his reputation without tarnish, mostly because no one knew much about him. He'd simply arrived in the neighbourhood. All anyone knew was that his antecedents were of the murky country-gentry sort with a baronial great-grandfather buried somewhere in his past. He was polite to the ladies and good-looking. But *she* knew that, at least in one thing, Archibald Redfield was not honest.

Alixe gazed up at the ceiling. It shouldn't have been enough to sway her from Merrick's standard. She *knew* Redfield was not a genuine man. Redfield had been after her money. She'd overheard him talking with his solicitor when she and her mother had come to call at the manor. Her mother had been outside, having forgot something in the carriage. It had been the day before Redfield had proposed to her in private. Wanting her money wasn't precisely scandalous in the way Merrick's knife wagers in a bordello were, but it was still intolerable to her. Up until that overheard conversation, she'd thought Redfield had genuinely liked her. She'd known he wasn't in love with her, but he'd liked her, respected her work. It had all been a ruse.

Which was why it had been so easy to believe Redfield today. Didn't it take one to know one? Like Redfield, Merrick, too, pretended to like her, had shown respect for her work and he'd been entirely convincing. Much more convincing than Archibald Redfield had ever been.

Even now, it was hard to believe Merrick had designed all this for his benefit while stringently maintaining that he was unattainable. But his presence marked her room. The fan he'd given her lay on her vanity. The ribbons he'd bought her dangled from her bonnet. The faint smell of coumarin-laced *fougère* lingered on the gown she'd worn to the alfresco party. In small ways, he'd made himself unforgettable and ever present while agreeing to all her demands. He'd acquiesced to her silly requirement that he teach her no more of his unconventional lessons. But that hadn't stopped them, merely changed their context. In hindsight, lessons would have been better. She could have understood their place. There would have been no confusion.

He loves me, he loves me not. If she'd had a rose handy, she would have denuded it. A thought occurred to her in the midst of her melancholy: she was working the wrong end of the equation. Perhaps it didn't matter if he loved her or how much. Perhaps what mattered was whether or not she loved him.

The dangerous idea that had begun to bud last night amid champagne and fireworks was in full bloom now. *She loved him.* It was hard to say when precisely it had happened. But one thing she was certain of: this was not an impulsive decision, not something that had occurred overnight. In spite of her best efforts, it had crept up on her. Alixe sat down hard on her bed, letting the discovery rock her very being.

She loved the murmur of his voice enticing her to

wickedness. She loved the feel of his body beneath her hands. She loved his laughing eyes that took nothing too seriously. It wasn't just his good looks. It was his soul, which wasn't nearly as dark as he liked to pretend. He was a good man who'd worked beside villagers, who shared her interest in history, who didn't despise her mind, who carried with him a thoughtful intellect. He was extraordinary in ways London had not recognised.

Most of all, she loved how she felt when she was with him. He made her feel... She groped for the word in her mind. Alive. He made her feel alive in a way she'd never felt before and, for that, she loved him and it didn't matter if he loved her.

All she knew was that she felt ashamed of her doubt, ashamed of the way she'd treated Merrick. He deserved so much better. She wanted to apologise. She wanted things back the way they'd been that morning when she and Merrick had kissed behind a tree and he'd pledged all he could offer. If she'd believed in him, she might be off somewhere right now with him, indulging what time they had left instead of moping about her room, wallowing in her regrets.

A frenzy of resolve engulfed her. Within moments she was striding out of the house. Merrick had not stayed once he'd dropped her off. But she knew where she could find him and what she'd do with him once she did.

Merrick dived into the water, letting the water close over him, letting the cool rush of it drown out all else.

He wanted to forget. He'd momentarily been a fool and it hurt. Alixe Burke had made him believe he was finer than he was, for a few hours at least. But Alixe had not believed him over Redfield's lies. The knowledge of it stung.

This was the problem with virgins. With his usual women, it was all straightforward: pleasure for pleasure with no complications afterwards, no expectations. No one mistook those encounters as a prelude to love. Everyone involved knew the rules of those engagements.

Alixe Burke did not play by those rules and yet the pleasure she'd brought him had far superseded any he'd known. There'd been an indescribable completeness to the release she'd given him. But it hadn't been enough. It had merely whetted his appetite for more. After the fireworks, he'd entertained indecent thoughts of her all night and most of the day. Walking beside her at the fair had been an exquisite sort of torture. Limiting himself to a kiss behind a tree had been another when all he'd wanted to do was toss up her skirts and bury himself in her until he was cured of the wanting.

The coolness of the water did nothing to subdue his arousal. He could imagine her writhing against the tree trunk near the shore, screaming her release as he took her. She would be glorious in her abandon, her hair streaming about her. She would call his name…

'Merrick.'

His imaginings were getting fairly vivid. Her voice sounded as if it were here in the grove with him.

'Merrick!' The call came again, more insistent this time.

Merrick opened his eyes. There stood the object of his musings on the bank of the swimming hole, beckoning him with the curl of one outstretched hand.

He neared the shore and she raised her arms to her hair where it lay in the loose chignon she preferred on warm days. She tugged and it fell loose about her, a coy smile on her lips. His heart thumped at the universal signs of a woman with seduction on her mind.

Merrick grinned, arms crossed as he floated on his back in the water, his head up just enough to keep her in view. 'Why, Alixe Burke, did you come here to seduce me?'

Her smile widened. Her hands dropped to the fastenings of her gown. 'Absolutely, although I might need you to get out of the water and help me.'

'With the seduction? Gladly.'

'No, my dress. Perhaps I should have planned better and worn something a little easier to get out of.' Alixe gave a charming laugh of helplessness.

He rose up out of the water and Alixe sucked in her breath. A warm sense of pride filled him at her admiration. He spun her about and set to work on the dress, his wet hands leaving watery tracks down the back of her gown. 'Are you sure you want to do this?' he murmured in her ear, pushing her long cascade of hair to one side, leaving her neck bare to his kisses. He hoped the question was merely rhetorical, but he had to ask. That streak of honour Alixe was convinced he possessed was hard at war with his desire.

He pushed the dress off her shoulders and she turned in his arms to face him, her own arms wrapping about his neck, her head thrown back to look up at him. 'I want this and more, Merrick. This time I want it all. With you. No more individual pleasure, Merrick. I want us to find pleasure…together.'

Her words would undo him before they even got started. His erection pressed against the thin fabric of her chemise. 'Alixe, I am flattered by your offer, but I cannot ruin you for a few hours of pleasure.'

'I do not care,' she said with a confident ferocity that made him smile.

'Your future husband might.' He had to know she understood what she was asking, what she was doing. God knew he wanted her beyond reason, but he had to cling to the shreds of that reason as long as he could for her sake.

'I've enough money to make him forget,' she whispered, reaching a hand between them to cup him with a light squeeze that sent a jolt of fierce, raw desire ricocheting through him.

There was nothing for it. He would give her something to remember. And himself, too.

The dusky summer evening closed around them as he took her down to the ground. At his kiss, she'd begun to burn; now she was fully consumed, revelling in the weight of his body over hers, the muscled sinews of his arms where they bracketed her in the place between her shoulders and head. His pale hair had darkened from the water and dripped erotic droplets on her breasts. She could feel his erection pulse against her thigh and she arched against him in her hurry to find relief from the building inferno. But Merrick would not be rushed, his damp skin cool against the heat of her own. His hand was at the juncture of her thighs, massaging, stimulating her body into ready compliance for what came next, his mouth at her breast, teasing with his tongue until she could bear the twin points of pleasure no more.

'Open a bit more for me, my love,' Merrick whispered at her ear, his knee gently widening the space between her legs and then he was there, poised at her entrance. She strained towards him, her heat rising again, her breath coming in gasps as he plunged.

She could feel him sliding inside her until the easy sensation stopped, replaced by a razor-sharp stab of pain. She cried out. She'd not expected that. There'd been no allusion to pain in their previous encounters.

'Shh,' Merrick hushed her. 'Be still, it will pass in a moment and then the pleasure will come. I promise. It only hurts the once.'

Already the pain was ebbing, her body relaxing around him, a new sensation starting to grow as he began to move inside her. Merrick took her mouth in a kiss, his hips pressed to hers, coaxing her body to join him in the rhythm. She moaned, her body moving with his, her need rising. Merrick's blue eyes were midnight-dark with passion, his body straining as his own desires spiked. Her body careened towards release, Merrick thrust once more, surging them over an unseen edge and they soared. There was no other word for it.

Somewhere, somehow, they were flying in a world that had fractured into a kaleidoscope of sensation.

Her only thought as she floated back to earth was that she'd been right. She'd been right to do this most intimate act with Merrick. It was nearly inconceivable to think of doing this with another. Yet when Merrick rose and held out a hand to her, she took it, letting him lead her to the pond, neither of them abashed by their nakedness.

In the gathering dark, they swam and bathed, basking in the sunset filtering through the trees. There were more kisses and gentle love play in the water, but Merrick did not take her again no matter how she pressed him. She would be too sore, he said.

At last, Merrick rose from the water and searched for his clothes. *This is what Eden must have been like,* Alixe thought, taking her fill of his nakedness while he dried, appreciating the lean curve of buttock descending into long thigh. Lord, how she'd become wanton. Two weeks ago, the sight of his nakedness had sent her stumbling over logs. Now, she could not get enough. He pulled on his trousers and she made a disappointed mewl.

'Sorry, love. Convention demands I wear trousers.' Merrick shifted his hips, adjusting the fit of his trousers, his hands at the waistband to work the fastenings. Alixe sucked in her breath. Even the way he put on his trousers was erotically fascinating. It was as sensual and intimate to watch him dress as it was to watch him undress.

Merrick threw her a knowing smile. He'd done that

on purpose. 'I should splash you for that,' she scolded. 'You were teasing me.'

'I was teasing *you*? My dear, I think you have that wrong. You're the one who's still naked.' Fully garbed, Merrick walked to the pond's edge and held out a hand. 'I'll play lady's maid. Let's get you dried off.'

Twenty minutes and several kisses later, they walked out of Eden, hand in hand. Everything had changed and nothing had changed. Merrick could not marry her, or want to marry her, any more than he had that morning. But Alixe suspected he most definitely had ruined her for other men far beyond the technicalities of having lain with her.

The house came into view and Merrick squeezed her hand. 'Shall you go on? They'll be missing you.'

'I'll tell them I stayed at the fair. No one saw me come back.' They were the first words they'd said since they'd left the pond.

Merrick nodded. 'It's as good an excuse as any.'

Silence followed. She wasn't ready to go in. The moment she crossed the lawn, everything would revert to normal. She wanted to ask if he would come to her again, but she feared sounding too desperate. Perhaps it would have to be she who went to him. She searched for something to say, but found nothing.

'I'll see you inside.' Then she started walking.

Straight into hell.

Chapter Fifteen

Alixe's mother saw her first as she was 'just coming down' to join everyone in the drawing room. Alixe had wisely opted to use the servants' stairs and return to her room undetected. She was doubly glad for the decision now that it was clear her mother's sharp eyes had been on the lookout for her.

'There you are, my dear.' Her mother beamed at her and Alixe's suspicions rose. Alixe smoothed the front of her skirt, thankful she'd had time to change into one of Merrick's new gowns, a lightweight summer silk in deep apricot that highlighted the healthy glow of her skin and the rich walnut hues of her hair.

'You look lovely, the new wardrobe is perfection itself.' Alixe could not recall the last time her mother had complimented her clothing. She searched her mother's smiling face for clues to this transformation. Ever since she'd turned down the last offer, her mother had treated her with an air of polite disregard. She'd been left to her own devices once it became clear she did not mean to return to London, her mother in clear despair of seeing her daughter married.

Tonight was a most glaring exception.

'I came back late from the fair and lay down for a moment. I must have dozed off,' Alixe improvised hastily to explain her tardy arrival.

Her mother shooed away the need for apology with a wave of her hand. 'No matter, you're here now. Your father and I have exciting news for you. Come join us in the study. Jamie can play host in our absence.'

Her father was already there, having taken up his customary place behind the massive desk where all important business was conducted. But he was not alone. Sitting comfortably in a chair in front of the desk was Archibald Redfield. Redfield had not spent the last few hours rolling about a swimming hole. He was turned out in his country finest, looking neatly barbered and self-confidently handsome with his dark-gold hair and alert hazel eyes. He rose when she entered and strode forwards to take her hand. 'My dearest Alixe, you look ravishing. I dare say a day at the fair has put some colour into your cheeks. When I saw you earlier, you looked a trifle pale.'

What was going on? Alixe's first thoughts were that Redfield had reported Merrick's kiss from the fair or, worse, that Redfield had somehow known what she and Merrick had been up to at the swimming hole. But her mother looked far too happy for anything calamitous to have occurred. Redfield was a rat, but not tonight. Tonight he was playing the indulgent gentleman to the hilt and that worried her greatly. She preferred the rat.

'Have a seat, my dear.' Her father gestured for her to take an empty chair. 'We have fabulous news. Just this afternoon, our Mr Redfield has asked for your hand in marriage.'

'This is wonderful,' her mother gushed. 'He's our neighbour, after all, and you won't live far from home. It's the most perfect of arrangements.'

Redfield smiled and humbly studied his nails while her mother outlined the benefits of the match. Alixe listened in growing horror.

'What about St Magnus?' She managed to slip the words in when her mother stopped to draw breath.

'You're absolutely correct, darling.' Redfield looked up from his nails with a benevolent smile that bordered on patronising. 'He should be told immediately. You and I have much to thank him for.'

Alixe bristled, but Redfield acted quickly. 'If it's all right, I would like a moment alone with my fiancée.' He gave a wide, white-toothed grin as he said the word, looking every inch the pleased bridegroom.

He dropped his act fast enough once her parents had exited the room. 'I know what's going through your pretty head, Alixe Burke,' he began. 'But you needn't worry. St Magnus can't harm you now. I won't allow him to slander my wife. I explained the entire situation to your father, how St Magnus was overly exuberant after winning the competition.'

He was talking about Merrick's ill-advised kiss, but that was merely the tip of the iceberg. 'St Magnus has been "overly exuberant" before this, I suspect, hasn't he? But I don't care, such is my regard for you.'

Alixe was not fooled about the nature of his 're-gard'. It had nothing to do with his affections. 'You've become quite desperate for my fortune.' She held his gaze steadily.

'Your parents have become quite desperate to see you married. Far more desperate than they were this spring. St Magnus has surprised us all. To my way of thinking, this works to both our benefits. I am desperate to wed, they are desperate to see St Magnus as far from you as possible.'

Redfield made an off-handed gesture. 'You should not be so surprised. This is how these alliances are made, my dear. Driven by my regard for you, I went about it all wrong this spring by asking you first. If I had gone straight to your father from the start, this might all have been settled long before now. I could have saved you from the ignominy of St Magnus's attentions.'

'I am not "your dear",' Alixe ground out.

'You're not St Magnus's either.' Redfield gave a mirthless laugh. 'He will be disappointed I've beaten him to the prize. But that is all. Men like him don't care to lose. He played a deeper game with your father's terms and lost. I'll have your money, he'll have his freedom. I suspect in the end, he'll be happy enough knowing that he's "lived to fight again another day" and all that. He will recover from this. There's always another woman ready to support the St Magnuses of the world.'

His cold analysis was revolting. She wanted to flee this room, wanted to throw herself on her parents' mercy for whatever it was worth and tell them Redfield only wanted her money. More than that, she wanted to throw herself into Merrick's arms and hear him tell her it wasn't a lie, that he hadn't wooed her for himself with the intention of claiming her dowry for his own, that he hadn't used her body against her.

'You disgust me.' Alixe turned on her heel. But Redfield caught her fast, his face close to hers.

'When you realise I'm being honest, you'll thank me. You know precisely why I want you. St Magnus, on the other hand, has served you a platter of lies. This isn't the first time he's traded pleasure for funds and tried to dress it up as something more. Ask him about the Greenfield Twins some time.'

Alixe wrenched her arm free. It wasn't true and she would prove it just as soon as she could find Merrick.

Merrick scanned the gathering in the drawing room. Alixe was nowhere to be found. It was not lost on him that the earl and countess were not present either. He hoped there hadn't been any difficulties. Lost in his concerns, he startled at the sound of Jamie's voice beside him.

'Looking for Alixe?' Merrick didn't care for the tension in Jamie's tone. It wasn't like him.

'Is she not here?' Merrick queried carefully.

'I need to tell you some news, news I hope you'll be happy to hear.' Jamie was drawing him outside onto the verandah, away from the other guests.

'I know you've been spending a lot of time with Alixe these past weeks and I haven't said anything.

She's been happy and she's starting to dress as she should again. You've been good for her, although I can't fathom why you've done it. She's not your type of woman.'

'Ashe doesn't think so either,' Merrick said with a touch of grim cynicism. He was getting tired of hearing about how unsuitable Alixe was for him. Did people actually think he didn't know that? Even so, did anyone think knowing it could stop him from wanting her?

Jamie shrugged in agreement and then elbowed him playfully. 'It's no secret what type of woman you like.'

A walnut-haired one with sherry eyes who swims naked and cries her pleasure to the sunset skies. But he could not say that to Jamie, nor could he seek Jamie's counsel about what to do next. He was feeling Ashe's absence keenly.

'Your news?' Merrick pressed.

'Archibald Redfield, our neighbour, has asked for her hand.'

The news was like a physical blow. He should not have been stunned. He knew Redfield coveted her fortune. 'But she's to go to London and have her pick of the Season.' Merrick managed to get out the words without exposing the scheme behind it. 'Surely she will decline.'

'Not this time. My father will not tolerate her refusing any offers at this point. He's over the moon about it. They're in the estate office discussing it right now. Redfield came right after his return from the fair.'

Merrick supposed there was veiled reproach to his poor behaviour at the knife-throwing contest in there somewhere, but he was still reeling. He wasn't ready to lose her so soon. He'd thought there'd be more time. He'd thought losing her in London would be easier, surrounded by his usual entertainments. Merrick placed a pleading hand on Jamie's arm.

'Do not allow this, Jamie. If you have any influence with your father, let her go to London and find someone better. The man is a fortune hunter. Do any of you know a thing about him?' He was thinking quickly now. He couldn't save himself, but perhaps he could still save Alixe. At the moment, it was the only thing that mattered.

Jamie stiffened at the request, the reference to fortune hunting finding purchase with him. 'What do you know, Merrick? Do you know something unsavoury about him?'

Merrick shook his head. 'Ask Alixe. Did you know she refused his overtures last spring? She didn't say anything about it out of fear of your father's wrath.' Merrick drew a breath and pressed on. 'The man doesn't even have a title. What is your father thinking to marry Alixe to him without trying London once more?'

'He's thinking of his daughter's well-being,' a harsh voice broke in. Redfield emerged from the drawing room, shutting the French doors behind him. 'Better to marry her to an upstanding landowner of the county than turn her loose in London where you can continue to lead her astray with your debauched ways and useless promises.'

'That is libellous!' Merrick roared.

'What is this?' Jamie looked from Redfield to Merrick. 'What have you done?'

'Do you have to ask? You know him better than any of us,' Redfield accused smoothly, arms folded confidently over his chest. 'What do you think he's been doing with your sister all this time? He's used your friendship to gain entrance to this gathering of decent people. In return, he's paid court to your sister in hopes of claiming her for himself and all the money that goes with her. He accuses me of what he's done himself.'

'You're a liar!' Merrick had enough. He was not the villain here. He lunged at Redfield, forcing him back to the wall with a body-jarring thud against the sandstone. He landed a solid punch to Redfield's gut before Jamie got a hold of him and dragged him off the other man, pulling him on to the lawn, away from the light.

Redfield was bent double, panting in his pain, milking it for all it was worth when the earl barrelled out on to the verandah, bellowing a phrase Merrick was coming to associate with him quite readily. 'What is the meaning of this? James?'

'There seems to be a difference of opinion over Alixe's engagement,' Jamie managed, fighting to keeping a restraining grip on him, much to Merrick's disappointment. If that scum Redfield wanted to moan in pain, he'd damn well give him something to moan about.

Folkestone raised his greying eyebrows and focused his cool gaze in Merrick's direction. 'Oh? Is that true? St Magnus, your work here is done. You've fulfilled your end of the agreement. You've won your freedom.

That is all you were promised. I have bargained with you in good faith; I trust you have returned the favour and not reached above yourself.'

'What is going on?' Jamie demanded. Merrick felt his heart sink. It was all going to come out and Jamie would not forgive him.

Redfield sneered, managing to stand upright at last. 'Your precious friend was caught with your sister in dishabille in the library. To avoid paying a gentleman's price for his indiscretion, your father allowed St Magnus to "help" Alixe find a more appropriate husband instead of marrying her himself. After all, why would anyone want Merrick St Magnus for a son-in-law if it could be avoided? However, there was a provision, that if St Magnus failed, he would marry her anyway. The longer St Magnus thought about it, the more appealing the idea of failure became. Why not claim her for himself? Why fix her up with pretty clothes and manners for someone else when he needs the money as much as the next man?' Redfield spat out. 'Your *friend* is as low as they come. Fortunately, I have offered for Lady Alixe to save her from being duped by St Magnus here.'

Jamie's grip relaxed slightly, probably out of stupefaction. Merrick took advantage and twisted free. 'You're a conniving rat.'

Merrick lunged again, but this time Redfield was ready for him and they both went down on the lawn, punching in a full-blown brawl.

It took both Jamie and the earl to separate them. 'Stop this, Merrick, for Alixe's sake,' Jamie murmured at his ear. 'This will only make a scandal for her.' It was the only argument that carried any weight with Merrick. Onlookers were starting to gather. Jamie and Folkestone would have to skilfully hush this up if they hoped to staunch any nasty rumours. Lady Folkestone would kill him for this. Instead of her house party being remembered for all the successful matches made, it would be remembered for this breach of propriety right at the last and it would be attributed to him.

'Let me speak with Alixe,' Merrick asked, tugging his waistcoat into place and relenting.

The earl shook his head. 'As I said, your work here is done and most admirably so. I would advise you to pack your things and leave. You can take rooms at the inn for the evening and then go on to wherever your kind goes when you aren't disturbing decent society.'

Merrick was gone. Alixe knew it without Jamie having to tell her, although he had quietly taken her aside before the dinner bell and told her Merrick had left on urgent business.

Redfield had taken up residence beside her for the duration of the evening. He'd been late coming into dinner and when he had arrived, he'd been wearing a different shirt than the one he'd worn in her father's study. Alixe couldn't help wonder if Merrick's urgent business was in some way connected to Redfield's change of clothing, as was the after-dinner disappearance of Jamie and her father into the study.

The only good to come of the evening was her father's decision to hold off announcing a formal engagement. She expected she had Jamie to thank for the reprieve. They would go up to London as planned instead of announcing the news at the midsummer ball the next evening. The delay would give Alixe a chance to enjoy the Season before the wedding and time to put together a fashionable trousseau. Besides, her father said, the contracts still had to be drawn up and there was no hurry now that things were settled.

Redfield had agreed to the arrangements with a tight smile that suggested he wasn't truly pleased. Alixe smiled at him smugly behind her father's back as they shook hands, but Redfield was not content. He cornered her on her way up the stairs, a proprietary hand on her arm that tightened painfully.

'St Magnus has left and I am still here, my dear. I defended your honour tonight with my fists and my proposal when that scoundrel St Magnus would have defamed it. You owe me. Don't ever forget it.'

Alixe fell asleep to sobering thoughts. It was hard to believe she'd lain in Merrick's arms just six hours ago. It was harder still to believe he'd only been part of her life for two weeks. She'd felt more alive in those two weeks than she had in the last two years and now it had all come to an end. Merrick had deserted her. Whatever his reasons, he was gone and she was alone once more. She wished she'd told him what she'd so recently discovered: that she loved him. But it was too late now. It was all over.

Chapter Sixteen

The juicy truth was all over London. Merrick St Magnus had been expelled from the Folkestone house party for brawling over a lady. *Brawling,* mind you, the matrons said behind fast-fluttering fans. Gentlemen might covertly duel, but gentlemen *never* lowered themselves to an all-out fist fight on a host's lawn, over the host's daughter none the less. It just went to prove Merrick St Magnus was no gentleman, no matter who his father was—a fact that made those fast fans reach gale proportions. More than one matron was entertaining libidinous fantasies behind those fans. What would it be like to be in the arms of a man who gave full vent to his passions? To his tempers? Women shivered in London's hot ballrooms at the very prospect.

It was the same wherever he went. Their minds were fairly transparent, as were the charms of some of the more forward ladies, Merrick noted, striding through Lady Couthwald's ballroom with Ashe at his shoulder. He returned the inviting smile of a popular lush-

figured widow with a curt nod of his own. There was
little variation in their thoughts except that some of
the more ambitious entertained ideas of having both
he and Ashe warming their beds.

'The conquering hero returns,' Ashe murmured.
'Is there a woman in the room who doesn't want you?'

'Only the ones who want you,' Merrick replied drily.
Such lust was not as amusing as it had once been.

'The widow wanted us both. It might have been
fun. We haven't done that for a long time.' Ashe
Bedevere was the only person Merrick knew who could
talk about a *ménage à trois* with the same casualness
he spoke of picking out a new waistcoat.

'*We*'ve never done that,' Merrick corrected.

'Are you sure? What about the time—?'

'I'm *very* sure.' Merrick cut him off, not about to
argue in the middle of a ballroom about whom Ashe
had engaged in one of his *affaires*. Ashe had been his
constant companion since he'd returned to town three
days ago. Ashe had opened up his rooms to share and
Merrick was grateful, but not *that* grateful. Ashe's debaucheries weighed on him. Somewhere between Kent
and London, his friend's habits had become tiresome.

'Are you in danger of becoming a prig?'

'Just because I don't want to "share" with you
doesn't mean I'm becoming a prig.' But maybe it did.
Maybe Ashe was right. He was changing and it frightened him. He didn't know what to make of it. It was
why he hadn't hurried straight back to London after
the fight with Archibald Redfield.

He could have come earlier. He'd delayed in the

hopes that time would dull the edge of scandal that was sure to precede him. But absence had only heightened the anticipation of his arrival and London society was certain he would arrive. Alixe Burke was here, after all, looking lovely and dazzling the young men. Surely St Magnus would not have risked a brawl only to retreat from the field, not when he'd been dancing attendance on the former jilt for two weeks in Kent, depriving the women of London of his presence? He didn't need a great sense of intuition to know this. The betting book at White's was full of wagers: when would he arrive, when would he seek out Alixe Burke at a venue and when he did would he stake his claim?

He had yet to see Alixe. There was no reason to. He'd done his duty for her and for her father. She was the Toast of London. His fisticuffs had ensured her initial popularity. Everyone was waiting to see the woman who'd brought two men to undignified brawling. Alixe Burke must be transformed indeed from the girl society remembered.

The rumours told the rest of the story. She'd gone from being on the shelf to being a highly contended prize. Men wanted to win the woman who had made St Magnus "decent" for even a short time. The last bit was Jamie's invention. Merrick wasn't convinced he'd been decent where Alixe was concerned. That was the other reason he hadn't hurried back to town. He'd hoped his ardour might have cooled and brought perspective.

It hadn't. The remedy had failed miserably. If anything, it had only increased.

He needed to see her. He wanted to assure himself she was well—that was what he told himself. In his more honest moments, he knew he wanted her—craved her, in fact; craved her dark eyes, her hair slipping through his fingers, her body pressed against his. That was not all he craved. He craved sitting in the library with her, talking with her, listening to her stories of history. But that was a craving he could not succour. There was nothing honourable he could give her in exchange for what she gave him. Because of that, he could not seek her out. People could speculate on what happened in the country away from society's collective eye. But what happened in London became fact. He could not indulge with her here.

Fate decided to tempt him and his hard-won logic. The crowd thinned at the far end of the ballroom and there she was. Alixe Burke in her newfound glory, gowned in soft peach with pearls at the base of her neck, a familiar fan dangling closed at her wrist and surrounded by gentlemen. She gave a laugh at something the gentleman to her right was saying. She leaned towards him, a gloved hand skimming his sleeve ever so lightly. There was nothing improper about it. The gentleman beamed, encouraged.

Merrick felt his gut tighten. He'd taught her that little trick. She'd been loathe to practise such measures that day, but this evening she employed it with enviable ease. He'd not anticipated feeling a proverbial blow to the stomach when she used it on someone else. Merrick recognised the gentleman with her, a Viscount Fulworth, who'd just happened to bet at White's that

Merrick would ask her to dance before the sixth of July. He wanted to pummel the man for wooing her while betting on her next move.

Behind him, Ashe cleared his throat. 'I think I'll see if the widow would settle for just one of us. Excuse me.'

Merrick nodded absently. By now others had noticed that he and Alixe were in close proximity to each other. The swell of conversation faded and covert glances darted his way. Alixe looked away from the gentleman she was conversing with, her gaze following the trail of silence until her eyes found him, wide and full of warm emotion for a brief instant before it was replaced with wariness.

He moved towards her. He had to act quickly, naturally, before onlookers started to speculate what any hesitation on his part might mean. On his periphery, he saw Jamie start to move, too, detaching himself from the nearby group he'd been with. He was grateful for it. Jamie's presence would sanction the interaction. But he knew, too, that Jamie would be there to protect Alixe. Merrick didn't imagine he was anything but *persona non grata* in the Folkestone household these days.

'Lady Alixe…' Merrick bowed over Alixe's gloved hand '…it is a pleasure to encounter you here.' He mentioned nothing about any prior meeting.

'Thank you, are you enjoying the ball?' Alixe replied.

'Yes, and you?'

'Yes. The decorations are quite fine.'

The banality of the conversation was stultifying. He didn't want to talk about the ball or the decorations. He wanted to ask her how she was, whether or not she regretted their decision at the swimming hole and did she understand why he'd left the house party; he wanted to explain he'd had no choice, that it had been in her best interest that he leave. He wanted to apologise for not being able to contact her, assuming she wanted to hear such things from him.

There was only one place that provided any privacy at a ball. He doubted she had any dances left, but he had to try. The orchestra was striking up the early refrains of a popular waltz.

'Would you care to dance, Lady Alixe?' Merrick asked.

Alixe looked flustered for a moment. She sought refuge with a glance to her dance card. 'I'm afraid this dance is spoken for.' She cast a quizzing glance at Fulworth.

Merrick's sharp eyes moved to the viscount. 'I don't mean to intrude, forgive me.' He was all politeness, but he could afford to be. He was about to help Fulworth win. Fulworth had a large sum riding on the wager.

Fulworth bowed. 'If Lady Alixe would not mind, you may take this dance, St Magnus. I find my supper has not settled as well as I'd hoped. My dear Lady Alixe, would you forgive me?'

What a ninny the man was. But Merrick merely offered Alixe his arm and swept her on to the floor before Fulworth invented another lengthy show of chivalry.

'He's no good for you, Alixe,' Merrick began, fitting his hand easily to the small of her back.

'Why is that?' Alixe enquired.

'He bet on you at White's. He wagered that I would dance with you before the sixth of July. Lucky for him, tonight's the fifth.' Merrick swung them through a turn, taking the opportunity to draw her closer.

'I'm coming to discover men are not so very different from one another, regardless of station,' Alixe said with a touch of coolness.

'How have you been?' Merrick moved to safer conversational territory.

'Do you mean, how have I been since you left so abruptly?'

'I understand you're upset. I would like to explain.'

'There's nothing to explain.' Alixe sighed. 'I'm not even sure I'm angry at you, precisely, except that you left without saying goodbye. But you'll be glad to know that Jamie picked up the pieces admirably.'

'And Archibald Redfield?'

'He has been temporarily thwarted. I have been given a London Season to enjoy the city and put together my trousseau while my father draws up the contracts and looks into Redfield's background. Father and Redfield stayed in the country, but I expect them to arrive any day.'

'London agrees with you. You look lovelier than ever.'

'I have to. It's my last chance to find someone better than Redfield.' She looked up at him, her gaze touching him at his core. In that brief moment he acknowledged what he'd been avoiding all those days on the road, putting off his return to London. He *loved* Alixe Burke.

'You were right, Merrick, I have only the freedom to

choose who my husband will be. Redfield tried to take that away from me. He may still succeed unless I find someone else. A titled young gentleman with a decent background would sway my father, I think. So you see, marriage has become a jail and an escape all at once.'

'You could marry me.' The words were out before he could stop them, before he could think about all the reasons he was unsuitable for her, before he could think about his fear that he would fail her.

Alixe stumbled against him in her surprise.

'My father has released you from your obligations. Jamie told me. You're no longer the husband in waiting.' Alixe shook her head. 'I don't mean to be cruel, but you haven't any money, no title. You are no better a candidate than Redfield, perhaps worse. My father would not accept you.'

'I'm not marrying your father. I'm marrying you. Would you accept me, Alixe?'

Her face froze, her whole body tensing in his arms. 'I cannot discuss this here.'

'Then where?' He unashamedly leaned close to feather her ear with a soft sensual breath. He would fight with everything in his arsenal, be it a sin or no. 'Name the place and I'll be there. I've thought of nothing else but you since I left Folkestone. I dream of you, I wake hard and ready with the wanting of you. Tell me you don't think of me, that you don't remember the magic we can make together.'

Her pulse leaped beneath the strand of delicate pearls and Merrick smiled. 'Admit you want me, Alixe Burke.'

'I will admit no such thing.' But she trembled as she said it and her eyes could not help but fall on his lips.

'You don't have to. Your body has done it for you, my dear.' They passed the doors to the verandah. 'Shall I sweep you outside and kiss you senseless?'

'Merrick, please don't,' Alixe begged. Her fingers had buried themselves in the fabric of his jacket at the shoulder. She was wavering.

'Why not? Why should I not ask for what I want? Why should you not take what you want?'

'Because wanting is not marriage. Marriage is for ever, Merrick, and wanting is…' She moved her bare shoulders in a delicate shrug. 'Wanting is not for ever, Merrick, and you know it better than any of us.'

Merrick gave her a final turn and the music ended. They stood facing each other, Merrick unwilling to release her. 'What if you say yes and we find out if you're right or wrong?'

'No more wagers, Merrick. Why don't you return me to my court of gentlemen?'

'And then what? Shall we make conversation about things we don't want to talk about? All the while I'll be making love to you in my mind and you'll know what I'll really be thinking.'

He returned her, but he didn't get a chance to flirt any further. Jamie quickly removed him from the circle of admirers moments after their return under the pretence he wanted to catch up with his old friend. Merrick wasn't fooled.

Outside, Jamie did not spare words for niceties. 'I think it would be best to leave her alone now. You've made your appearance to satisfy society's curiosity. There's no more reason to patronise her court.'

'Is this a warning?' He'd expected no less. Jamie had a sister to protect and Jamie knew what he was. But his tone was sharp with Jamie. His own emotions were on edge. In the last fifteen minutes he'd discovered he was in love, proposed marriage and been refused. It was quite a full evening even for him.

'Merrick, we're friends. This is an awkward spot for me to be in. She's got a decent proposal from Redfield and all these fellows to choose from now if she doesn't want him.'

'Don't forget my proposal,' Merrick added.

'You haven't proposed to her,' Jamie countered.

'I have, too—just now on the dance floor.'

'The dance floor?' Jamie breathed in disbelief. 'Merrick, really.' Then he paused, groping for the right phrasing. Merrick felt a stab of sympathy for his friend. Jamie was struggling to find proper words for a most improper betrayal.

'As friends, Merrick, tell me—is Redfield speaking the truth? Did you think to claim Alixe for yourself?'

Merrick leaned against the balustrade. 'No. I would never play such a game with your sister.' Or with any woman. That was his father's style, not his.

'Then why?'

Why propose to Alixe Burke when he could have any woman of the *ton* for any myriad pleasures without the office of marriage?

'Because, Jamie, when I look at her, I can't imagine her as anyone's but mine.' It was the single reason that had overcome years of reservation and belief that he'd never be suitable in that capacity for any worthy woman.

Jamie's hand was strong on his shoulder in commiseration. 'Then I am sorry.'

Sorry that he wasn't a better sort of man, a man who hadn't lived his life earning a reputation for questionable behaviour. Sorry for not having the funds to afford a wife like Alixe Burke. Sorry for falling in love with the one woman he could not attain.

Alixe couldn't concentrate on anything Fulworth was saying. Whatever wit he'd possessed before the waltz had vanished upon her return. Merrick and Jamie had gone out to the verandah. Only Jamie had come back in. She hoped they hadn't quarrelled. She hoped Merrick hadn't gone to seek comfort somewhere else. She hoped so much, the list was getting rather long and distinguished by the time she dragged her attention back to the conversation. Fulworth was going on about lobster patties on buffet tables.

Was that what he was truly thinking? Surely the very proper Fulworth wasn't thinking improper thoughts. If Merrick had been there, she was certain he would have flashed her a private look, one of his half-smiles that sent a hundred messages at once, all of them sinful. She couldn't help the small smile that crept across her mouth at the thought of Merrick. He'd been outrageous on the dance floor, but it was hard to stay angry with him for long. Even when she should.

He had proposed! She had refused and rightly so.

The idea was preposterous. It took more than wanting to make a marriage, just as it took more than connections and money. Redfield would say the proposal
proved Merrick was after her money and had been all
along.

'By my calculations, at two lobster patties a piece
at an attendance rate of two balls an evening, the av-
erage gentleman consumes two hundred and fifty lobster patties a Season,' Fulworth said with a flourish.

'Oh, that's quite a lot,' Alixe exclaimed with enough
verve to hopefully sound impressed with his mathe-
matic prowess.

The other gentlemen were arguing now—was two
really a fair approximation? Wouldn't three be better?
What was he considering as the start of the Season,
the week after Easter or the Academy art showing?

Did they care that much? They were certainly putting up a grand impression of caring greatly about the
consumption of lobster patties among English peers.
Alixe mumbled an excuse about visiting the retiring
rooms to Fulworth, who hardly gave her a glance, and
slid into the oblivion of the ballroom, glad to have
made her escape.

Alixe found a quiet retreat in the dark haven of the
Couthwald library. She sank on to the sofa and kicked
off her slippers, flexing her toes in relief. She was tired
of dancing, tired of smiling, tired of pretending any of
London's finest held an iota of appeal. They were nothing but a way out of a bad situation and into a mediocre
one. She would resist marriage to the fortune-hunting

Redfield however she could, even if meant taking one of those lobster-patty experts out there.

You could marry Merrick. To his credit, he had seemed in earnest tonight. But that didn't change facts, and she knew all too well every reason Merrick should be refused, from social considerations to her own personal happiness. It would kill her to watch him stray once the 'wanting' had waned.

But until then, it could be wonderful, came the dangerous counter. Perhaps a little bit of pleasure was better than none at all.

Alixe took a deep breath to relax. It was the first clue she wasn't alone. She caught a faint whiff of *fougère*.

'We have to stop meeting like this,' came the familiar seductive tones of the devil himself. Merrick emerged from an alcove hidden from view of the sofa. His very stance was one of insouciance. His cravat was off, his waistcoat unbuttoned, a snifter of brandy dangling casually in one hand.

Fleeting panic struck. Alixe stood up in a rush, slippers forgotten. 'Please tell me you're alone.' Alixe's gaze travelled past him to the alcove, praying no one else emerged. She didn't want to see him with another woman tonight.

Merrick gave a wicked grin and stepped closer. He gave the brandy an indolent swirl. 'I could, but it would be a lie since I'm here with you.' Blue hunger raged in his eyes. This was not the tamer, flirtatious version of Merrick St Magnus who talked a harmless scandal on a picnic blanket. This version was wild, a barely leashed original of the other paler imitation. His hunger was for her and it roused her most outrageously. A wanton heat pooled between her legs, tingling and sharp.

When he spoke, his voice was nothing more than a growl, hoarse with desire. 'You've refused my decent proposal. Can I offer you an indecent one?'

Chapter Seventeen

One three-letter word and he would be her lover. It would be rough and beautiful and there would be no going back. Once could be excused as spontaneous, but twice was deliberate. Alixe lifted her hands to her coiffure and pulled the pins from her hair until it shook free. 'Yes.'

Her voice was the slightest of whispers but it was all the confirmation Merrick needed, all she needed. She was in his arms, her hands working the fabric of his shirt loose from the waistband of his trousers as his hands worked the folds of her gown up her thighs. It would be folly to disrobe. This decadence would have to be enough. Alixe strained against him, hands slipping beneath his shirt, palms running up the planes of his chest, revelling in the feel of him beneath her fingers.

His mouth was buried against her neck, his kisses sending a *frisson* of heat through her. She offered up a moan of both desperation and completion. Nothing

had been right since she'd left his arms. Everything was
right now. In this moment nothing mattered but the feel
of him, the taste of him, the smell of him.

'I missed you so much,' came the simple words, the
inadequate words. Would he understand all they en-
tailed? Were there words enough to convey what he'd
meant to her?

'God, Alixe.' Merrick breathed against her, hands
tangled in her hair, pulling her head up to meet his
hot gaze. 'Wanting you is killing me.' He lifted her
against him, whispering hoarse instructions. 'Wrap
your legs about me.'

She did so, tightly, as if she could hold him for ever.
The library wall was at her back, a bulwark against
the rough onslaught of passion that followed. He took
her in a single stroke, hard and forceful, and she welcomed it. *Welcomed him.* She could do nothing but
moan her pleasure as he claimed her again and again,
branding her with each thrust, his own need for her
every bit as great as her need for him. Alixe thought
dimly, as their desire crested, how would once, twice,
three times, ever be enough, how would she ever get
over the wanting of him? She knew only one thing: she
was lost. Lost to pleasure, lost to want, lost to him and
she could do nothing about it except give in for however long it lasted.

With a final thrust, Merrick surrendered to the madness of want, letting the sensations of ultimate release
thunder through him as he poured himself into Alixe.
This was what he'd sought during those interim days

while he roamed aimlessly between Kent and London. He'd been waiting for something and this was it. This was definitely it: loving Alixe.

Alixe's face was dreamy as she lifted her head from his shoulder where she'd buried her cries, but her eyes were questioning. 'What shall we call this, Merrick?'

'Madness, utter madness.' It was the only answer he had for her. He couldn't fully explain any of these feelings to himself, let alone another, and certainly not while he was still deep in the throes of satiated climax. 'We could end the madness with marriage, Alixe,' Merrick ventured.

'A most proper option under the circumstances. I am surprised, Merrick, but only a little,' came a cynical voice from the door. The door shut with a quiet snick behind the intruder. 'Tsk, tsk. I would have thought after the incident with Lucy the upstairs maid you would have learned to lock the door.' The figure stepped forwards into the dim light of the room.

'Perfect timing, as always.' Merrick made no move to restore his dishabille, his voice barely veiling the sneer of contempt beneath it.

'And this must be the ravishing Alixe Burke. Or would it be more accurate to say the "ravished" Alixe Burke?'

Merrick balled his fists. He was going to hit someone. Soon.

To her credit, Alixe didn't flinch. 'Unfortunately your reputation doesn't precede you. You would be?'

Merrick stepped in. 'This is Martin St Magnus, my brother.'

'I've had the devil's own time tracking you down—' Martin began.

'There's a reason for that,' Merrick cut in swiftly. He wanted Martin out of the room as quickly as possible. He and Alixe had things to work out. Now was not the time for a family reunion.

'If you ran from scandal the way you run from Father, your lot in life might be considerably improved.'

'I do not run. I have made it clear to him that he does not have the ordering of me. I go where I please, when I please.' This was not proving to be an expedient exit.

'From your tone, I must deduce that you think I do not enjoy such luxuries.' Martin flicked his dark gaze towards Alixe. 'You've outdone yourself this time, Merrick. Debauching an earl's daughter? You may have overreached yourself at last. You have to marry this sort of girl.'

He felt Alixe tense beside him and his protective instincts surged. She did not need to be dragged into the mire of his distorted family. Merrick crossed his arms and widened his stance. 'You may insult me all you like, but you will not slander Lady Alixe.'

'Or you'll pummel me the way you pummelled that Redfield fellow at the house party? If you keep it up, Merrick, you won't be invited to any decent places.' Martin feigned a sigh and took up residence in a chair with a wave of his hand. 'Then again, that list is probably fairly short as it is. I hear you aren't even keeping your own rooms these days. You're sharing rooms with that degenerate Bedevere. That's got to be a pit of depravity if ever there was one.'

'Don't get too comfortable in that chair, Martin. You need to leave.' Merrick took a menacing step forwards. 'Lady Alixe and I were having a conversation before you interrupted.'

Martin's eyes roved over Alixe. 'Perhaps, Lady Alixe, I could escort you back to the ball before any more damage is done. Surely you know you shouldn't be without a chaperon under such circumstances.' He stood and held out a hand to her. 'Come with me. Walk away from this folly while you still can.'

Merrick's gut clenched. Would she take that hand? Would she take a look at him and realise how reckless they'd been? Would she regret it? *Don't go with him, Alixe,* Merrick willed her in his mind.

Alixe did not hesitate. 'I believe you've been asked to leave.'

Martin nodded knowingly. 'I see. You're in love with him. I pity you, Lady Alixe.' He strode to the door, calling his message over his shoulder. 'I came looking for you because Father has asked you to call on him tomorrow at three. Show up. I believe there's money and property to discuss. You shouldn't miss it.'

At the door he paused and turned back. 'Lady Alixe, make sure you know what you're getting into. There's nothing but heartache down any road he leads you. He's not capable of anything more. You know it's the truth.' Then he was gone, leaving a malevolent silence in his wake.

'His interruption doesn't change what I'm asking you, Alixe.' Merrick pressed what was left of his advantage. Martin may have been right in one respect.

He had overreached himself this time. A woman of Alixe's calibre would think twice about taking on a man with his history. That history was staring her in the face. It was easier to disregard rumours in the country when London was far away. Somehow, they seemed less real than messages delivered in person by heirs to marquisates.

Alixe offered a wry smile and shook her head. 'Am I supposed to say it doesn't matter? What about all the things you said in Kent about not being able to love? What has suddenly changed you to a marrying man capable of faithfulness? Which one is the real you, Merrick? The faithless rogue or the solid family man?'

Of course. Alixe Burke would demand complete faithfulness from a husband. She would not tolerate dysfunction in any guise. Merrick did not like the coldness of her tone. She was slipping away from him; the heat of their passion had chilled.

She moved to push past him. He could not let her leave just yet. She would not seek him out after tonight. She would try to avoid him as she'd tried to do at the house party.

Merrick took her arm in a gentle grip. 'Alixe, I will always be at your disposal should you need me.'

'I won't. Don't you see, it's not enough for me. I would avoid being the wife you've tired of as you pursue the latest woman who's caught your very fleeting attentions.' She drew a deep breath and gathered herself. 'I could not live with myself, knowing I sold myself so cheaply. I don't know how you do it.'

* * *

At promptly three o'clock, Merrick presented himself at his father's town house, a magnificent Greek Palladian structure four storeys high on Portland square. He had not set foot inside the family residence in seven years. It had not changed from the images in his memory. The huge urns in the entry were still filled with enormous amounts of fresh flowers. The marble tile of the floor was enviously devoid of any scuff marks left by errant boots.

In short, the place still felt like a museum. It made him want to stomp his foot on the floor just to leave a clod of dirt behind. But there would only be short-lived victory in that. A servant would immediately sweep it up and pristine order restored. Messes of any sort were not tolerated in the St Magnus household. Which was why he'd bothered to come at all. There was one mess that had lingered overlong and Merrick meant to see himself extricated from it.

The butler ushered him to the study where his father liked to conduct business. Merrick did not miss the message. He'd been relegated to 'business'; perhaps he even rated a 'family business' label.

The walnut doors pushed open into the earl's domain. Gareth St Magnus, the fifth Marquis of Crewe, sat behind his massive carved desk, imposing and austere. Merrick had forgotten how big everything in the house was. The desk, the chairs, the vases in the front foyer.

'Merrick, it's so good of you to come.' Gareth rose halfway from his chair and gestured for him to take the chair set opposite—the business side of the desk. The rules for the interaction were clearly established. There was no 'son', no welcome home embrace. His father might have been talking to an investment partner or a casual acquaintance.

Gareth pushed a packet of papers towards him. 'A great-aunt on your mother's side has left you a small bequest. Apparently, she found you to be quite charming. The papers are all in order, although you can have a solicitor of your own choosing look through them. The property is near Hever. There is one stipulation.' There was a challenging glint in Gareth's eye. 'You cannot sell it to cover gambling debts and you must be wed to inherit it.'

There was a moment's elation. He was a landowner, something he'd never thought he'd be, something he'd never aspired to be. Alixe would be pleased. Then there was a moment's deflation. There was no more Alixe. Alixe had left him last night, hurried towards the inevitable by his brother's cold reminder of reality.

'Perhaps now you can properly offer for the Burke chit.' A curious flame sparked in the marquis's blue eyes, far too like his own. He and his father were genetic imprints of the other. Even at fifty, with gold hair fading to the dull sheen of harvested wheat, his father bore a remarkable resemblance to him. He'd always resented that resemblance. He had spent most of his life fighting against it. He did not want to be his father—a man who'd made marriage miserable with his faithlessness for a decent woman like his mother.

'You wish to marry her. Is she breeding or are you after her money since you refuse to spend mine?'

'That is none of your business.'

'Has she refused you?'

He must have betrayed himself with a slight movement of his eyes.

Gareth crowed, 'She has and rightly so. She's far too good for a wastrel like yourself. This is rich. The infamous lover of London has been refused. Perhaps you're losing your touch? It's not been a good year for you. I hear you can't pay your rent, that you've moved in with Bedevere. All that money in the bank would set your world to rights.'

'I won't touch a penny of it. I want nothing to do with you or anything that's yours.' Of course, his father knew. His father knew everything.

The marquis gave a cold smile. 'Take your estate and go. Find a bride if anyone will have you without my money. Remember, it's fine to have a poor man in bed, but don't fool yourself, Merrick. No woman wants a poor man for ever.'

Chapter Eighteen

It had been two weeks since she'd seen Merrick and Alixe was starting to fear she was going to need him, after all. Alixe pushed a needle through the fine Irish linen she was embroidering with a delicate border of flowers. Her bravado had been only that the night she'd left him in the Couthwald's library. She'd been angry and stunned, although in hindsight she shouldn't have been.

Alixe rummaged in her bag for a strand of blue silk and carefully threaded her needle, letting the routine of the activity and the warm sun in the garden soothe her rampant thoughts. Her mother had offered to sit with her and sew, but Alixe had wanted to be alone, afraid she might betray herself in the company of another. Her mother would be mortified if she knew the direction of Alixe's thoughts, nearly all of them bent on the person of Merrick St Magnus.

She'd known the truth about Merrick from the beginning. Jamie had seen to it with his discreet warnings. Even without Jamie's warnings, London had seen to it. Merrick's reputation could not be hidden in town. She'd heard about it in juicy bits and pieces behind fans at teas where the ladies would pretend to report his antics in appalled tones when they were really titillated. And she'd seen what he was for herself. He was handsome, charming, wickedly dashing in his behaviours and a second son with no other prospects than the ones purchased by his searing blue gaze and well-displayed physique.

She knew men like that. She'd been warned about them all her life. Every heiress possessed of a fortune the size of hers knew who was acceptable and who was not. But she'd wanted to believe Merrick was different. For a time that had been possible. No one expected or wanted her to marry him. He'd not been thrust in her path as a suitor. He had been given a very defined role to play in her life for a very brief period of time. That made him safe.

Then he had kissed her and everything had changed, for her at least, and nothing had been safe any more: not her dreams of freedom through self-imposed spinsterhood, not her determination to avoid fortune hunters and not her determination to avoid a marriage for the convenience of an alliance. If she married at all, she had her standards: respect, fidelity and perhaps even love.

Those were not items Merrick could offer and yet she found herself willing to forgo them in return for the extraordinary pleasures he did offer and the astonishing moments of connectedness that came with them.

In fact, she'd already risked forgoing those ideals twice and it appeared there were going to be consequences.

Oh, yes. Alixe feared she was going to need him very much. She was late. It was early days yet, only five days past the expected arrival of her monthly flow. She could still pretend there were any number of reasons for it: the hectic stress of the Season, the personal stress of her own matrimonial drama, the heat of London in July. There was no reason to panic. But she needed to make plans for the worst, of which there were only two possibilities. Accept Merrick's offer of marriage or accept Archibald Redfield's and push to marry quickly, which shouldn't be a concern in either case.

Archibald wouldn't care; perhaps with his own blond looks, he wouldn't even notice the child wasn't his. He wanted only her money and all the prestige she represented. There was security in knowing what that marriage would be from the start. There would be no illusions, no pretences towards romance, no wounds to heal later when the pretences were stripped away. But that marriage would represent all that she'd fought so hard to avoid.

If she had to choose, would marriage to Merrick be any better? There'd be pleasure, to be sure. There would be moments when all would be well. But there'd be moments of heartache, too, when the reality, once obscured by bouts of pleasure, would shine through and she would realise Merrick didn't love her. There would be doubt, too. Had he engineered this from the start? Had he seen the opportunity to snare her fortune for himself as Redfield had so inelegantly suggested?

Perhaps he'd even hoped she'd become pregnant and forced to marry him. But she was hard pressed to view him in such a devious light. No matter what the scandalmongers said about him, she did not think many of his pranks were undertaken with malicious intent or with those who didn't understand the risks.

What to choose? Illusion or reality? Merrick or Archibald? How could she choose either and still be true to herself? Alixe prayed she wouldn't have to choose at all. But it might be too late to escape all damage. She highly suspected Merrick had already broken her heart.

'Miss, you have a caller. Will you be receiving?' It was Meg and Alixe noted immediately that her maid's colour was high. Her voice quivered ever so slightly with excitement and her hands were clasped tightly together at her waist. Alixe's suspicions rose, her own pulse leaping irrationally at the prospect that Merrick St Magnus was waiting in the foyer, further proof that she had not escaped unscathed.

Alixe smoothed her skirts with her hands, gathering calmness. 'You may send him to me, Meg. Bring him to the garden and ring for lemonade,' she said in her most placid tones.

'Shall I tell your mother?' Meg asked.

Alixe thought quickly. 'No. You shall be our chaperon and that will be enough.' Merrick had a certain amount of audacity to come calling at the town house after her father had summarily dismissed him at the house party. She also suspected Jamie had reiterated that same dismissal in, she hoped, more polite tones at the Couthwalds' ball. Merrick had fulfilled his purpose and the Earl of Folkestone had no more need of him.

It also raised the question of what could possibly bring him here. He was not oblivious to having been given his *congé*. He knew the reception he'd likely receive. A small flicker of hope leapt low in her stomach. Had he come for her? What a wonder it would be if a twenty-six-year-old heiress, relegated to society's shelf, had stirred the honourable passions of a veteran rogue like St Magnus. What a wonder indeed. If he could love her, it might change everything.

If she would accept him, it would change everything and for that, Merrick was willing to risk it all. It had taken some time to wrestle his answer to Alixe's question. Who was he? But now that he had, the path seemed straight, although no less dangerous for its simplicity of direction.

Merrick strode behind Alixe's maid, who was beaming with barely contained excitement. She hurried him out to the garden with all the haste decorum allowed. He understood the reason for it and it both inflated his hopes and reminded him of the risk he took in coming here. Alixe had consented to see him, but he was still *persona non grata* in the Burke household. He was not Folkestone's choice of a proper husband for his daughter.

But he was through the door. He'd been received. One hurdle overcome. One risk conquered. The next was Alixe. He must conquer her inhibitions in regards to marrying him. To that extent he'd taken great pains in the past weeks. Merrick gave his waistcoat a final tug and followed Meg out into the sunlight of the Folkestone garden.

Alixe was sewing at a stone bench, surrounded by lush roses. Her dark head was bent to the needlework and she looked the veritable portrait of genteel English womanhood in a light muslin gown of celadon: beautiful, refined and calm. The illusion brought a smile to Merrick's lips. His Alixe was so much more than that and seldom was she calm. His boots crunched on the gravelled path and she looked up, her sherry eyes unable to hide the questions bubbling beneath the calm surface.

'Why, Lord St Magnus, what brings you out so early in the day?' She rose and let him kiss her hand, all a great show for Meg's benefit. Her gown did her figure all sorts of favours. The neckline enhanced the fullness of her breasts and the skirt flared ever so slightly over the curve of her hip. She looked entirely womanly and he felt himself stir at the sight of her.

Merrick made a show of his own, consulting his pocket watch. 'It's not as early as all that, Lady Alixe. It's nigh on eleven.'

'Not too early for lemonade at least.' Alixe sent Meg a not-so-subtle look and the maid scurried off. The moment she was gone, Alixe dropped all pretence.

'What are you doing here? Surely you know you're not welcome.' Alixe took up her needlework, keeping her hands busy.

'By you?' Merrick sat beside her, drinking her in.

Two weeks had seemed an eternity, but he could not see her until he'd been sure of himself.

'You know what I mean. My father has dismissed you.' Alixe bit off a length of string between her teeth. Merrick found the motion delightfully erotic.

'But *you* haven't, Alixe. I find that I am not satisfied with our last conversation. We have not finished it. I asked you a question and you have not answered it,' Merrick forged ahead. Lemonade would only keep Meg occupied for so long.

'Correction, I did answer your question. You simply did not care for it.' Alixe stabbed the linen with uncharacteristic roughness.

'Hence, my dissatisfaction with our conversation.' Merrick reached over and took the embroidery hoop from her hands. 'Lay this aside for a moment, Alixe. You'll kill the cloth otherwise.' His hands closed over hers to forestall any of her fidgets and it gave him strength, too, to feel the warmth of her skin beneath his.

'You asked me a question at the Couthwalds'. I've come to answer it. You asked me who I was, the rogue or the husband,' he began. He could feel her hands clench beneath his as she tried to pull away. 'You were right to ask. I had no answer that night.'

Meg returned with the lemonade. Merrick waited for her to set the tray on a nearby table and take herself off a discreet distance before continuing.

'I believed because I looked so much like my father I would act like him, too. I would only be capable of being like him. But I'm not him. He has no hold over me. I haven't spent a penny of his allowance and I hadn't set foot in the family town house for seven years, until two weeks ago.' Merrick paused here to pull out a sheaf of papers from inside his jacket. 'I haven't been a perfect gentleman…'

Alixe squeezed his hands. 'I've told you once before I don't believe you're as awful as all that.' Something born of innate goodness shone in her sherry eyes, a refusal to believe someone was so inherently flawed.

'You should. There's plenty of proof.' He was tempted to tell her about the Greenfield Twins, but an errant sense of decency poked at him.

'Could this be enough for you, Alixe? This chance that I could be a better man *for* you, *because* of you?' He handed her the papers he held. 'I hope this is further proof that I can be redeemed. I want to be redeemed, I want to be all you need.'

Alixe took the papers and scanned them. 'You've come into property?'

'From a great-aunt. It's mine upon marriage,' Merrick began. He wanted to be honest about the conditions, but he didn't want Alixe to think he'd come begging for her hand simply to get his hands on the property with the added benefit of her money. 'It could be ours, Alixe,' he said. 'I would have something of my own. I wouldn't be entirely reliant on your fortune. It's not a big estate, but it would be our place. It's not too far from Folkestone. You would be able to keep an eye on your historical projects.'

'What are you asking me, Merrick?' Alixe ventured cautiously, handing the papers back.

'I am asking you to reconsider. In all fairness, I have overcome your initial objections at no small risk to myself.'

'You would have made a fine barrister, Merrick.' Alixe smiled softly in the wake of his closing arguments.

'Well?'

'I am fully cognisant of the honour you do me.'

His heart sank. She was going to refuse. That's how refusals started. Not that he knew firsthand, but he'd heard others talk about it at the clubs. No one had ever refused him. Then again, he'd never proposed anything honest like this to a decent woman before.

'It will not be enough,' Alixe said sadly. 'I wish I could accept, but it will not be enough.'

'Then tell me what it will take.'

'Love and fidelity, Merrick. That is my price.' Alixe squared her shoulders, her chin going up in piquant defiance. 'Can you be faithful to me, Merrick St Magnus?'

How could he promise permanently something he'd barely experienced temporarily? The right answer would be yes. But the honest answer was, 'I'll try, Alixe.'

'There can be no "try" in this, Merrick.'

'I will not bind you to me with a lie, Alixe. Would you prefer I say "yes" for the expedience of gaining your agreement without knowing it absolutely for the truth?'

'No, of course not.' Alixe rose, signalling it was time for him to leave. But she rose unsteadily and swayed. Merrick caught her by the arm and righted her.

'Are you unwell?' Merrick gestured for Meg. 'Pour some lemonade, please.'

'It's just the sun.' Alixe attempted a smile. She sat down and took the cold glass from Meg.

But Merrick thought differently. 'Meg, perhaps a parasol might help. Would you be so kind as to fetch your mistress one?' Surely Alixe would have said something.

'Alixe, is there something you'd like to tell me?' he said gently, although his insides were a sudden roiling mess.

She shook her head and sipped the lemonade. It occurred to him that she might not know. He tried again, forgoing any delicacy. 'Alixe, have you bled since we've made love?'

She looked up, startled by his bluntness. 'No.' It came out in a rueful, breathy little sigh.

'Is there a chance you may be pregnant?' Merrick pressed.

Alixe would not look at him. She kept her gaze fixed on the trellis of climbing roses across the path. 'It is too soon to know. I am not so very late.'

But she was late and Merrick had seen other signs: the smallest of changes in her body barely visible to the casual eye beneath her gown. He would wager her courses would not come. 'You should have told me.'

She looked at him with eyes that threatened to tear and it stabbed him to his core that his Alixe should be suffering. He'd been careless with her, caught up in the magical madness of her and now she had no choices left. It seemed she'd have to settle for 'try', after all. He'd speak to her father this afternoon whether she liked it or not.

Chapter Nineteen

Admittedly, Merrick had little experience with being proper, but women were mainly the same whether they were proper or not when it came to courtship. He presented himself sharply at four o'clock at the Earl of Folkestone's town house, flowers in hand for Lady Folkestone and a box of chocolates for Alixe. Gifts usually went a long way in smoothing rocky paths, as did a clean appearance. A clean, well-kempt man bearing gifts was hard to refuse.

Always careful with his grooming, Merrick had taken extra pains that afternoon to be turned out at his sartorial best. A sapphire stick-pin glinted in the snowy folds of his cravat and a thick band of antique gold adorned the middle finger of his left hand—both pieces a quiet testimony to what he hoped would be perceived as his 'wealth'.

Lady Folkestone received him first in the front parlour, offering him a polite, albeit empty, smile as she took the flowers. But mamas were women, too. Mer-

rick employed a compliment about the wallpaper and
the general good taste of the room, drawing her into a
lively discussion of the latest trends towards more or-
nate furniture. 'Being a man, naturally, I prefer a sturdy
chair. Those spidery-legged baroque pieces are lovely,
but they're hardly able to support a man's weight. Every
time I sit down in one I find myself waiting to hear it
crack,' Merrick confided in a conspiratorial tone, letting his eyes smile with the sharing of a secret. 'They're
not at all like these chairs. Now, these chairs are hardy
and yet elegant with the upholstery you've chosen. The
light colours of the striping detracts from what might
be seen as their heaviness.'

'That's precisely what I was thinking. My husband
did not agree. Folkestone thought the lighter colours
would show wear and dirt more quickly, but I insisted,'
Lady Folkestone exclaimed, obviously thrilled to have
a male divine her reasoning *and* agree with it. She
was warming to him, although Merrick thought such
warmth might fade if she knew what her daughter and
he had been getting up to. But surely Lady Folkestone,
with all her matchmaking abilities, was not oblivious
to the reasons he was here in a home where he'd been
all but banned.

A footman arrived to announce the earl was ready
to see him. Merrick rose and bowed graciously to Lady
Folkestone. 'It's been a pleasure speaking with you.
I've enjoyed your insights on decorating very much. I
hope to have some property of my own shortly in which
I might employ your talents.' Lady Folkestone smiled,

a much more genuine smile than the one she'd given him upon his arrival.

The earl was another matter. Folkestone couldn't be wooed with chocolates or flowers or comments about cushion colours. He sat stoically behind his desk, not unlike Merrick's own father, and glared. 'You are not welcome here,' he said baldly.

Merrick took the empty chair across from him, acutely aware he'd not been invited to sit. He sat anyway and crossed a leg over his knee. 'I am here to offer an honourable proposal of marriage to your daughter.'

Folkestone drew a deep, irritated breath. 'You're not what I want for her, as you have been made aware on several occasions now.'

Those were harsh words to hear to one's face, but Merrick merely smiled to show the haughty earl he was not bothered by the rude comments. 'Things have changed since then.' That was putting it mildly. 'I have come into a property, a modest estate near Hever. It passes to me upon my marriage. I would be able to give your daughter a home on my own terms.'

There. Let that quash any concerns over fortune hunting. There was a slight flicker in Folkestone's dark eyes. He had not known about the inheritance. It *did* make a difference, but only a slight one.

Folkestone toyed with an obsidian paperweight. 'A property is important. A man does not want to live off his in-laws' largesse.' What he meant was a 'real' man. 'But there are other implications besides the practicalities of supporting Alixe.' He gave Merrick a hard stare.

'There are social considerations that cannot be swept away with a property.'

'Such as?' Merrick enquired in a blithe tone. He knew full well what Folkestone was hinting at, but he would be damned if he'd give way to implied meanings. If Folkestone wanted to point out his inadequacies, the man would have to do it in explicit terms.

Folkestone's face hardened. 'Don't play games with me, St Magnus. We both know what social concerns I speak of. Your relationship with your family is strained, to put it politely.'

'That's by choice, sir,' Merrick said levelly.

'You have no title of your own, nor any prospect of coming into one. She's the daughter of an earl. Marriage to a second son is a step down for her, especially when you come to her with nothing.'

Merrick stiffened at that. He'd not ever been a direct recipient of the negotiating process Alixe claimed to abhor. He could see why she despised it now. He was being sized up for his assets as if that was all that mattered. 'Is my genuine regard for Alixe such a small thing, then?' Merrick replied.

Folkestone coughed at this. 'St Magnus, your sense of "genuine regard" for a lady is legendary among the *ton*. You've held quite a few ladies in this so-called genuine regard and you've married none of them. It does lead me to wonder why you'd want to marry my Alixe. She's the richest, of course. Perhaps that is what appeals to you?'

'What appeals to me is her intelligence, her compassion, her beauty.' Those were not things he could prove to Folkestone. How could he explain how Alixe made him feel? How did he convey that when he was with her, he was a better sort of fellow than he'd ever been. When he was with her, he didn't miss his old life and its misguided revels.

Folkestone set down the paperweight. 'It seems to me that there are other women who might be glad of the chance to be recipients of your genuine regard and, in turn, save your new-found estate by marrying you. However, my daughter isn't one of them. Even if I found your suit appealing and trustworthy, I would decline. As you also know, there is a very nice and legitimate proposal on the table from Mr Redfield, whose situation I find acceptable. He already has a manse. He doesn't need marriage to claim his property and he'll live nearby so that Alixe will be close to family. I think, under the circumstances, Mr Redfield is exactly the kind of grounded countryman Alixe needs as a husband.'

'He has no title, no wealth of his own. You are holding me to a double standard here,' Merrick argued. He could feel hope slipping away.

'He is a self-made man, which is more than I can say for you. He started with nothing and from it has created something. I find I respect that. You, on the other hand, are the son of a marquis, with many options open to you. But you've chosen none of them.' Folkestone's eyes narrowed.

'Then Redfield has truly fooled you. He may have fashioned something for himself, but at whose expense? How many women has he ruined or exploited to climb this high?'

'None that I know of. The same cannot be said for the Greenfield Twins.'

And that was that. Merrick heartily wished he'd never heard of the Greenfield Twins. His notorious wager was all over town and he hadn't even done anything, technically speaking. He managed to exit the town house with a show of dignity, but his heart was sinking.

He'd hoped Folkestone would have accepted his suit and allowed things to follow their proper course. It would certainly have avoided difficulties. He and Ashe had failed to turn up anything shady on Redfield. Whoever he was, the man had covered his tracks exceedingly well. That option had come to a dead end. The other option was exposing Alixe's pregnancy. It would force Folkestone's approval of the match, but the costs were enormous. Folkestone would never believe after such a revelation that Merrick had offered in good faith. There would always be doubt that Merrick had deliberately seduced her for her fortune and to claim his estate. Under such a cloud, what kind of future could he and Alixe expect to build?

He said as much to Ashe at White's in the quiet of the late afternoon. They had a corner of the main room to themselves. Most gentlemen wouldn't put in appearances until after seven and the evening entertainments began. Merrick was glad for the solitude.

'You have two choices,' Ashe said thoughtfully,

swirling brandy in a crystal snifter. 'You can forget about her or you can marry her.'

'Have you been listening? I don't have Folkestone's permission *and* she's pledged to Redfield.'

'Have *you* forgotten how to play outside the rules?' Ashe shook his head ruefully. 'Spare me the idiocy of fools in love.'

He drank and swallowed. 'You don't need permission to marry her, you dolt. I'm talking about elopement. She's twenty-six, for heaven's sake, and you're thirty. It's not like you're two green children come to town for the first time.'

'There will be a scandal.'

Ashe sprayed his brandy in a choking fit that brought a footman running to his side. 'A scandal? You're afraid of a little scandal *now*?' He coughed. 'It wouldn't be your first and it certainly wouldn't be your worst. This would be your most "decent" scandal, however, since it ends in the noble state of marriage.'

But it wasn't what he wanted for Alixe. He wanted to prove to her that he could be decent. He didn't have to live surrounded by scandal and notoriety. Merrick St Magnus could be something more than the *ton*'s most charmingly wicked rake. He'd liked the man he'd discovered inside himself at Folkestone. He'd liked translating the manuscript, and building fair booths and exploring ruins. That man could build a life worthy of her.

No, he wouldn't embarrass Alixe with an elopement. A dash to Gretna Green in the dark would only confirm suspicions that he'd been hunting her fortune.

A baby appearing early would be the icing on a very bittersweet cake. Society would dine out on the two of them for years. But Ashe had given him an idea. There was a way to decently marry Alixe, but for that he'd need two things: a special licence and her consent. He was certain he could get the former. He wasn't as sure about the latter.

Alixe sank gratefully on to her bed and kicked off her dancing slippers. The night had been beyond tedious. The best thing that could be said about it was that it had ended early. She was thankful. Her feet hurt and her mind had been in a constant state of turmoil since Merrick's surprise visit the day before.

He'd shown up that afternoon, too. He'd left chocolates for her, but apparently the focus of the visit had been to see her father. She'd been apprised of Merrick's proposal over dinner that night before her father's assurances that she'd be safely married to Redfield as soon as the banns could be called.

That meant three weeks. Not very much time at all. Alixe reached up and began pulling pins out of her hair. She'd dismissed Meg, wanting to prepare for bed in private, a decision she might regret when trying to get out of her gown, but not yet.

If she didn't act soon, she'd be married to Redfield and carrying Merrick's child. She was growing more certain of it by the day. It was the stuff of Gothic novels or a theatrical drama. Her life had been so very ordinary, so very predictable and staid not that long ago.

One fateful act had led to another and here she was, so far from the path she'd laid out for herself.

But that path was devoid of love, of certain elemental human experiences. Yet the price of love was exorbitant and it came with no guarantees, not even the guarantee her love would be returned. Merrick loved her for now, but what of later? That very doubt had stopped her tongue at dinner, from declaring she preferred St Magnus over Mr Redfield, after all.

Lost in her thoughts, Alixe struggled with the fastenings at the back of the dress, a summer night's breeze catching her bare skin where the dress lay undone. She turned sharply towards the draught and stifled a yelp of surprise just in time. Standing in the doorway of the little balcony that led off her room with an air of casual confidence, shirt sleeves rolled up, cravat undone, was Merrick.

'What are you doing here?' Alixe hissed in a hushed whisper.

'That's quite a greeting,' Merrick said with his usual casual ease. 'Not "how did you get here"? Or how glad you are to see me?'

'It's rather obvious how you got here.'

'Obvious doesn't make it easy. I will admit climbing up to your room is a bit ill advised. It will be a while before I try it again.' Merrick stepped into the room, filling the feminine abode with his masculine presence.

'No maid?' He looked around for Meg.

'No, you're lucky,' Alixe scolded. 'What would you have done if she was here?'

Merrick gave a cocky shrug, drawing her atten-

tion to the broadness of his shoulders. 'She likes me.
I wouldn't have done a thing except let her go to bed
early. It does look like you're in need of some help,
though. Perhaps I could stand in for your maid.'

He swept the long skein of her loosed hair forwards
over one shoulder, the feel of his warm hands against
her skin, intimate and relaxing as they worked the remaining fastenings. 'Lock your door, Alixe,' he murmured at her neck once he had finished.

'I locked it earlier,' Alixe managed. She was already
trembling for him.

'Good, I want to look my fill of you.' He slid the
gown off her shoulders, letting it cascade to the ground
in a spill of sea-green silk.

That drew her out of her stupor. 'You can't mean to
stay! Redfield is downstairs talking to Father.'

Merrick chuckled, a warm soothing sound that
reeked of his confidence. 'Are you expecting him?'

'No, of course not. *I* wasn't even expecting you,'
Alixe retorted.

'Then we won't be interrupted. Stop worrying,
Alixe.' His whisper was at her ear, his kisses light on
the column of her neck.

She arched her neck to the side, giving him full access to it, startled by the glimpse of them in the vanity
mirror. Merrick stood behind her, a veritable Adonis in
the evening light of the room, his attire less than perfect, the mussed quality only enhancing his sensuality, his buttermilk hair a pale halo, his eyes devil-dark
with desire. She barely recognised the wanton princess
in the reflection as herself: her hair loose and hanging

to one side, one shoulder of her chemise falling down her arm, the outline of her breasts visible through the thin material, Merrick's hands just below them, tantalisingly close. It was a provocative image.

Flustered by the sight, Alixe moved to turn into his arms, but Merrick held her fast. 'Watch us, Alixe. Watch how good we are together.'

And she did watch. It was wicked and yet riveting. Merrick pulled the chemise over her head, leaving her entirely unclothed. His hands cupped her breasts, his thumbs moving up and over the fullest part of them, caressing and stroking in a languid rhythm that had her leaning into him with a small moan of delight.

But after a while, it seemed patently unfair that he should be clothed and Alixe turned in his arms. This time he permitted it. She stripped away the cravat and made short work of his waistcoat and shirt. He sat down briefly to pull off his boots and allowed her to slide his trousers down his hips.

He was naked beneath the clothing and she revelled in the sight of him. The lamplight limned the fine sculpture of his chest, the square bones of his hips and abdomen. Alixe ran her hands over the flat of his stomach. 'I think this is the best part of a man.'

'Truly? I would have thought you might prefer other parts,' Merrick said mischievously, moving her hand lower.

Alixe grinned up at him. 'I like this part, too.' And she did. She liked that part of him very much. 'Did you come here to seduce me?'

'Most definitely.' Merrick turned her back to the

mirror, his voice husky with wickedness. It sent a
shiver of anticipation through her, her need rising.
'Brace your hands on the vanity, my dear, I will show
you how I mean to seduce you.' The moment of play
was gone; he was all serious lover now as he bent her
to him. 'I shall be your stallion.'

Oh, this was wickedness unleashed! He was hard
against her backside and she felt her body respond,
wanting him in her. Her gaze was riveted on the mirror now, watching him mount her from behind, watching him drive deep inside her, a warm hand splayed
on her stomach to offer support. Again and again he
drove until she could feel the surge of passion grow in
its intensity, pushing them higher towards some enig-
matic apex and then shatter like thin crystal against a
wall. He fell against her in his completion. She could
feel the pounding of his chest at her back, the heat of
him wrapping her in the blanket of his body.

He found the strength she lacked to guide them
both to her bed. She nestled against the hardness of
his chest, her head at his shoulder, his arm around her,
drawing her near.

How easy all this was with him. Being with him,
naked and playing, sharing the intimate pleasures of
their bodies, was entirely natural. She could not fathom
how it would be with Redfield or another.

'You were right when you said this was madness,'
Alixe said slowly after a while. She drew a tiny circle
around the flat aureole of his breast.

'We have a whole lifetime to work it out, Alixe, to
see if it is truly madness.'

Alixe shook her head. 'It's more complicated than that, Merrick. I know my father has refused you.'

'Will you allow his decision to stand? I came here tonight, Alixe, for you. I've never been one for convention and tradition. I don't need his permission. But I do need yours. There's a special licence in my trouser pocket. I would come for you tomorrow night and take you to Folkestone and marry you at St Eanswythe. Alixe, will you have me?' He was all seriousness. She could feel his body tense beneath her as he awaited her answer.

'You don't have to do this for the baby, it's still too soon to tell,' Alixe murmured, trying to stall until she could make up her mind. Did she dare risk it all on Merrick St Magnus?

'Whether there is a child or not is immaterial to me. I came here tonight for you. I would have come anyway.'

'Why?' Alixe breathed, daring to hope.

'Because, Alixe Burke, I have discovered that I love you. It's not a discovery a man makes every day.'

There could be no doubting him. The honesty of his confession brought tears to her eyes. 'Well, that changes everything,' Alixe managed, trying for levity.

She felt him relax beside her. 'I should hope so. But I still want to hear you say the words.'

There in the darkness, Alixe gathered all her courage. She was a smart woman who'd thought much about what she demanded from a marriage and what she demanded of herself. She understood the world even though she'd chosen to shun it in the hopes of a better life. Her hero, St Eanswythe, had attempted the same. But St Eanswythe had died at twenty-six and Alixe Burke was going to choose to live. She whispered the two most important words of her life for better or worse.

'Yes, Merrick.'

Chapter Twenty

Alixe stretched, a long languid movement that started in her toes and went all the way up to her arms. She arched her back and let the morning sun bathe her in its warmth. Everything was right with the world for the first time in weeks. She pushed her eyes open. Today was her wedding day.

Sort of.

Today was the day she'd embark on the journey that would culminate in her marriage to Merrick. He was gone already. He'd left at dawn, waking her briefly for a kiss before departing out her window. But he'd be back tonight with a carriage. Twelve hours to wait. He would send instructions this afternoon regarding where to meet.

A trill of excitement coursed through her at the prospect. She would simply disappear. After tonight she would no longer be Lady Alixe Burke. She would be Lady St Magnus. There was a certain fairy-tale quality to it; the self-proclaimed spinster with her shapeless gowns had captured the attentions of London's most sought-after lover.

Alixe blushed in the morning light, recalling the wicked passions of the night. She was most thoroughly ravished. She dropped a hand to the flat of her stomach. Child or not, she was ready to take on whatever lay ahead. She did not fool herself that marriage to Merrick would be perfect. There would be social shoals to navigate. The circumstances and haste of the marriage would be much talked about. She did hope timing might be on their side. The Season would wind down in a couple of weeks. People would return home to their country houses and forget about the events of the Season. By next spring, their marriage would be old news and there'd be juicier bits of gossips to occupy society.

Society wasn't the only hurdle they'd face. There would be her family's outcry to contend with as well. Her father would be furious that she'd gone against his efforts to see her married to Redfield. Her mother would consider this a blow to her social status, having a daughter married to a scoundrel. She didn't know what Jamie might think. She hoped he might forgive her. She hoped he wouldn't blame Merrick for this. This was her decision. She was going to have a try at love and see where it led.

With conviction in her choice, Alixe tossed back the covers and rang for Meg. It was time to embrace the day. Nothing would stand in her way now.

Nothing would stand in his way now, Archibald Redfield thought smugly, his booted toe tapping impatiently on the tiled reception-hall floor of Lambeth Palace. In a few minutes, he'd have the special licence in hand and the road to claiming his heiress would be clear of its last hurdle.

The traditional Folkestone talked of calling the banns, but Redfield wanted a surety should anything go awry. Banns meant three weeks of waiting. A special licence meant instant permission to marry should he need it and he just might. Nothing had gone according to plan where Alixe Burke was concerned and he would not take any chances here at the end with his goal nearly attained, especially not with St Magnus in town.

It had been galling to hear St Magnus had been in town while he himself had been detained with the earl, drawing up a marital contract. But it had been important that he be there. He couldn't be in two places at once and he couldn't risk the earl uncovering anything questionable about his past that might skew the acceptance of his proposal. If he was present, he could explain away any unpleasant discoveries. There were benefits to drawing the papers up in Folkestone, too. The country solicitor was competent, but less likely to have access to the information networks of London. The last thing Redfield wanted to do was draw up papers in London where the risk was larger that someone would know something unsavoury about him. So he had stayed with Folkestone to secure his match. Meanwhile, Merrick St Magnus hadn't given up. Which only meant one thing: the man must feel there was still some hope.

That fear was confirmed last evening when he'd driven home with the earl's family from an early night out at Lady Rothersmith's musicale, a venue he'd not been disappointed to depart. Folkestone had let it drop over brandy after the ladies had retired that the disreputable St Magnus had had the audacity to make an appointment. Of course, the earl had assured him, St Magnus had been refused out of hand. To which Redfield had politely reminded Folkestone with a smile that they had an agreement complete with legal papers. But just in case, perhaps with circumstances being what they were, a special licence would be a useful precaution.

He needed Folkestone's approval on this. An ordinary fellow like himself couldn't simply walk into Lambeth Palace. He'd need a letter of introduction from Folkestone to expedite his case. He had elegantly pleaded a gentleman's prerogative: a poor man might have to wait three weeks while banns are being called, but a man of funds could forgo that necessity. It was an especial honour for the bride to be married by special licence and while money was exceedingly in short supply for Redfield these days, he considered the twenty-eight guineas well spent if it meant procuring Alixe Burke's dowry. Folkestone had seen reason and acquiesced.

At last the heavy doors opened and the clerk reappeared, bearing papers in his hand. 'Do be careful, sir, the ink is barely dry,' he warned, handing over the papers. 'There must be something in the air. This is the second one that's been requested in as many days,' the clerk said congenially.

Redfield didn't care if it was the fifth. He only cared he had what he wanted. But he could afford to be generous in his success so he made polite conversation anyway. 'Who might the lucky fellow be?'

The clerk chuckled at that. 'Someone we'd never thought to see enter these hallowed halls.' He lowered his voice. 'I suppose it's not discreet to tell you, but we all had a good laugh after he left. Lord St Magnus.'

The elation of victory faded. Redfield kept a smile pasted on his face. 'St Magnus, that old dog? What does he want with a special licence?' he said with a congeniality he no longer felt.

The clerk shrugged. 'No idea, but he's got one now. Came in yesterday, late afternoon, and caught the archbishop at tea.'

Right after the visit to Folkestone, Redfield thought. He made a hasty exit. His instincts had been right. St Magnus hadn't taken 'no' for an answer. A new game was afoot. He could guess what it was. St Magnus meant to take the decision away from Folkestone. A *frisson* of anger shook him almost visibly as he strode down the pavement. All this trouble for snobbish Alixe Burke, who thought she was too good for the likes of him. She hadn't even dressed well until St Magnus had forced her to it. He did have to admit, she looked lovely these days. Bedding the shrew would be less of a hardship than he'd originally thought. St Magnus might have taught her some interesting tricks there, too.

Archibald Redfield was a practical man. Love

couldn't buy you a thing, but money could. He wasn't so much troubled by the thought that St Magnus had been tupping Alixe Burke behind the scenes as he was about the prospect that Alixe Burke had permitted it. Therein lay the danger. Such permission implied she preferred St Magnus over him. If so, St Magnus wouldn't have to steal her away, she'd go willingly unless he could stop it.

Archibald Redfield would not go away, Alixe thought with no small amount of irritation that afternoon. He'd taken her out for a drive in Hyde Park, which she'd hadn't been able to refuse, and now they sat in the shade of the garden with her mother, sipping lemonade and talking about the various improvements he wanted to make at Tailsby. The list was long, which no doubt accounted for the lengthy conversation.

'A gentleman's home must mirror his values,' he told her mother. 'I want a place of light and beauty, a place that will be a perfect setting for my family.' He looked her way with a warm smile that she was sure was affected. 'A prospective bridegroom must be indulged in his own fancies.' He laughed. 'While the ladies talk of gowns and flowers, gentlemen plan their home.'

Gentleman, my foot, Alixe thought. If he used the word 'gentleman' one more time, she was going to throw her lemonade glass at him. Then they could see what a 'gentleman' did with lemonade all over him. He might aspire to be a gentleman, but he had not attained such status yet.

'A gentleman?' Alixe queried perversely. 'I was unaware there was a title in your family.'

Her mother shot her a tiny frown of disapproval and quickly moved to restore tranquillity. 'Didn't you once say, Redfield, there was a baronetcy among one of your great-grandfathers?'

Redfield gave a casual lift of his shoulders. 'The family tree is so very tangled I can scarce keep it all straight for three generations, let alone four. I leave that sort of work for nimbler minds such as yours, Lady Folkestone.'

The compliment worked well in placating her mother. Her mother gave her a smile as if to say 'what a nice fellow, he wasn't even put off by your snide and inappropriate remark'.

'Lord St Magnus has a title,' Alixe continued her needling. 'That definitely makes him a gentleman.' She watched Redfield's smile tighten infinitesimally.

'I should like to think it takes more than putting "lord" in front of a name to make a gentleman,' Redfield responded. 'It takes knowledge of certain nuances, demonstration of certain behaviours, a certain restraint. Gentlemen are the bedrock of good society. I do not consider St Magnus to be a model citizen.'

'My brother cares for him a great deal,' Alixe shot back, letting Redfield know he was in grave danger of offending Jamie.

'Your brother is kindness itself.'

Alixe knew what that comment really meant and she neatly turned the tables. 'As you have been. Surely you have other obligations than dancing attendance on the two of us.'

'We are to be married. Nothing gives me greater pleasure than spending time with my fiancée. The only greater joy would be allowing me to announce that happiness tonight.' He was asking her mother for permission, but he was looking at her, his eyes hard and assessing as if he was searching for something, as if he knew something.

Alixe tensed, panic taking her as her mother glanced between them and said, 'Yes, I think tonight at the ball would be perfect. If we wait too much longer, the Season will be finished and there won't be a chance to celebrate.'

He did leave after that. But the damage was done. Alixe's first reaction was to run straight to Merrick. But if Redfield suspected anything, he would also suspect that. He meant to flush her out. She must do nothing to give away her anxiety. That meant she could only wait until evening and hope nothing else went awry.

Even if she'd thought it safe to send for Merrick, there was no chance for it. Her room was the scene of chaos. She was not alone for a moment. Meg was there with her mother and her mother's maid. 'It's not every night my daughter gets engaged!' her mother all but crowed as she bustled about Alixe's room, giving instructions for her hair, her gown, her slippers. Three gowns already lay discarded on Alixe's bed, none of them deemed right for the occasion.

'Meg, bring out the deep-cream gown with the forest-green sash.' It had been one of Alixe's favourites when it had arrived and she hadn't worn it yet. 'I think that one will do nicely, Mother,' Alixe put in, trying not to swivel around while her mother's maid put up her hair. How would Merrick get word to her when she couldn't contrive to be alone? She had thought word would have arrived earlier. It was after seven and no word had come.

A thousand thoughts rioted through her head, adding to the chaos. Had Merrick changed his mind? Had he been delayed? At last she was proclaimed 'ready'. The woman in the mirror looked dazzling, if not a trifle pale.

'I'll just help her with some powder and rouge,' Meg said, shooing the others out. 'She'll be downstairs in just a moment.'

Alixe was grateful for the quiet that followed. She let Meg touch up her face with a light application of cosmetics. 'I don't know what's been going on, miss,' Meg began as she worked. 'But Lord St Magnus sent a boy to the back door asking for me today. Asked me where you'd be tonight and I told him. He said a carriage would be waiting at ten o'clock outside the back-garden gate.'

Relief washed over her. Merrick hadn't forgotten, hadn't changed his mind. Now it was up to her. All she had to do was elude Redfield. She didn't fool herself into believing it would be an easy task. Redfield suspected something was up. How he could have guessed, she didn't know. It was immaterial. The only thing that mattered now was getting to Merrick.

'Is everything all right, miss?' Meg eyed her carefully in the mirror.

'Everything will be all right, Meg. You didn't tell anyone, did you?'

Meg gave her a solemn look. 'No. Are you sure this is what you want? Lord St Magnus is a handsome fellow, but…'

'It's what I want, Meg.' Alixe smiled and rose, giving the maid a quick hug. 'Everything will be fine, you'll see. But if anything goes wrong, tell my brother what you know. You can trust Jamie.' She hoped she was right on that account.

Alixe swept up a matching green wrap and gave her room a final survey. It would be a long time before she was back here and by then everything would be different.

She was late. Merrick checked his pocket watch a fourth time. The minute hand had slipped past the three, edging towards half past the hour. He didn't want to ponder what could be keeping her. There were plenty of doubts that were taking up residence in his thoughts. Had she changed her mind? Had she started her courses and decided against marriage now that the danger had passed? Had the clear light of morning altered her passion-influenced decision the night before? Or was she in need? Had something occurred to prevent her making their appointment?

He hadn't been able to get close to the house today. Redfield had been there nearly the entire afternoon. He'd opted for sending a message through Meg. Had she been able to deliver it? Originally, he'd planned to slip a note into a bouquet and leave it for Alixe, but that seemed too risky with Redfield's presence. Redfield's presence had concerned him greatly, especially with what Merrick had learned that morning. His enquiries had turned up unsavoury information at last. Redfield made a habit of preying on middle-class women of comfortable means. He'd not aimed so high before and Merrick would see to it he wouldn't again by whatever means necessary. The proof was in his pocket.

But that didn't allay his present worries. Had the messenger boy got the time right? The sooner he had her out of Redfield's clutches, the better he'd feel.

There was no way to know short of going inside. That was one thing he couldn't do. He wasn't dressed for it. He was dressed for travelling. For another, he hadn't been invited. Besides, making a scene would hardly assist a discreet getaway.

That line of logic held until ten-thirty. To hell with discretion. He was going in there. Whatever happened inside would be far better than the not knowing going on outside. Merrick climbed out of the coach and called up to the driver, both of which were borrowed from Ashe, who'd called him a fool but loaned them anyway, saying, 'My driver's a good shot if it comes to that.'

'Bring the carriage around to the entrance. I'll be leaving by the front door. And, John, be ready to drive.' He tossed up a bag of coins. 'Bribe 'em for a good spot at the kerb if you have to and have the lanterns lit.'

'Will do.' The coachman nodded, having been fully

briefed on their purpose. 'But pardon me saying so, how are you going to get in? You're not invited.'

Merrick winked, the prospect of action raising his spirits. 'You don't need an invitation when there's a perfectly good fence to climb.' With that, he leapt up on a pile of discarded crates, scaled the railings with an agile ease born of too much practise escaping forbidden boudoirs and disappeared.

Merrick jumped down on the other side, thinking how odd it was to climb railings to get *in*. Usually he climbed them to get *out*. The garden was nearly deserted and he kept to the shadows to avoid drawing attention to himself. The verandah was another matter. Footmen abounded with trays of champagne and lobster patties. It wasn't long until the butler, accompanied by two tall footmen, cornered him at the back of the ballroom and demanded to know his business.

'I have a message for Viscount Knole,' Merrick replied, using Jamie's title. If Alixe was here, there was a good chance Jamie was, too.

The butler's narrowed gaze suggested doubt, but he sent someone in search of Jamie and Jamie turned up quickly, looking less than pleased. 'It's all right,' Jamie dismissed the butler, but the stare he fixed on Merrick told a different story. 'You're not wanted here, Merrick.'

'Where's Alixe?'

'She's up front.'

Merrick stepped forwards, determined to cut a swathe through the ballroom to reach her, but Jamie put a restraining hand on his chest. 'I don't pretend to know what happened between you and Alixe. Whatever it was, it's over now. You need to accept that. She's chosen Redfield. They're going to announce the engagement momentarily. You have to let her go.'

All Merrick said was, 'No.' The woman who'd writhed in his arms the night before would not be swayed from her promise so easily. He plunged into the crowd, making his way to the dais. Folkestone was ringing his champagne flute for attention and Alixe stood pale and desperate beside a beaming Archibald Redfield, her eyes darting through the crowd, searching for something, for someone. That someone was him. *Hold on, Alixe, I am coming*—although he had no idea what he'd do when he got there.

Chapter Twenty-One

Alixe searched the crowd for a last-minute miracle. Fate had conspired against her in the most agonising of ways. Redfield had not left her side all evening. He'd even escorted her to the ladies' retiring room and waited for her. She'd watched the hours slip away. Ten o'clock came and passed and she remained tied to Redfield. She wanted to kick him, wanted to rail at him for ruining her plans, but that would admit there'd been plans at all. Now it was too late. Unless Merrick guessed at her distress and came for her. Even then, there'd be a scandal to pay. There would be no quiet getaway that her family could choose to unobtrusively hush up. Instead, there would be public drama. She would have succeeded in giving her family fits again after she'd tried so hard to avoid it.

Her father was tapping his goblet for attention. Redfield had her arm in the discreet vise of his grip, firmly holding her rooted to him on the dais. Her mother was smiling and, somewhere in the back of the ballroom, there was a surge of movement swirling through the press of people, the crescendo of murmurs rising as the motion moved forwards. She caught a glimpse of pale-gold hair and broad shoulders pushing forwards.

Merrick.

He had come.

Her father cleared his throat. 'My dear friends, I want to thank you all for joining us this evening and allowing us the opportunity to make a most heartfelt announcement. At long last, I am pleased to share with you the engagement of my daughter to Mr Archibald Redfield, lately of Tailsby Manse. I have been proud to call him neighbour and now I will be able to call him my son-in-law as well.'

Polite applause broke out. Redfield preened. Alixe shot a desperate look at Merrick. He neared the dais, but looking at him was a mistake. Redfield followed her gaze, his grip tightening on her arm. 'My dear, he is too late if he means to claim you. Whatever plans you might have had, they've been successfully rerouted,' he whispered at her ear.

Alixe wrenched her arm to no avail. His grip held. 'Don't make a fool of yourself. You'd look ridiculous up here struggling,' Redfield said in low tones.

'You're late, St Magnus,' Redfield called out. 'Too late, some would say.'

There was some nervous laughter at the base of the dais, but Alixe noted wiser souls stepped back, clearing the space between Redfield and Merrick.

Her father's gaze flicked to Merrick. 'How dare you come to disrupt good society.'

'I come to oppose this announcement.' Merrick's voice rang out, silencing the murmurs that seethed behind him. 'If you ask the lady in question, I think you will discover she prefers another.' Merrick held out his arm, his hand so near she could almost touch it. His eyes turned to her, blue and blazing. 'Come with me now, Alixe.'

'You go with this blackguard, Alixe, and you won't see a penny of your dowry,' Folkestone hissed. Alixe could see the fans near the dais flutter faster. This was rich drama indeed. Drury Lane could do no better. 'Do you want her, St Magnus, now that she hasn't a penny to her name?'

Merrick's eyes held hers, his hand beckoning. 'I'll always want her.'

Tension eased from her shoulders. Alixe stepped forwards. She wanted only to get to Merrick and scandal be damned. She didn't care a whit for what anyone was thinking. Merrick had come for her. Merrick had publicly declared his affections in front of all these people. Nothing else mattered.

But Redfield didn't release her. Instead, he yanked her hard to him, an arm imprisoning her against his chest. The cold press of steel swept across her throat and Alixe gasped. Dear God, he had a knife. Those in the front row screamed in alarm. She vaguely heard her father attempt to reason with him. 'Redfield, what are you thinking?'

It was Merrick who answered. 'He's thinking his chances are gone. Once Alixe is lost to him, he won't be able to pay his bills.' Merrick waved a sheet of paper. 'Archibald Redfield is one of his many names. Under the name of Henry Arthur, he's wanted for defrauding three widows in Herefordshire and two older ladies in York.'

Redfield tightened his grip and Alixe shuddered. 'Don't do anything foolish, St Magnus, or I'll cut her and we'll both be the poorer for it.'

He marched them down the steps, using her as a constant shield, heading towards the garden door where there'd be no one to impede their progress once they gained the street. Alixe tried to struggle, but her efforts were short lived. He hauled her against him with a vicious tug. 'As for you, if you'd like to end up dead, keep it up.'

Alixe could feel the alarming trickle of blood work its slow way down her neck. Her struggles had done that, causing the blade to nick her. He meant business. Something inside Redfield had snapped. He'd become more than a fortune hunter. He'd become lethal.

What was supposed to have been an escape had now become a rescue and an inept one at that. Pandemonium reigned in the ballroom once Redfield slipped out the door. People raced every which way to depart, impeding Merrick's ability to follow Redfield into the night. 'Jamie!' he shouted above the din. 'We cannot let him leave the premises.' With a mixture of fear and hope, he thought of his carriage parked in the street. Ashe's coachman could be a surprise ally. But the last thing he wanted was Redfield to find the carriage and take Alixe into the night.

Jamie nodded and they pushed through the crush together, gathering a phalanx of supporters as they went. Merrick's concern for Alixe fuelled him. The man had shown his true colours tonight. Whatever hopes Redfield had of living the life of the country gentleman and rubbing elbows with the peerage had vanished the moment he'd drawn the knife. Merrick understood what the others present might not. There was still a chance Redfield could earn a ransom if he could get away.

They gained the verandah steps and Merrick caught a glimpse of Alixe's light-coloured gown. 'Over there!' he called to Jamie, dipping down in a fluid motion to retrieve his own weapons. Some men carried a knife in their boot. Merrick carried two, one for each boot. He carried them out of habit. One could never be too careful in the gaming hells or with jealous husbands. Tonight he was glad for it. There might be twenty men behind him, but it wouldn't matter if there were sixty. This confrontation was about who would die first, not about how many. Merrick wondered if anyone else understood that.

Redfield had reached the railings, but was slowed down by the cumbersome task of unlatching the gate while still holding Alixe captive. Merrick threw his first knife with unerring accuracy, sending the whistling blade over Redfield's shoulder and effectively pinning the gate shut.

'You're trapped, Redfield.' Merrick halted with twenty feet between them, the mass behind him stopping as well. He could see the madness in Redfield's eyes and the fear in Alixe's. He would kill the man for that alone. Then he caught sight of the trickle of blood seeping down Alixe's neck. Killing the bastard wouldn't be enough. He palmed his second knife and let cool clarity flow over his red-hot rage.

'You're the one who's trapped,' Redfield sneered. 'My freedom for her life. That's the only deal we have now. I've already cut her once.' The blade pressed again and Alixe gave a gasping scream.

'You're wrong, Redfield.' Merrick considered his options with lightning speed of mind. There was a square section of Redfield's shoulder not protected by Alixe's body. It was his best chance of a good throw. 'There are too many of us. You won't get out of the garden alive.' Perhaps Redfield hadn't realised the game wasn't about numbers yet.

'She'll be dead first,' Redfield countered. 'Or maybe it will be you. Care to bet on that?' Something shifted ever so slightly in Redfield's eyes, Merrick barely had time to react. In an enviously fluid move, Redfield shoved Alixe away from him and threw the knife. Merrick's own response was hasty, but no less accurate. His blade found purchase in Redfield's body just as Redfield's blade embedded itself in his right side. He heard Alixe scream his name as he fell, the force of the blow bringing him to his knees, and then he knew nothing, only that Alixe was safe.

In the week that followed, the Folkestone town house thrummed with stealthy activity. Doctor's orders were for peace and rest, but even those strict commands couldn't keep the halls empty while London waited with a communally held breath to see if its latest hero would survive.

Redfield's knife had struck dangerously close to a lung and Merrick had lost copious amounts of blood along with consciousness. Alixe had taken charge from the start, scrambling to Merrick's side in the garden and ordering he be taken into the house. She'd seen he was given the best bedroom, although her mother had feared the sheets would never recover. She'd seen him tended and had not left his side for any extended period of time since, except for an occasional rest and to update the visitors who seemed to throng the reception rooms.

Ashe Bedevere was there constantly, although he remained in the drawing room playing endless games of chess with Jamie while he worried over his friend. Her father was still in a state of disbelief: how could they not have known about Redfield? The other regular company haunting the drawing room was Martin St Magnus. He sat by himself for hours, usually reading, but he would look up expectantly whenever she entered the room, hungry for news. He was tired and drawn, as they all were. Alixe had not forgotten the disdain he'd shown Merrick at the Couthwalds', but his concern was sincere. She regretted she had no better news to give him day after day. Merrick remained the same: unconscious except for the briefest, most unpredictable moments of lucidity, which lasted only seconds.

Nursing was tiring work. There were those who would help her and at times Alixe accepted their assistance, but for the most part, she insisted on being his caregiver. He had nearly died for her. He might die for her yet and there was no deeper proof Alixe could ask of his fidelity. He'd faced Redfield in the garden, knowing full well what the risks were, and he'd taken them fearlessly, never questioning what might be required of him. All for her.

Alixe knew as she toiled over his broken body that she had not guessed at the depth of affection he held for her or the tenacity to which he clung to it. She'd been too caught up in her own feelings to see that he was struggling with the same emotions. Merrick St Magnus loved her. Truly loved her. Every time she thought of it, the incredible and undeniable truth of it washed over her anew. It was a staggering realisation to make at a staggering time. *You can't die now, not now that I know,* ran like a litany through her mind day and night.

But she had to prepare herself for the worst. The doctor had told them that morning if Merrick didn't rouse to more complete consciousness soon, it wouldn't be his wound that killed him, it would be the lack of nourishment. He would grow too weak. It had been five days since he'd last eaten. They'd made efforts to feed him, necessarily. But there was only so much broth that could be delivered via a hollowed-out reed, only so much water they could force past his unresponsive lips.

The doctor came that evening and she watched him check the bandage. He shook his head as he rose. 'It won't be long now. His pulse is not as strong as it was this morning and even this morning it was less than what it had been.' He put a kindly hand on her shoulder.

'If he wakes, those who need to say goodbye should be ready.'

No. It wasn't possible. He couldn't die now. Not when he loved her and she loved him. Not when they had a lifetime ahead of them. Not when they had a child on the way. She was very sure of it now.

Alixe locked the bedroom door with slow determination. She had wanted to do this all week, but decency didn't permit it. She crawled in bed beside him and lay next to his good arm. There was solace in being with him like this, physically close. She carefully laid her head on his shoulder and closed her eyes. She imagined they were back at St Eanswythe, lying beneath the trees and he was very much alive, his body thrumming with vitality and passion.

She let the tears come, let them fall on his bare chest in her grief. He had changed her and for the best. They'd talked of his redemption, but they'd never once talked of how he'd redeemed her. He'd reclaimed her from a life of isolation, she saw that now. He'd taught her about the transforming power of love, whether he'd intended to or not. There would be those who might say St Magnus was the one transformed, but in her heart she knew it was the other way around. If only she could tell him.

Damn him. How dare he leave her, she thought not for the first time, but this time the thought was tempered with anger. How dare he, she thought again, her temper rising. Then Alixe Burke did the unthinkable. She kicked him.

'Ow! Always…kicking…me,' came the hoarsest of murmurs.

Alixe screamed and shot bolt upright. She had not expected an answer and yet there it was after days of silence. It was a raspy answer to be sure, but it would do. 'You're awake!' she crowed exultantly before panic set in. 'You mustn't go back to sleep,' she babbled. 'If you do, the doctor says you won't wake up again.' Alixe pressed a hand to the side of his throat like she'd seen the doctor do. The pulse that met her touch was solid and stronger. She breathed a little easier.

'How do you feel?' She studied his face. His blue eyes seemed more alert than they had on prior occasions. She touched his forehead, feeling for the dreaded fever, but there was none.

'Hungry.' One-word answers were all his voice could stand at the moment after his initial outburst.

Alixe grabbed for the bell pull and yanked with ferocity. She didn't dare take her eyes from him for fear he'd slip away if she blinked. She felt the touch of his hand on hers and looked down. His touch said what his voice could not. 'I'm here, Alixe. It will be all right now.'

Her tears fell afresh. She was still sobbing when she unlocked the door to let the food in. But the worst was over. Merrick was going to live.

Over the next few days, Merrick improved steadily, defying the doctor's earlier prognosis. He was able to receive visitors for brief periods of time. Ashe came. Jamie came. Martin came; although the words they exchanged were few, both were affected by the reunion of sorts. Alixe had hopes that whatever differences lay between the brothers, this might mark a new chance for them. Last of all, her father came.

'It seems I owe you an apology,' Folkestone began, settling himself wearily into a chair. Alixe had never seen her father look so very worn out. The ordeal had taxed him not so much physically, but mentally. Merrick's actions had challenged her father's assumptions and required him to draw new conclusions, a task Alixe knew was not easy for him.

'I may have misjudged you. You did my daughter a most honourable service. You saved her life nearly at the expense of your own. That is not something I can overlook. If you still intend to marry her, you have my permission.'

Merrick nodded and shifted on his pillows to sit up straighter. He shot her a warm look. 'I do intend to marry her as soon as I am able. I find now that I have a future to look forward to, I am anxious for it to begin as soon as possible.'

'Well…' Her father coughed, uncomfortable with the level of emotion suddenly present in the room. 'I'll leave you two to work out the details.'

Merrick smiled at her and beckoned, patting a space on the bed beside him. 'Come, let me hold you. That's at least something I can do with one good arm.'

Alixe sat quickly beside him, revelling in the feel of him. After almost losing him, she knew she'd not take the presence of his body for granted again. They had not talked of the evening in the garden since his recovery, but she ventured it now. She traced a circle around his nipple, watching it tighten in response, and smiled softly to herself. 'You're London's latest hero, you know,' she began. 'Everyone's talking about how brave you were, how bold. I think there's even a bit of verse circulating. I was so frightened and there you were, taking charge. You knew exactly what you were doing.' She paused.

'He would have killed me, Merrick, if it hadn't been for you. He was different that night. Something had snapped in him, I could sense it. I couldn't tell you what it was, but it was something. I think now, he'd never been right in the head from the start. He was always watching people.'

Merrick's arm tightened about her. 'I was scared, too. I didn't think about being brave. I only thought about you.' His hand reached up to trace the tiny white scar left by Redfield's knife. 'When I saw that you were hurt already, my only thoughts were to set you free, it was all that mattered and then I realised nothing had mattered for a long time. There'd been nothing to fight for. Now there was—there was you.' He played with her hair, a twinkle in his eye. 'I do believe, Alixe Burke, the London gossips have it all wrong. It was not me who saved you. It was you who saved me.'

Alixe shook her head. 'I disagree. You have saved me in ways far beyond what happened in the garden.'

'Well…' Merrick sighed happily '…then it looks like we're even.'

Chapter Twenty-Two

The ruins of the church of St Eanswythe was hosting its first wedding in centuries. The early autumn sun shone pleasantly through the leaves of the trees and the small gathering of guests hummed with excitement as they sat amid the crumbled stones of the cathedral.

The handsome groom, Merrick St Magnus, stood impatiently at the impromptu altar with Vicar Daniels. Jamie Burke stood beside him along with Ashe Bedevere, who was looking far more decent than he actually was, a fact not lost on several ladies in attendance.

Local flowers and ribbon looped down the aisle on poles mounted into the dirt between the old flagstones, making a pretty setting. But Merrick had eyes only for the woman who waited at the far end of the aisle, gowned in a dress the colour of gold leaves, a wreath of autumn flowers crowning her dark head. In Alixe, he had his very own saint. Not bad for a sinner of such glorious proportions.

The vicar gave a slight nod and she began a slow

procession towards him. He offered her his hand and held it throughout the service, barely hearing the words of the ceremony. His hands trembled a bit when he slipped the gold band on her finger. She was his. The enormous wonder of it was not lost on him. He bent to kiss her, sweeping her into his arms and kissing her full on the mouth until even Ashe felt the urge to intervene. If anyone thought it unseemly, Merrick didn't care. He wanted the world to know he loved his wife, a fact he demonstrated quite publicly throughout the wedding breakfast that followed and more privately later that night.

'I have something for you.' Merrick rolled over to snatch a scroll tied with a small ribbon from the bedside table. They'd chosen to spend the night at an elegant inn on the road to Hever.

'What is this?' Alixe asked, her eyes lighting up at the prospect of a gift. She slid the ribbon off and unrolled the paper. Merrick waited for her reaction. He'd thought a long time about what would be most meaningful to her. The usual gift of jewels didn't suit her and, even if they had, Merrick was determined not to spend her dowry so frivolously.

'Oh!' A gasp escaped her. 'How did you ever manage this, Merrick?' Her eyes moved to his face.

'It looks like your farmer lived happily ever after with his "sow".' He reached over to gently push the hair back from her face where it had fallen forwards.

Alixe put the paper aside. 'It's the perfect gift. How did you know?'

'Because I know you,' Merrick said, pleased the gift

had touched her. He wanted to spend his life pleasing her. She was beautiful in the candlelight of their room.

'How did you ever find out?' she began again.

'I managed a few visits to the village and helped Vicar Daniels go through some old records.' Merrick shrugged, making little of his efforts. He didn't want to talk about a Norman farmer in detail at the moment. His mind was already on wanting to take her again.

Alixe snuggled next to him. 'It's the ideal wedding gift. Thank you.' She traced circles on his chest, her favourite pastime while she waited for better things to come. 'I have a gift for you, too.' She stretched up and whispered one word in his ear.

'Are you certain?' Merrick felt his heart thud.

'Yes. I met with a doctor in London before we left.'

The pronouncement might have undone a lesser man. But Merrick St Magnus threw back his head and laughed.

Twins.

Of course.

He didn't doubt it for a moment. He was Merrick St Magnus and he did nothing by halves.

* * * * *

REQUEST YOUR FREE BOOKS!

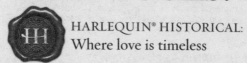

HARLEQUIN® HISTORICAL:
Where love is timeless

2 FREE NOVELS PLUS 2 **FREE GIFTS!**

YES! Please send me 2 FREE Harlequin® Historical novels and my 2 FREE gifts (gifts are worth about $10). After receiving them, if I don't wish to receive any more books, I can return the shipping statement marked "cancel." If I don't cancel, I will receive 6 brand-new novels every month and be billed just $5.19 per book in the U.S. or $5.74 per book in Canada. That's a savings of at least 17% off the cover price! It's quite a bargain! Shipping and handling is just 50¢ per book in the U.S. and 75¢ per book in Canada.* I understand that accepting the 2 free books and gifts places me under no obligation to buy anything. I can always return a shipment and cancel at any time. Even if I never buy another book, the two free books and gifts are mine to keep forever.

246/349 HDN FEQQ

Name	(PLEASE PRINT)
Address	Apt. #
City	State/Prov.	Zip/Postal Code

Signature (if under 18, a parent or guardian must sign)

Mail to the **Reader Service:**
IN U.S.A.: P.O. Box 1867, Buffalo, NY 14240-1867
IN CANADA: P.O. Box 609, Fort Erie, Ontario L2A 5X3

Not valid for current subscribers to Harlequin Historical books.

Want to try two free books from another line?
Call 1-800-873-8635 or visit www.ReaderService.com.

* Terms and prices subject to change without notice. Prices do not include applicable taxes. Sales tax applicable in N.Y. Canadian residents will be charged applicable taxes. Offer not valid in Quebec. This offer is limited to one order per household. All orders subject to credit approval. Credit or debit balances in a customer's account(s) may be offset by any other outstanding balance owed by or to the customer. Please allow 4 to 6 weeks for delivery. Offer available while quantities last.

Your Privacy—The Reader Service is committed to protecting your privacy. Our Privacy Policy is available online at www.ReaderService.com or upon request from the Reader Service.

We make a portion of our mailing list available to reputable third parties that offer products we believe may interest you. If you prefer that we not exchange your name with third parties, or if you wish to clarify or modify your communication preferences, please visit us at www.ReaderService.com/consumerschoice or write to us at Reader Service Preference Service, P.O. Box 9062, Buffalo, NY 14269. Include your complete name and address.

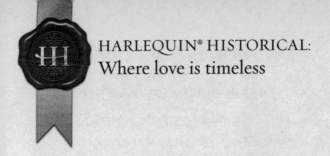

HARLEQUIN® HISTORICAL:
Where love is timeless

BOUND BY ROYAL COMMAND!

A dangerous mission at Queen Elizabeth's bidding is Celia Sutton's chance to erase the taint of her brother's treason. Her life is at risk if she's discovered—and so is her heart when she learns her co-conspirator is also her one-time seducer: brooding and mysterious John Brandon!

Will Celia fulfill her duty to Queen and Country or risk it all for love?

Find out in

Tarnished Rose of the Court

by Amanda McCabe

Available October 2012
from Harlequin® Historical

Ashe Bedevere's eyes glittered dangerously, his tone forebodingly quiet. "You shouldn't say things you don't mean, Mrs. Ralston." The faintest hint of a wicked smile played on his lips.

"And you, sir, should know better than to scold a lady." Genevra opted for the high road.

"Why is that?" He stepped closer to her. He was all man and there was no place for her to go.

"Because you are a gentleman." At least he was dressed like one. Up close, she could appreciate his impeccably brushed jacket stretched elegantly across an impressive breadth of shoulder. But other than the clothes, she had her doubts.

"Are you sure?" His voice was low and he gave her a sensual half smile, his eyes roving her face, flicking down ever so briefly to her throat and perhaps slightly lower. His attentions were perilously arousing.

"No." Her voice came out in a hoarse tremor. She wasn't sure of anything in that moment, least of all how they'd arrived at this point.

"Good, because I can think of better things to do by moonlight than quarrel, can't you?"

His next move startled her entirely. Before she could

think, his hand was at the nape of her neck, warm and caressing, drawing her to him until his mouth covered hers in a full kiss that sent a jolt of heat to her stomach.

She arched her neck, letting his kiss travel the length of her throat. This was not the hesitant kiss of a moonstruck dandy. This was the kiss of a man proficient in the art.

Her arms were about his neck and she breathed deeply of him. If temptation had a scent, it would be this.

Without warning, Ashe stepped back, releasing her, his eyes a smoky green.

"I don't know what you're doing here, Mrs. Ralston, but I will find out."

"What makes you think I'm doing 'anything'?"

"A woman doesn't kiss like that unless she wants something. Badly."

It took a moment to comprehend, so unexpected was the comment. "If I were a gentleman, I would call you out for that." Genevra fairly shook with rage. She'd never been so insulted. If he wasn't careful, she'd call him out anyway.

"We've already established there are no gentlemen here at present," he drawled. "And you, Mrs. Ralston, are no lady."

Don't miss
HOW TO RUIN A REPUTATION
by Bronwyn Scott

Available September 18 from Harlequin® Historical

HARLEQUIN Blaze

red-hot reads

Two sizzling fairy tales with men straight from your wildest dreams…

Fan-favorite authors

Rhonda Nelson & Karen Foley

bring readers another installment of

Blazing Bedtime Stories, Volume IX

THE EQUALIZER

Modern-day righter of wrongs, Robin Sherwood is a man on a mission and will do everything necessary to see that through, especially when that means catching the eye of a fair maiden.

GOD'S GIFT TO WOMEN

Sculptor Lexi Adams decides there is no such thing as the perfect man, until she catches sight of Nikos Christakos, the sexy builder next door. She convinces herself that she only wants to sculpt him, but soon finds a cold stone statue is a poor substitute for the real deal.

Available October 2012 wherever books are sold.

www.Harlequin.com

HB79715